Praise for the Author of
A HIGHLANDER CHRISTMAS

Dawn Halliday

"Dawn Halliday is the *hottest* new voice in Scottish romance."

—national bestselling author Monica McCarty

Sophie Renwick

"Sophie Renwick cooks up a spicy romance hearty enough to satisfy any appetite." —Megan Hart, author of *Tempted*

Cindy Miles

"When it comes to delivering charming, funny, and tender romances, Miles is at the head of the class." —*Romantic Times*

A Highlander Christmas

DAWN HALLIDAY

CINDY MILES

SOPHIE RENWICK

A SIGNET ECLIPSE BOOK

Signet Eclipse
Published by New American Library, a division of
Penguin Group (USA) Inc., 375 Hudson Street,
New York, New York 10014, USA
Penguin Group (Canada), 90 Eglinton Avenue East, Suite 700, Toronto,
Ontario M4P 2Y3, Canada (a division of Pearson Penguin Canada Inc.)
Penguin Books Ltd., 80 Strand, London WC2R 0RL, England
Penguin Ireland, 25 St. Stephen's Green, Dublin 2,
Ireland (a division of Penguin Books Ltd.)
Penguin Group (Australia), 250 Camberwell Road, Camberwell, Victoria 3124,
Australia (a division of Pearson Australia Group Pty. Ltd.)
Penguin Books India Pvt. Ltd., 11 Community Centre, Panchsheel Park,
New Delhi - 110 017, India
Penguin Group (NZ), 67 Apollo Drive, Rosedale, North Shore 0632,
New Zealand (a division of Pearson New Zealand Ltd.)
Penguin Books (South Africa) (Pty.) Ltd., 24 Sturdee Avenue,
Rosebank, Johannesburg 2196, South Africa

Penguin Books Ltd., Registered Offices:
80 Strand, London WC2R 0RL, England

First published by Signet Eclipse, an imprint of New American Library,
a division of Penguin Group (USA) Inc.

First Printing, November 2009
10 9 8 7 6 5 4 3 2 1

Library of Congress Cataloging-in-Publication Data:

Halliday, Dawn.
A highlander Christmas/Dawn Halliday, Cindy Miles, Sophie Renwick.
p.   cm.
ISBN 978-0-451-22872-7
1. Highlands (Scotland)—Fiction. 2. Supernatural—Fiction. I. Renwick, Sophie. II. Miles, Cindy.
III. Title.
PS3608.A54835H55 2009
813'.6—dc22   2009024595

Set in Goudy
Designed by Ginger Legato

Printed in the United States of America

Contents

Winter Heat

DAWN HALLIDAY

For Lawrence

Chapter One

A tiny bud of hope bloomed within Maggie MacDonald as she peered out the frosty pane of her window. A storm approached—the air was thick, heavy with the promise of snow. Meager light from inside the cottage dappled the gray graveled path leading toward the village road. Fog wisped lazily above the ground, and the clouds hovered low enough to caress the thatched eaves.

Perhaps Innes Munroe would leave her alone until the storm passed. Perhaps Innes would spend the next ten days sotted, the drink would wipe his wish to claim her from his memory, and the New Year would dawn with new hope for Maggie's independence.

A pretty dream. It'd take a cudgel to the skull to make Innes forget his intentions when it came to her.

A puff of cold air brushed Maggie's face, and she closed the curtain against the chill that swept through her. Pulling a plaid tight across her chest, she knelt to tug on a second pair of stockings.

Beyond the partition dividing the cottage into two rooms, one of the servants moaned softly in her sleep. It was late, and tomorrow would be a long day, for they'd planned to make the three-mile journey to her cousin Torean's castle for her annual fortnight-long

5

visit. Every December, the MacDonald laird summoned family members to his castle, where they observed Christmas prior to the raucous revelry leading up to Hogmanay and the New Year.

This year Maggie thought the festivities might be muted, for the recent uprising against the Hanoverian King hadn't proved to be the great success they'd all anticipated. Yet the MacDonalds of Beauly had lost none of their men in the Battle of Preston, and that in itself was a cause for celebration.

Maggie snuffed out the two oil lamps and returned to her bed. Leaving her plaid wrapped around her body and pinned at her shoulder for additional warmth, she slipped beneath the heavy wool blankets, shivering.

Crack!

The sound of splintering wood jolted through the cottage, jerking Maggie awake. She bolted upright, but before she could decipher what had happened, a big masculine hand clamped over her face.

Every muscle in Maggie's body went stiff. The taste of mud washed over her tongue. She bared her teeth and bit down hard on the thick flesh padding the man's palm. Snarling a curse, he released her mouth, and Maggie let out a pealing scream.

The intruder bent over her, a looming black shadow with yellow-hued teeth gleaming in the dimness, and hefted her from the bed.

"You don't wish to make this easy for me, do you?" he spat into her ear.

Maggie recognized the voice instantly, for it belonged to Innes Munroe. His familiar oniony smell overlaid with the essence of whisky washed over her, and the greasy ends of his pale hair brushed over her cheeks.

"Damn y—"

He dropped her lower body, and again his hand clapped over her lips, filling her mouth and nose with the coppery taste and scent of blood.

"I've waited too long, Maggie MacDonald. My patience is at an end. You're coming with me."

Something sharp prodded her between her collarbones. Maggie glanced down at the glinting blade of a dagger, its point probing her flesh.

"Dare to bite me again, and I'll sink it deep, I promise you," Innes growled.

She realized he'd already pulled her halfway to the gaping doorway. He'd splintered her door and pulled it from its hinges, and its remnants lay on the snow just beyond the henchman who loomed at the threshold, leering at her. He gripped his sword hilt, ready to impale anyone who attempted to hinder his master.

"Ah, what have we here?"

Maggie followed Innis's gaze to see her three servants hesitating at the partition opening. Her man-of-all-work, Naughton Campbell, stood in front of his daughters, who stared from each side of his body at Innes and Maggie with wide, terrified eyes.

The blade at her neck pressed deeper, breaking her skin, and Maggie gasped. Tears collected behind her eyes, but she refused to cry, refused to give Innes the satisfaction of even a whimper.

"Come one step closer, and I'll kill her." Innes's voice, as always, was a harsh rasp, like the words had been dragged over hot coals before emerging from his mouth.

He shifted, and Maggie found her arm, which had been pinned between her body and Innes's, was now free to move. Her hand shot up to grip his wrist. With all her might, she tried to yank the dagger away from her tender skin.

She couldn't budge him. He was too burly, too strong, his strength heightened by drink and determination. He jerked her another step backward, tugging her toward the cold outside air.

"Ma'am?" Naughton asked, his question a low rumble. Fear clouded his eyes as his gaze darted from Maggie and Innes to the man standing at the threshold. Maggie didn't blame him. Innes alone was younger and stronger than Naughton, and twice his size.

"Stay put, all of you," she ordered. It would only cause more bloodshed were Naughton to put himself at risk.

She sucked in a breath, and in an abrupt move, she twisted in Innes's arms to free herself from his iron grip. The action did nothing but drive his blade deeper. A trickle of blood flowed down her chest and collided with the edge of her shift.

"Oh, ma'am!" Lizzy, the younger of the two girls, began to cry. Naughton held his arms out to block the girls, ensuring they remained at a safe distance.

Closing her eyes, feeling nothing but the sharp sting on her neck, Maggie stilled. She must save her strength—attack Innes and run when he least expected it.

With his arm like a band of steel clamped around her middle, Innes dragged her backward. He hesitated at the threshold, pausing to sneer at Naughton and the girls. "Good night, then."

Maggie braced herself against the chill as he yanked her into the night air.

Logan Douglas hadn't yet found shelter for the night. Locked in nightmarish memories of the battle at Sheriffmuir, he'd lost track of time and simply kept going on his endless march north as the gloom of dusk darkened into a velvety night. When cold flakes of snow began to drift into his eyes, he snapped back to himself. He stopped in his tracks; took in his surroundings.

"Hell," he muttered.

This far north, the towns were scattered few and far between, and though villagers brought their animals up to graze in the summer months, these mountains were virtually uninhabited at this time of year.

Logan strode resolutely onward, ignoring the increasing pain of the bayonet wound in his thigh, keeping his keen eyesight trained on his surroundings. Despite the cloak of darkness, he could make out the shadowy terrain, the barren trees, and the evergreens. If there was shelter, he'd find it. He'd survived so far, and no mere winter storm would best him. If he had to, he'd walk through it. He didn't need the stars or the sun to guide him. These were the Highlands—his land, his home—and he could find his way north by smell, taste, and touch if need be.

Soon he glimpsed a potential shelter. Just beyond a ledge to the east, the thatch of a roof peeked out from beneath a thin layer of snow. He walked toward it, and gradually the small, stone-walled circular structure came into view.

It was more than he'd hoped for. Its owner had probably abandoned it for the winter only a month or two ago. Logan trudged around to the tightly woven wicker door and pushed it open, making out the dark shapes of furniture—a table, chairs, and bed—in the deep shadows of the room.

He felt his way to the hearth. The wide fireplace possessed the added luxury of a stone chimney, rare for so small a place in such a remote location, with a generous amount of dry peat stacked beside it.

After lighting a fire, Logan rose to more fully assess his surroundings by the light of the flames. A low stone table and two chairs occupied the room's center. Fresh provisions—a measure of oats, a pan full of dried meat, dishes of butter and cream, a bucket of eggs, and several bottles of whisky and ale—sat on the tabletop. The wood-frame bed with a heather-stuffed mattress was pushed against the far wall, with clothes, linens, and plaids stacked in an open chest at its foot.

This cottage hadn't been abandoned for the winter—in fact, the opposite appeared to be true. Someone planned to move in. Not tonight, though, Logan deduced. Not this late, and not in this storm.

Logan would light a fire and sleep, but he wouldn't take anything from this place. When he went on his way in the morning, he would leave the cottage as he'd found it. The owner would never realize anyone had spent the night.

All that kept Logan alive was the act of moving forward, constantly striving toward his goal: his brother's lands in the far northern Highlands. They were Logan's lands now, and Logan's responsibility, for his brother had died at Sheriffmuir.

Home had seemed as remote as China less than a month ago. Every day, however, he grew closer.

A few hours' rest and he'd be on his way.

Innes Munroe was drunker than he'd originally appeared, Maggie realized. The henchman had started whining about the cold not ten minutes after they'd left her cottage, and Innes had sent him home. Now they sat astride an exhausted horse, Innes holding Maggie tightly against him, her wrists bound with rough twine, her shift riding up her thighs.

Blood still trickled from her chest, and her left eye had swollen to a slit, for he'd hit her hard enough for her to see stars the last time she'd tried to escape.

As soon as Innes had tossed her onto the horse, a light snow had begun to descend, and as they traveled on, the world turned a solid gray-black beneath the cloudy sky.

Innes slipped his arm beneath her plaid, and his callused red hand closed over her breast. "Aw, that's nice, isn't it? Just big enough for my hand, aren't you, Maggie girl?"

Renewed fury stormed through her, and she twisted, ramming her elbow into his gut. "Stop pawing at me, you animal!"

His breath left him with a whoosh. Releasing her breast, he snagged one of her wrists over the twine he'd used to bind her. He squeezed until the small bones rubbed together. Maggie gasped. If he squeezed any tighter, surely he'd break her wrist.

"You'd best let me go, Innes Munroe," she said through clenched teeth. "Torean will see you hanged for this."

At that, Innes released a booming laugh. "I don't think so, woman. It was his idea that I take you—show you who your master is."

"You're a liar!" Yet a sick feeling churned in her gut. For some unknown reason, her cousin had befriended this lout. Couldn't Torean see how despicable he was? Was he so blind as to have sanctioned Innes's abominable acts?

Torean's father had died suddenly last winter, and Torean was a young man—younger than Maggie by four years. He hadn't been prepared to take on the responsibility of the lairdship, and some of his actions as their leader had taken the clan aback. Nobody understood why Torean would befriend the belligerent younger brother of the Munroe laird.

Maggie blinked against the sting of snow in her eyes. She

couldn't see much farther than a few feet in front of them, but she knew they were heading uphill and had drawn far from the village. As they ascended the mountain slope, the clouds grew ever thicker. Yet Innes continued to force the tiring horse through the snow flurries. The animal's hooves sank into the freshly fallen powder with each step it took.

Maggie gave thanks for her thick, long-sleeved shift, her two pairs of stockings, and her plaid. Thank the Lord she'd taken her plaid to bed, otherwise she'd surely be an icicle by now. At least she was dry, and though not warm by any stretch of the imagination, she wasn't near frozen to death either. Innes, dressed in thick wool trews, boots, layers of shirts and jackets, and covered by a plaid, hadn't given her condition a second thought.

He dropped her wrist and fumbled in his coat. She heard the glugging noise as he gulped down more of the drink. Hopefully he'd drink himself into a stupor, she thought bitterly. Then she could shove him off the horse and escape.

Returning his flask to his pocket, he switched arms, taking the reins in his right hand and clamping his brawny left arm around her torso. His thumb rubbed rough circles over her breast, and she tensed but this time she didn't flail.

"Where are you taking me?" she said through clenched teeth.

His only answer was a low chuckle, but pinned against him as she was, she could feel his body responding in anticipation. Wherever their destination, she had a fair idea of what he intended to do to her once they arrived.

That was something she couldn't countenance. She'd die before giving herself to this brute.

Carefully, she inched her bound hands upward over her plaid, ever so slowly so the drunken man behind her wouldn't notice. In any case, he wasn't paying attention—he was far more interested in pinching her breast. His arousal poked at her bottom, and his pungent breath puffed over the top of her head.

Her fingers touched the cold silver of the brooch at her shoulder. It was the only weapon she possessed, surely not as effective as a pistol or a sword, or even a dagger, but she prayed it would be enough.

Her brooch was different from the usual circular brooch worn by the women of the clan. About the length of Maggie's hand, it was long and narrow and shaped like a sword. A dragon stood just below the hilt, its wings unfurled, its body ringed by a flat silver circle etched with the words, *"Per mare, per terras"*—"by sea, by land"—her family's motto. At the bottom of the ring, the dragon's talons curled over a large, dull amber agate.

On her deathbed, Maggie's mother had handed her daughter the brooch, saying Maggie must keep it with her always; for it possessed the magical ability to detect a MacDonald woman's lifelong soul mate.

Her mother was as superstitious as they came, though, and Maggie didn't believe any such nonsense. The brooch certainly hadn't detected anything before Maggie had married Duneghall, whom she'd loved wholeheartedly during their brief time together.

It was just a trinket, and an odd one at that. But her mother died when she was fifteen years old, and out of respect for her memory, Maggie always kept it near. She enjoyed that it earned her a raised brow whenever she encountered a stranger—for what kind of a woman pinned her plaid with a miniature weapon? But more than that, it was the only possession Maggie had to remember her mother by.

Maggie fumbled with the brooch, finally releasing the pin

and sliding it free from the wool. She clutched it between her palms, its sharp point facing her, and returned her hands to her lap.

The sword tip and the pin together weren't truly dangerous. They couldn't inflict permanent damage. Yet Maggie knew where a man was his most sensitive, and Innes Munroe was drunk as a drum. This was her last hope.

She took a deep, fortifying breath. Then she clenched her knees, scooted her bottom forward over the rise of the saddle's pommel, twisted her body, and stabbed her hands backward, plunging the tip of the brooch into Innes's groin.

He howled. Dropping his hand from her breast, he slapped it to his crotch, simultaneously jerking on the reins. The horse reared its head back in discomfort and skidded to a stop.

Maggie yanked her brooch from Innes and scrambled awkwardly off the animal, falling on her face in the snow. She commanded her body to straighten by sheer force of will, for her leg—Innes had kicked her thigh earlier when she'd tried to slip off the horse and run away—protested vehemently.

Keeping her bound hands before her, she ran. Only a few seconds passed before she heard the sound of Innes and the horse advancing on her. She dove into the shelter of a snow-covered cluster of evergreen bushes, praying Innes was too drunk to heed her deep footprints in the snow.

The horse thundered past, but then Innes shouted, "Whoa!" and Maggie squeezed her eyes shut, willing her footsteps invisible as horse and rider turned and once again drew near.

"Maggie!" Innes shouted, his crusty voice raw with pain. "Damn you to hell, where are you, you bloody witch?"

She gripped her brooch in her shaking fists, prepared to use it as a makeshift weapon again.

He circled the area over and over, shouting, threatening her with everything from rape to disembowelment. Then he stopped the horse directly in front of the bushes she cowered under. The animal nickered, and Maggie clenched her teeth to prevent them from chattering.

"Don't be stupid, lass." Innes sounded somewhat levelheaded for the first time all night. "You'll catch your death. You don't want to die out here tonight, do you? It's going to be a mean storm, Maggie girl. Already you can scarcely see your hand before your face. I'll take you somewhere nice and warm."

Over her dead body, she thought grimly. She'd gladly freeze to death before returning to that bastard.

"Come on now," he crooned in his grating voice.

She remained still, resolute. She would find shelter on her own, find a way down the mountain, back to the village. She would *not* go to Innes Munroe. She'd be damned if she'd sacrifice her pride and be raped. No matter how slim they were, she'd take her chances with the storm.

Innes dismounted nearby, and she heard the streaming sound as he pissed in the snow on the opposite side of the bush. Mumbling to himself about crazy women not being worth the effort, he returned to his horse.

"Very well then, Maggie," he shouted, trying to regain control of the animal, who tossed its head and whickered in a mild complaint. "I offered you a warm bed with me tonight, but since you'd rather die in the snow, so be it." He gave a long-suffering, dramatic sigh and flicked the reins. "Goodbye, then. I'm going to Malmuirie's, where the lasses know how to treat a man like a king."

Malmuirie was the madam of the nearest brothel, and as Innes turned his horse, Maggie pressed her lips together to prevent herself from wishing him luck getting it up after what she'd done to his testicles. She remained motionless until the sound of retreating hoofbeats faded, leaving the world in silence save the whisper of the falling snow.

Using her teeth, she worked at the twine binding her wrists. Innes was ultimately a stupid man, for he'd tied her tightly but not expertly, and slowly, surely, she worked the knot loose.

The loop suddenly went slack, and she shook off the twine. Finally free, she flexed her stiff, cold fingers and rubbed her raw wrists.

Rising from her hiding place behind the bush, Maggie turned the way they had come, marveling at the fact that her footsteps had nearly disappeared. She could barely make out the path they'd taken, but that didn't matter. She knew what direction to go: downhill, where she'd find the village, protection, warmth. Home.

She covered her head with her plaid and pulled it tight around her, thanking Providence for her second pair of stockings and for their ability to keep out some of the wetness of the snow.

Sometime later, as the first gray light of dawn edged through the thick cloud cover, Maggie's weak legs could hardly drag her through the snow. She knew she hadn't been walking for long, but she'd lost the ability to distinguish uphill from down. Each stride took her up to her ankles in snow, and sometimes she stepped into deep drifts and sank to her thighs. She was so tired. So very, very tired. The pale white snowdrifts called to her like warm, downy beds, and she craved nothing more than to lie down upon one of them and have a rest.

Just a short break, she thought. Blocked on three sides by a shoulder-high granite bluff that would keep her safe from the elements, a high rise of snow just ahead looked like the perfect bed.

It would be like sleeping on a cloud. Her brooch slipped from her fingers as she stumbled to the drift and fell to her knees. She'd just have a short rest; then she'd retrieve her brooch and continue on her way.

Pulling her plaid tightly over her shoulders and wrapping it around her hands, she lay on the snow, curled her body into a ball, and embraced the warmth of slumber.

Logan woke before dawn, as was his habit. Quickly and efficiently, he boiled a pot of water, cooked some of the porridge from his small bundle of possessions, and ate. He left the cottage as he'd found it, silently thanking its unknown owner for his hospitality.

Snow fell tranquilly now, for the wind had calmed. The going was more difficult this morning, however, for deep snowdrifts had gathered over the terrain. The thick cloud cover had broken, and Logan hoped it would stop snowing soon. He was still a few days' journey from home, and though he would if he must, he'd rather not trudge through waist-deep snow to get there.

Sweat broke over Logan's brow as he made his way downhill. Given the location of the cottage, he guessed there would be a village at the valley floor where he might find shelter tonight.

Something caught his eye—a shimmer in the gray light. All his senses on alert, Logan drew himself to a stop. Silently raising his musket, he turned toward it.

The small object lay half buried in the snow, but a rainbow of glittering light cascaded around it. Following behind the barrel of his gun, Logan approached it cautiously. When he had drawn close, he flicked it with the butt of the weapon, revealing a long silver pin in the shape of a sword. On the blade stood some kind of bird perched upon the largest clear multifaceted gem he'd ever seen. He'd be damned if that wasn't a diamond.

A soft groan drew his attention from the bauble. Tucked beneath a cleft of a short ridge of granite, a figure lay half covered in snow. A pale white cheek offset by black hair, lashes, and brows. A red plaid covered the slight body.

Holy hell, what was a woman doing out here? A tiny, harmless woman, huddled beneath a plaid, with nothing covering her head? Rage swelled through him. Whoever had allowed this to happen should be shot.

He'd have thought she was dead if he hadn't just heard her. He took two angry steps toward her. "Lass?"

She didn't respond.

"Can you hear me?"

Nothing. Her eyes didn't so much as flutter.

He sank to one knee beside her. She was beautiful, exquisite, with a fall of raven curls cascading around her pale oval face. Logan's fury deepened when he noticed the red, swollen area around one of her eyes and the bit of dried blood caking her lower lip. She looked like a fragile porcelain doll, utterly serene, utterly helpless. Used and tossed away.

An emotion he'd thought dead roared to life deep within him, caught in his chest, and sent the blood raging through his veins. Gently, he pushed aside her stiff, frozen plaid. His breath caught. Christ . . . she wore nothing but a shift beneath, its neckline stained with blood. He shrugged out of his coat and wrapped it around her before gathering her pale limp body in his arms. Her skin was cold as ice.

As lifeless as she appeared, though, he knew she lived. As he cradled her in his arms and bent his face down to her, he felt the soft whisper of her breath against his cheek.

"Come, lass," he murmured gruffly, wondering if she heard him at all. "I will warm you."

Chapter Two

Warmth washed through Maggie. It pushed through her muscles, combating the frozen knots in her shoulders and neck. "Mmm." She shifted her body, turning beneath comfortable, heavy blankets. Seductive heat pressed in on her from all sides. Warm air brushed over her cheeks, and she opened her eyes to find herself gazing into a peat fire.

But the fire wasn't the source of her warmth—a solid source of a heat hotter than any fire pressed into her back, its earthy male scent mingling with the peat. Bare skin cradled her bare skin.

Awareness slammed into her.

Someone—a man—lay behind her. And she was utterly naked.

Her languid muscles tensed. A strangled cry emerged from her throat. With her heart pattering like a frightened rabbit's, she lunged away, falling from the bed, then scrambling to an upright position on a hard-packed dirt floor.

He was faster than her. As graceful as a cat, he leaped to his feet, trapping her between his body and the hearth.

She stared up at him in openmouthed horror. This wasn't Innes Munroe. This man was harder, taller, darker. Even more frightening in appearance. His face was untainted masculinity, with a high forehead; wide, lush lips; a blade of a nose; and narrow, dark eyes topped by menacing brows. Midnight black hair descended in silky waves to brush broad shoulders. Other than the plaid he wrapped around his waist as he rose, he was naked too.

Maggie flattened her bare feet on the floor, tightened her fists at her sides, and looked up at him in brazen challenge. Though her insides had turned to jelly—no man had seen her unclothed since her husband died—she refused to show him her fear. She was no weakling.

In any case, she thought with an inward flinch, she needn't hide her body from him. Clearly the man had already familiarized himself with it. Without moving, she rapidly assessed herself. The only pain she felt radiated from the places Innes had hurt her— her chest, her leg, her wrists, and her face.

Still, that didn't necessarily mean this man hadn't touched her, hadn't violated her. Why on earth else would they both be naked?

She tried to control her fear while squelching the shivers that built just beneath her skin. She'd been warm a moment ago, but now the cold prickled over her skin like tiny knives, painful in its intensity.

Glaring up at the tall stranger, she couldn't determine whether she was more or less appalled than if she'd found herself in bed with Innes. At least with Innes she knew her enemy. This man was an unknown entity, intimidating in both size and demeanor. Everything else in the room seemed diminutive and unimportant when compared to him.

"I found you in the snow." His voice was a low, rumbling growl that sent a tremble crawling down her spine. "Come back to bed. It's still storming outside, and you're chilled."

"What did you do to me?" she demanded.

His lips thinned. "Nothing."

She raised a brow.

"I brought you here."

"Naked?"

He shrugged. "Your clothing was wet."

She glared at him. "What have you done to my clothes?"

"Wet." With a swift movement of his arm, the stranger motioned behind him. Beyond the bed, her shift, plaid, and stockings dangled from the rafters.

"Now come back to bed." His hard voice sent renewed shivers through her. The cold seized her body, gripped at her with painful talons. Raising her hands, she flexed her stiff fingers, staring in fascination at the disconnected way in which they moved.

Beyond her fingers, she saw something flash in his dark eyes. Something dangerous.

Slowly, she lowered her hands, curling her fists at her sides. She must gather her wits, keep them close. Despite the compulsion to study her whereabouts, Maggie kept her focus solely on the stranger. Wind rustled the eaves outside, but the peat fire sighed behind her, warm and inviting. It took every ounce of her will not to collapse to her knees and crawl close enough to it to singe her hair in the flames.

Struggling to keep her voice even, she asked, "Who are you?"

"Logan Douglas," he replied shortly. He held out his hand. "Return to bed. It is too cold."

She held her ground, curling her toes into the frigid, hard-packed dirt. "Where are we?"

"In the mountains."

She swallowed down the surging panic. The man just stood there, stiff and unyielding, blocking the path to the exit. She was

at this big stranger's mercy. As much as she tried not to show it,
she was afraid.

"Who are you?" she pushed out.

"I told you . . ."

She shook her head. "I know everyone within miles of Lub-
fearn. Where did you come from, Logan Douglas?"

"Far from here."

Slowly, the recollection of what had happened to her drifted
into Maggie's mind. A drunken Innes Munroe had abducted her
from her cottage. He'd tied her wrists and carried her up the mountain on his horse. She'd escaped, Innes had abandoned his search
for her and headed to Malmuirie's, and she'd started the long walk
home. After that, her memory faded to a blur.

"Where did you find me?" she asked hoarsely.

"Less than a mile from here," Logan said. "You were unconscious."

"When?" Maggie's voice wavered.

"This morning."

No outside light seeped in from the cracks in the stone walls
and the door, and the only light inside was the flickering gold
glow cast by the fire. It was nighttime. She'd been absent from the
village an entire day. By now, her servants would have informed
the laird what had happened. Would he come after her? But Innes
had said her cousin had approved of his abduction of Maggie.
When Innes returned to the castle without her, what would he
tell Torean?

Knowing Innes, he'd stay deep within the warm carnal haven
of Malmuirie's at least until the storm had passed, which meant
Torean wouldn't come searching for her anytime soon. Her knees
trembled, knocked together, and though she tried to still her body,
she shook like an autumn leaf in a gale.

She gritted her teeth. She must remain upright. But even as she commanded herself not to crumple, her legs simply melted from beneath her. Before she slammed face-first onto the hard-packed dirt, Logan scooped her against his chest. She tried to stiffen in his tight embrace, but her body wouldn't obey her.

"Put me down," she managed to say through her chattering teeth.

He ignored her command. "Come to bed. I'll warm you."

"N-n-no!"

Gently, he laid her down and tucked the blankets over her. Still, her whole body shook, and the sound of her knocking teeth resonated like booming drums in her ears. She'd never be warm again, she was certain of it.

Logan's hand curled over her shoulder. "I've seen this before. I need to lie beside you. I must give you my warmth."

She clenched her teeth in an attempt to control them. "I need—bring me my shift."

"No." A line appeared between his black brows as he hovered over her. "It is wet."

She groaned in frustration. "My stockings and plaid then."

"They won't help you." His voice washed over her, dark and rumbling and warm. "You require the heat of my skin."

"You—you'll . . ." She wrapped her cold arms around her even colder body. "I don't want you touching me."

"I must."

"I don't know you!" The pitch of her voice rose to a reedy screech.

Wearily, he sank to the edge of the bed. She saw his hand advancing, reaching toward her, but she gathered her strength and flinched away. He sighed. "I won't hurt you."

"How can I know that?" She sounded shrill and panicked, but she was too frightened—and too cold—to care.

"I don't hurt women."

She shook her head. "You—you look like you'd hurt anything that stood in your way."

"Not you," he said flatly.

She blinked at him, and he turned away, busying himself by piling more plaids on her body.

Perhaps she was being stubborn. This Logan Douglas, as solid and intimidating as he was, seemed to have no intention of hurting her. Yet it damaged her pride to know he'd taken her clothes off, had observed her bare form, and then had lain for Lord knew how long with his body pressed against her, both of them stark naked.

Staying in her curled-up position, Maggie forced her sluggish body to turn away from him, a clear signal of dismissal.

"I . . ." His voice was rough. He cleared his throat and tried again. "I wish to help you recover. That's all."

She burrowed more deeply into the blankets, seeking not only their warmth but their ability to hide her body from his dark, compelling eyes. "I'm completely recovered."

It was a lie. Her skin prickled with pain, and shivers continued to ravage her body.

He released a harsh breath. "No. You're pale. Your lips are more blue than pink."

"I'm well," she insisted.

"You are frozen."

"I said I am well." Her tone brooked no argument, but her eyelids felt weighted by steel. She was so, so tired. She couldn't think straight. She needed sleep. Only sleep could warm her.

He tried once more. "Allow me to lie beside you."

"No." It was becoming difficult to speak. "You—you must sleep on . . . on the floor." She sounded rather drunk, though she couldn't remember drinking anything. Had she?

Giving in to the pressure, she closed her eyes.

"You're exhausted."

Finally they could agree on something. "Will you sh-leep on the floor?" she slurred. "Please?"

All her strength had gone. Yet a strange man stood hovering over her. Valiantly, she struggled to open her eyes.

He stared down at her, but instead of the frustration and anger she expected, compassion filled his face.

"I'll keep you safe," he said, his voice low and soothing. "You must rest."

"I . . . Lord . . . so tired." And the cold . . . it hurt.

"You're safe, lass. Nobody will hurt you." The low-pitched words seemed to come from far away. "Sleep."

She'd curled herself into a tight ball beneath the plaids. Her teeth rattled. Logan had never felt so frustrated. She suffered and he could do nothing about it, because she'd ordered him not to touch her.

He lay still, staring at the hearth, his need to help her warring with his honor.

She whimpered.

Hell.

He rose from the hard dirt floor and stood over the bed. Crossing his arms over his chest, he gazed down at her face, the only part of her visible above the plaids. She was so damn pale, it made his gut clench. He could help her. Why hadn't she seen that?

Because she was distraught from her ordeal and not thinking straight. She was terrified of him—he was a man, and obviously a man had recently abused her. That combined with the cold had rendered her insensible. She had panicked.

Once she realized the purity of his intentions, she would understand.

The bed sank under his weight as he settled beside her, slowly sliding under the covers. He pressed his bare chest against her back, and, deep in slumber, she snuggled against him. He caught himself from releasing a sharp breath as his groin reacted to the cool softness of her body wiggling against it.

Slowly—he didn't want to wake her—he slid his hand over her bare hip and closed it around her waist, steeling himself against the chill. God, her skin was so cold. His own heat was a gift he'd gladly bestow.

"Mmm . . ." she murmured. Her teeth had stopped chattering.

He lay in silence, listening to the whisper of the fire and the increasing shriek of the wind, until every inch of her skin was as warm as his own. Then he slipped from under the covers and returned to his makeshift pallet on the floor.

Maggie awoke wrapped in a cocoon of pleasant heat. When she cracked open her eyes, she saw dim light had seeped into the cottage. A fierce wind whistled outside, but morning had arrived, and she felt so much better. So much warmer.

"How are you?" The rumbling voice came from the direction of the fire, and Maggie turned toward it, blinking at the tall figure sitting on a low chair. He swiped something through a bowl of water—a blade, she realized. He'd been shaving. His dark gaze met hers, and heat washed over her cheeks.

"Much better, thank you." Awkwardly, she rose to a seated position, clutching the plaids against her chest. For long moments, she sat in silence, remembering all that had happened as he continued to shave. Finally, she said, "Is it still snowing?"

"Aye."

"You were wrong about me requiring your body heat for warmth. The blankets were more than enough."

He made a noncommittal noise in his throat.

She gazed at the bedclothes that lay in disarray near his feet. "Thank you for sleeping on the floor."

He shrugged and dropped the razor into the water.

"And . . ." She swallowed, suddenly realizing she might have been somewhat harsh to him last night, considering all that had happened. "Thank you for bringing me to shelter. I am . . . very grateful."

Abruptly rising from the chair, he stalked to the bed. On instinct, Maggie cringed backward. He reeled to a halt, every feature in his face turning still as stone. "I told you I would not hurt you."

Breathless, she nodded. "Aye." And she believed him. "But . . ."

A muscle ticked in his jaw. He stared down at her. "You were ill used."

She looked away from him. How embarrassing it was to admit such a thing, yet her bruised body did it for her. There was no need to answer him.

"The bastard raped you."

"No," she breathed. "N-not that." Thank God. Although if Innes had managed to get her wherever he'd planned to take her, he would have raped her, and happily, too. Logan was right to call him a bastard.

"I would never harm a woman," Logan said, his voice tight.

Gazing at the far wall, she clutched the plaid more tightly about her.

He leaned toward her. His fingers brushed her cheek as he pushed away a curly strand of hair that had fallen across her face. Gently, his fingertip touched the tender bruised flesh surrounding her eye.

"Who did this to you?" An edge of steel laced his voice.

She shrugged, still refusing to look at him.

His fingers slid into her hair, and he cupped her cheek in his big, warm palm, forcing her to face him. "Tell me."

"It's over," she said quietly.

But it wasn't over. When she returned home, Innes would continue to pursue her. She doubted anything save death—his or her own—would thwart him. He never stopped, not since the day Duneghall died. And if what he'd said about Torean's involvement was true, she was doomed.

She took a deep breath. She wouldn't think on any of that now. The small victories were all that mattered, all that would continue to matter. If she could win those battles, perhaps in the end she would win the war. She must continue thinking so, otherwise she would lose the war before she finished fighting. And, when it came to Innes Munroe, she'd fight till the bitter end. She took a deep breath and forced her thoughts to return to her little victory.

"I stabbed him in the bollocks with my . . ." Slapping her hand to her bare shoulder, she scrambled onto her knees, looking wildly about. "My brooch! Have you seen it?"

Logan's dark eyebrows drew together as he frowned. "Brooch?"

"It was pinned to my plaid . . ." Wait . . . she'd been clutching it in her fist. She'd held on to it like a weapon as she'd trudged through the deepening snow. "No, I was holding it."

"You were holding nothing."

She shook her head. "No, no . . . I had it. It . . . it was my mother's . . ."

She would not cry. She swallowed hard against the lump building again in her throat.

Awareness dawned, softening Logan's fierce expression. "The sword pin with the bird and the diamond."

"Aye! Not a bird—it's a dragon. And not a diamond, an agate. Where is it?"

"It was lying in the snow a few feet away from you." Logan frowned. "I left it. Once I saw you, I forgot about it."

"I must find it."

Logan nodded. "I'll take you there."

Pulling a plaid over her shoulders, she jumped off the bed and went to her clothes. Everything was still damp.

"Not today, though," he added.

"We must go now," she insisted, though reason told her she couldn't walk anywhere in this weather, at least not until her stockings and shift had dried.

"No. It's snowing too hard, the wind is too strong, it is too cold, and you are still recovering. You must eat. I'll cook something."

"But—"

His eyes narrowed into slits. "You must eat."

Maggie snatched the ends of the plaid around her, closing them over her front, and raised her chin at him.

His gaze remained fixed on hers, but a subtle smile played over his lips. "You know I'm right."

She scowled, resisting the urge to stamp her foot.

He turned away and reached for his shirt, which hung on a peg beside the fire. Muscles rippled across his back, and Maggie stared, fascinated despite herself. When the shirt slid over his broad shoulders, she could no longer see his spectacularly muscled torso. Disappointment washed through her before she ruthlessly thrust it away, reminding herself that this man was a complete stranger.

She continued watching in silence as he rebelted his plaid then folded it over his shoulder and pinned it in place. Two steps took him to the table in the center of the room, and he rifled through the items piled on its top.

"Is this your cottage?"

Busy opening a small sack of oats, he didn't look at her. "No."

"Whose is it, then?"

"I don't know, but I expect him to return once the storm abates." Taking a pot from the table, he strode to the door. When he opened it, a blast of snow and cold whipped through the room. Quickly, he knelt to scoop some fresh snow into the pot and then stepped back inside, closing the door firmly behind him.

His dark gaze speared her. "Tell me if you become cold again."

She was already cold. Keeping her lips pressed firmly together, she nodded.

Kneeling beside the hearth, he hung the pot on the hook over the fire. "What's your name?"

"Margaret MacDonald. Everyone calls me Maggie."

He inclined his head and reached out to her. "Come, Maggie."

Lured by the promise of warmth, she stepped around the bed and sat on its edge, extending her legs toward the flames.

"Why do you think the owner will return?"

He gestured at the table with his chin. "Someone brought supplies in anticipation of his arrival."

"Oh." She gazed at the tabletop, at the bottles of whisky sitting upon it, and realization dawned. This must have been where Innes Munroe had intended to bring her. He'd had it all planned—he'd wanted to take her somewhere isolated so she couldn't escape. So no one could hear her scream. How long had he thought to keep her here?

Until she gave everything to him, no doubt. Her body, her soul. Her independence. A shudder racked her body. In an instant, Logan was at her side. "Cold?"

"No." But the tremble wouldn't go away.

Tentatively, he reached toward her, and when she didn't pull away, he tugged her close, fitting her against the side of his muscular body. This time, she didn't fight him. It was Innes who scared her, she realized, not this man. As big and intimidating as Logan Douglas was, if he'd intended to hurt her, he would have done it by now.

He was, in his harsh, masculine way, attempting to comfort her. To help her.

"Shhh." He patted her head awkwardly, but his touch was gentle and more soothing than she would have expected. "You needn't fear him any longer. I won't let him hurt you."

Logan touched his fingertip to the wound Innes's dagger had inflicted on her chest. The light skin-to-skin contact sent an unexpected prickle of desire rolling through her. Her breath caught, and for a suspended moment, she froze. And then her wits returned in a rush. She jerked away, tamping down the unfamiliar sensation.

She crossed her arms and gazed at the flames licking at the bottom of the pot. Logan sat beside her in silence.

"He thought brutality was the way to win my affections," she murmured eventually, moving her fingers to press over the dagger wound. She slid Logan a glance. "That approach never works with women, you know."

Logan nodded grimly. He didn't try to touch her again. "It doesn't work with anyone."

"He has wanted to marry me since my husband died in a hunting accident five years ago . . ." Maggie sighed. "It seems like forever."

She never spoke of this to anyone, and yet she wanted to tell Logan Douglas, stranger though he was. She forged onward. "His name is Innes Munroe. He's threatened, cajoled, coaxed, but I've refused him again and again. All I want is for him to leave me in peace."

Logan sat stiffly, staring at the fire. His fingers curled into fists. His face was hard, his expression angry. He truly felt protective of her, she realized. But that was absurd—he hardly knew her. Perhaps he was the kind of man who felt it his duty to protect the weaker set.

He spoke through tight lips. "What happened last night before I found you in the snow?"

A renewed shudder rushed through her. "I was asleep, and he and his man kicked in and splintered my door. I tried to fight him, but I . . . couldn't. He was drunk. He took me from my bed, threw me on his horse, and started riding like a madman up the mountain. I"—she sucked in a breath—"I think he intended to bring me here."

She glanced at Logan to gauge his reaction. He scowled down at her, his forehead creased. "Haven't you any men in your clan? To care for you? To look out for your safety?"

"I don't require a man to protect me."

"Of course you do."

She huffed out a breath. "Well, there are men in my family, of course. The MacDonald of Beauly is Torean, my first cousin. However, I've never asked—"

"Why didn't your laird protect you from this Munroe?" The growling threat had returned to Logan's voice.

"He believes I should accept Innes." She shrugged, thrusting away the dark feeling of betrayal that admission brought with it. "At least, that's what Innes said. He said my cousin approved of him abducting me from my home. That it—" Maggie swallowed the bitter taste of bile. "That it was Torean's suggestion."

Logan made a low, menacing sound, and his shoulder muscles bunched.

She shook her head in bemusement. Though it probably should have roused her independent nature and raised her hackles, she found herself lapping up Logan's attention like a starving kitten would a bowl of sweet cream. No one had ever been so protective of her—even Duneghall had left her to her own devices upon sensing her capability to care for herself.

"Why does that distress you, Logan Douglas?" She raised her hand and touched it to the solid bulk of his arm.

"I don't enjoy seeing a woman ill used."

"But you don't know me."

Logan's hard fingers pressed beneath her chin and lifted it until she faced him. "I know you, Maggie. I've lain beside you, flesh against flesh. I'd say I know you well." He lowered his head until their noses were inches apart, and his warm breath washed over her cheek. He stared at her with those deep black eyes, searching, studying. His pupils were dilated, his lips parted. Lord, what beautiful lips he had.

She'd lost every impulse to push him away. In fact, she wanted him close. *Closer.* Her lids descended, heavy from the anticipation of his kiss. As he drew nearer, she leaned into it. They were so close she could all but feel those lips on her. Taking her. Possessing her.

For the first time since she became a widow, she craved a man's kiss. That intimate sharing. That carnal embrace . . .

He dropped her chin. Then he rose and turned toward the fire.

"Porridge is ready," he said gruffly.

Chapter Three

Logan was no good with women. His mother had died when he was a babe, and he'd been raised among men. Women had always been vague, ambiguous creatures to him, mysterious as the kelpies that prowled the depths of the Highland lochs.

Maggie MacDonald wrought all kinds of strange sensations on him. It went beyond his regular befuddlement with her sex. Whenever he set eyes upon her slight frame, a violent protectiveness overcame him. Yet whenever he tried to act on those impulses, she thrust him away. Outwardly, she was as frail and delicate as a flower, but inwardly she was fiercely independent.

He didn't know what to do with her. The more he remained in close quarters with her, the more he wanted to touch her. Beyond that, to tame her. His self-control grew more tenuous by the minute. If he spent much more time in this cottage with Maggie MacDonald, he was going to crawl out of his skin.

Maggie certainly didn't supply any assistance in soothing his tormented thoughts, not with her hot and cold behavior. One moment, she'd brush her fingers over his arm or his shoulders, murmuring how warm he was—and arousing him nearly beyond endurance—and the next, she'd catch herself and put as much distance between them as she could in the small space they shared.

The blizzard raged on, and they sat near the fire through the day, sharing food and ale, and talking. She seemed cured of the effects of exposure to the cold, but bruises had deepened on her face and leg, and a scab had crusted over the area where Munroe had nicked her with a dagger—constant reminders that she'd been wronged. Just a glance at the black smudges circling the delicate skin of her eye was enough to make Logan itch to hunt down Munroe and drive him through with his sword.

Satisfied that she no longer required his body heat, Logan slept on the floor that night. The next morning, snow continued to fall and black tinged the clouds overhead, promising the storm would intensify yet again. The snow alone served as reason enough to stay in the cabin a while longer, yet even if the weather had cleared completely, Logan still wouldn't have taken her home. Though she appeared healed in body, he sensed the distress of her spirit, and he had no wish to lead her into danger.

He couldn't allow her to return to the Munroe bastard, Logan thought grimly as he pushed back from the table and took their breakfast dishes to rinse outside. He must see her home and ensure Munroe wouldn't trouble her anymore. He didn't relish killing, but if he had to kill the man to be certain, that was what he'd do.

Maggie didn't seem anxious to leave the cottage, either. Not to return to her home, in any case. When he'd announced he thought the weather too unpredictable to risk the journey down the mountain, she'd only spoken wistfully of the lost dragon pin that had belonged to her mother.

"How will we ever find it?" she'd murmured sadly. "It's probably buried under a mountain of snow."

It seemed to be all that she was truly connected to, all that she truly cared about, and he'd promised they'd search for it once her clothes had dried.

He stepped inside and went to the fire to warm his hands. Feeling her gaze on him, he glanced back at the table. "What is it?"

She shook her head. "Nothing."

She sat shrouded in shadow, yet light from the fire made her curls sparkle like black gems. She wore a plaid wrapped round her body, and he'd given her the use of his plaid pin so she wouldn't have to grip the edges to keep herself covered.

He lowered himself to the edge of the bed nearest the fire. As soon as he sat, Maggie gasped and hurried toward him, staring at his leg with wide eyes. The plaid had bunched up on his thigh, revealing the half-healed bayonet wound.

"Good Lord in Heaven," she breathed.

He yanked the edge of the plaid down to cover his wound. "It is nothing."

"You've been stabbed!"

"Aye."

"Who?"

"A governmental at Sheriffmuir."

"You are a Jacobite," she breathed.

"Aye." He searched her eyes, wondering whether she was a sympathizer. Many of the MacDonald clans had pledged themselves to the cause, so it didn't seem far-fetched to think she might be for King James.

"My cousin's men were at Preston to fight for James," she murmured, and he released a breath of relief. Logan didn't wish to analyze why her political bent should matter to him; it just did.

"They returned home weeks ago, though," she mused. "That is where you're going, isn't it? Home?"

He nodded.

"Is it because of the wound that you didn't return with the other men?" she asked.

"I lost consciousness during the battle and was captured by the enemy."

"The English?"

"No. The Duke of Argyll's men."

"Och," she murmured sympathetically. To be captured by the English would have been bad enough, but the sheer torture of being captured by one's own countrymen was an experience Logan never wished to repeat.

"I escaped," he said tonelessly. "About a fortnight ago."

"And you have been walking all this time."

He nodded.

Tentatively, she reached for his leg, but he captured her hand in his own. "No."

"I might be able to help."

"There is nothing to be done."

Nevertheless, she lowered herself beside him, and when she reached toward him again, he allowed her to pull up the hem of his plaid. A jagged scab covered part of the wound, but another part oozed clear fluid, and the area encircling it was red, angry, and swollen.

Maggie studied it, her fingers gingerly touching the outside of the wound. "It's going to fester, I think," she said with an edge of horror in her voice.

"It already has."

She didn't answer.

"It is healing now," he said.

She shook her head, seemingly unable to believe him.

"It is not going to kill me."

She glanced up, her fists curling, anger lending a steely gray hue to her blue eyes. "You intend to cheat death by mere force of will, do you?"

"I've done it before."

Maggie blew a coil of hair away from her face. "Foolish man. It requires washing. Then . . ." She glanced around the dim interior of the cottage, her gaze landing on the chest he'd pushed into a corner. She'd already explored its contents to search for something to wear, but had only found men's clothing and boots. "I know what to do. My mother taught me . . ." She broke off, blinking against the shine in her eyes. "I'll tear up some linens for a bandage."

He shrugged as she fetched a pot of snow and hung it over the fire. Then she knelt before the chest. Before long, the room filled with the shrieking sound of tearing fabric.

Finally, she returned to him, stopping at the table to retrieve one of the bottles. She held it up. "Whisky. This bottle is one of Torean's." Her lips twisted wryly. "I daresay Innes Munroe single-handedly keeps my cousin's distillers busy."

He simply watched her.

"I'm going to pour some of it over the wound. It'll hurt like hell."

His eyes widened at hearing such language from someone so refined and petite, but the strength of the word combined with the way she said it was enough to make him believe that she didn't exaggerate in her prediction of the pain she would in-flict.

"Too bad," he murmured. "I thought you'd brought it for me to drink."

Her lips curled as she turned to remove the pot from the fire. She bunched a piece of linen in her hand and dipped it into the hot water. Then she poured a generous portion of whisky into the pot, and Logan whistled out a breath, shaking his head.

"Too bad all this fine whisky must go to waste, eh?"

"Mmm, you read my mind." Though he doubted he was as enamored of whisky as the Munroe bastard.

"It isn't difficult. You're a man, and you think like one."

If she knew that so confidently, did she also know how she drove him to the brink? How hard watching her had made him? Beneath his plaid, his cock ached, begged for relief. It was enough to make him anticipate with relish the forthcoming sting of the whisky on his wound.

She raised the cloth. "You must hold still."

"I hardly think a tiny bit of a woman wielding whisky is liable to move me," he scoffed.

"Don't be so certain—MacDonald spirits make a formidable weapon. But"—she leaned forward and lowered her voice—"here is the family secret: A MacDonald whisky will prevent vile ill humors from attacking your body."

He raised a brow. "Is that so?"

"Aye. Now you must remain very still while I clean the wound."

He grunted and held his leg stiff, every muscle tensed to hold it in place, no matter what she intended to do.

She held the bottle over his leg, then upended it.

"Gah!" he yelled. He managed—just barely—to keep his leg from flailing and kicking her in the face.

He clenched his teeth. Hell, that stung.

She gave him a grim smile. "I told you."

"Just get on with it," he said through a tight jaw.

She bent down, pressed the cloth to the wound and . . . good

God . . . *scrubbed* at it. He curled his fingers, gathering fistfuls of plaids in his hands.

"Tell me about your family," she said, as if to divert his mind from the pain.

His stomach plummeted, and he very nearly groaned aloud. She couldn't know it, but this topic hurt worse than any physical pain she could inflict upon him.

Closing his eyes, he recited the basic information about himself. "My mother died when I was young. I was raised by my father and my older brother. My father died two years ago. My brother and I joined the rebellion this past summer."

"Where is your brother now?"

He fought not to grimace from the pain. "Dead."

Her hands stilled. "Oh, Logan. I'm sorry."

"His wife and children . . ." He paused. It was now his duty to care for his sister-in-law and her three daughters, just as it was his duty to manage his brother's tacksmen and tenants. Determination to do his duty for his lands and people—and the women who were now his only family—was what drove him to first stay alive, then escape from Argyll's men and trudge over two hundred miles north in the dead of winter.

"They are all alone now," she finished quietly.

He should still be moving, Logan realized. He'd already delayed too long. Guilt stabbed at him—he'd scarcely thought about his driving need to rush home since he'd encountered Maggie Mac-Donald in the snow. For the first time since the battle, he'd let go of his single-minded urgency.

Her brow furrowed as she focused on his leg and removed a tiny piece of gravel from his wound.

Maggie had softened him. Her presence had comforted him. Ultimately, he couldn't regret the interruption to his journey home. Seeing to Maggie's safety and well-being was worth the delay of a few days.

Gently, she folded the cloth over his thigh. "Did your brother die at Sheriffmuir?"

"Aye." He closed his eyes against the memory of watching the cannonball tearing through his brother's chest, and a shudder twisted through his body like a screw.

Maggie nodded tightly, then lapsed into silence as she painstakingly cleaned the wound, removing bits of debris he hadn't realized had been embedded in the injury since the battle.

As she worked, Logan studied her hair, her face, the way her lips pursed in concentration. A light sheen of sweat glistened on her forehead. A wee freckle near her left eyebrow disappeared in the crease between her brows when she frowned.

"There!" Rocking back on her heels, she tossed the soiled rag back into the pot. "Now we must give it a few moments to dry, and then I'll wrap it."

He began to rise, but she placed her hand flat on his chest, pushing him back to the bed. She scowled down at him. "What do you think you are doing?"

He gave her a sheepish look. "I could use some of that whisky now, I think."

"You stay right there. I'll fetch it."

She retrieved the bottle from the floor and went to the table to pour some into a cup. He studied her profile. The rounded shape of her jaw, the gently sloping nose. Her unruly hair fell across her face, and she shoved it out of the way as she turned to bring him the cup.

"Thank you." His lips curved up as he took it from her. It was such a rare expression for him, it felt odd, as if he were forced to crack through a thin layer of ice over his face before the smile could form.

She sat beside him and prodded his leg. "Good. It's dry. I'll wrap it, then." Taking a strip of linen from the pile at the bottom of the bed, she began to wind it round his leg.

Logan set his cup on the floor and eased onto his back, lifting his leg from the blanket so she could wrap beneath it. He nearly smiled again as he watched her, for she assiduously kept her eyes on his wound, not allowing them to travel higher to peek beneath his plaid, where his wayward cock, revived after its respite during the wound cleaning, grew more insistent by the second.

She finished wrapping his leg in silence, then went to tend the fire. She was so beautiful. Unconscious, she was the most precious thing he'd ever seen, but from the moment she'd opened those blue eyes and faced him without any semblance of fear, he'd been entranced.

"Tomorrow is Christmas, isn't it?" she said quietly, still facing the flames.

Logan frowned. The days had melded together since he had begun to walk north, but he tried to keep count. "Aye, I think so."

"Today, then, is Christmas Eve, and we don't have a Yule log to burn through the night." She turned to him, her eyes bright. "Nevertheless, we must keep the peat burning until dawn. My mother always insisted upon it when I was a lass, for she said the elves are out this night, and a strong fire is the only way to keep them away."

The way she smiled at him, slightly pensive, slightly wry, made Logan's body tighten all over.

When he'd first brought her in from the cold, he'd stripped her naked. Then, the need to save her had kept his baser impulses in check. As he worked, he'd resisted reacting to the curve of her hip, her narrow waist, the creamy mounds of her breasts. He'd kept his focus on warming her. Nevertheless, as he'd tried to infuse his body heat into her, he couldn't help but revel in the smooth softness of her skin, in her utter femininity. She was soft where he was hard, smooth where he was rough, narrow where he was wide, delicate where he was large.

Now, despite the bruises, she was whole and healthy, and as vibrant as anyone he'd ever seen. Just looking upon her, even clothed as she was in a shapeless plaid, made his blood heat to a boil. And right now, as she gazed up at him, the firelight haloing her head, a light flush drifted across her pale cheekbones and her eyes shone with some emotion—was it longing?

Was it possible she wanted him, too?

Logan nodded gravely. "Aye, we'll keep the fire going. Wouldn't want elves filching the whisky."

She grinned, and blood roared through his veins. Every inch of his skin burned with the urge to touch her.

Tearing his gaze away, he rose and yanked on his jacket, then gathered his plaid over his shoulder without returning his focus to her. If he looked, he didn't know what he might feel compelled to do. He had to get away from her, even for just a few minutes, to soothe the edginess crawling beneath his skin. The perfect excuse came to him as he worked the row of buttons on his jacket. "I must search for your brooch."

"No, you shouldn't. I didn't know about your leg when I agreed—"

"I told you I would search today, and I will," he interrupted her. "Stay inside, and I'll be back before dark."

"No!"

He turned to her, raising a brow.

"I . . . I'll go with you."

"It's too dangerous. It's going to storm again."

She shrugged. "You said the place where you found me wasn't far away."

"It's far too cold to risk it. And your clothes—"

"—are completely dry," she announced, smugly victorious. She yanked her stockings from the ceiling and pulled them on.

Sighing in resignation, he went to bank the fire. By the time he finished, she'd secured her stockings and dropped her shift over her head. Clearly she'd had much practice in dressing before others, for he only caught a glimpse of pale flesh as the plaid fell to the floor and the shift covered her nakedness. She retrieved the plaid and wrapped it around her body, finishing by fastening it with the borrowed pin. Then she strode to the trunk and removed the too-large men's leather boots.

Once she'd finished lacing the boots on as tightly as possible, she rose and smiled at him. "Are you ready, then?"

Logan opened the door and turned his face up into the gently falling snow, allowing the coldness to collide with the heat boiling through him.

Closing his eyes, he prayed for temperance.

The place where Logan had found her looked different in daylight, but from the recesses of her mind, Maggie dredged up the memory of the small, sheer rock bluff that she'd believed would shelter her from the storm.

She stared at the outcropping and shook her head in disbelief. "I must have been mad to think I'd be safe here."

Logan stood a few steps away from her, carrying the shovel he'd found leaning on the outside wall of the cottage. "The cold addled your head."

She wrapped her arms around her body, and Logan turned to her. His expression was guarded. Shuttered. "But you're safe now."

The realization struck her like a brick in the stomach. If it hadn't been for him, she would have died in the snow. She hadn't truly believed it until this moment. She blinked hard. "Thank you."

He shook his head, and a muscle pulsed in his jaw. "I lost your brooch."

"But you saved me." She gave him a tremulous smile. "I suppose that's more important."

She was human, after all. She'd never felt so vulnerable as she did at this moment, staring at the place she might have died if not for the stranger standing nearby.

She studied Logan's stiff, hardened features, tight lips, and dark eyes. He wasn't a stranger anymore. He'd saved her life. He'd suffered war, capture, injury, grief, and imprisonment in the past few weeks, but he'd rescued her from certain death and made certain she recovered from her ordeal. All along he'd listened to her. He'd treated her with respect.

She trusted him.

As she stared at him, she realized she was shaking. It was a deep shiver that originated in her bones.

Logan released a harsh breath, dropped the shovel, and in two long strides, he stood in front of her. Reaching out, he pulled her tightly against his warm, hard body.

She couldn't resist his touch anymore. She didn't want to. His powerful embrace was so welcome, so comforting. She wanted to crawl right into his heat and stay there.

Pressing his lips to the top of her head, he murmured, "You're more important than anything, Maggie."

She stiffened in shock. His words sucked the breath from her, leaving her unable to speak.

Abruptly, he pulled away, taking a step back. A light flush darkened his cheeks, and he cleared his throat. "We should search. Do you remember where you dropped it?"

"No," she murmured, suddenly unable to meet his eyes. "Do you remember where you saw it?"

"I was distracted. I forgot it completely once I saw you," he replied.

"All right. You take the area near the rocks; I'll look here."

Maggie knelt down and began to sift through snow until her fingers were red and numb with cold. She clomped back and forth in the too-large boots, combing the entire area before the bluff. Then she found a stick and dug. After an hour had passed, clouds muted the dull remains of sunlight, and the snow came down in thick flurries. She could hardly see beyond the ridge. Frustrated, she straightened and tramped over to Logan. "This is ridiculous."

He looked up from the deep groove he'd shoveled in the snow. He'd been working hard, and sweat beaded his brow despite the cold. "What do you mean?"

"We'll catch our deaths if we continue. It's hopeless." She clamped her jaw tight, but her lip trembled and a tear slipped from her eye. "Damn it." Angrily, she brushed the moisture away with the back of her hand.

"Ah, Maggie."

She'd never known how much that brooch meant to her, but losing it felt like she was losing her mother all over again. Emotion welled up within her, and then it overflowed. She buried her face in the woolen lapels of Logan's jacket. He dropped the shovel and wrapped his arms around her, enclosing her body in a protective cocoon, and she clung to him and sobbed.

Finally, exhaustion crept through her bones, and she brushed away the last of her tears. Darkness had chased away the last vestiges of daylight, and all was silent in the snowy gloom.

Wrung dry, she looked up at him. "Take me back to the cottage, please, Logan. Let's leave this place."

Chapter Four

Damn it—he'd wanted to find her brooch. With Maggie at his side, Logan strode through the snow in rising frustration, his wounded thigh throbbing. He'd return, search again. It was imperative he find it. The pin was important to Maggie, and therefore it was important to him. He wanted her to have it.

Through the flurries of snow, the cottage came into view, their tiny haven in a dismal, charcoal world. The idea of returning at dusk to a warm cottage and food appealed to him, but the idea of returning with Maggie at his side made an odd feeling flutter in his chest.

"Juniper!" she suddenly announced.

"Juniper?"

"Aye." She gestured at a clump of trees just beyond the cottage. "Every year for Christmas and Hogmanay, we decorate the laird's castle with wreaths of juniper and mistletoe." She glanced up at him. "May I borrow your dirk? I'll cut one small branch to hang from the rafters. Just to remind us it's Christmas."

"Of course. I'll cut one for you."

Her lips twisted. "I'm quite capable of cutting a branch of juniper."

"Nonetheless, I'd like to help."

When they reached the clump of shrublike trees, Maggie chose a long branch heavy with berries, which he sawed off and carried into the cottage. She helped him hang the branch from the center roof beam. Finished with the task, they both stared up at it, inhaling its sweet, woodsy evergreen fragrance.

"Perfect," she announced.

He grinned at her, and this time it came naturally, easily, without having to crack through that layer of ice he'd believed permanently encrusted his skin.

Outside, the storm gathered force. The temperature dropped severely, and wind blasted through the eaves. Within the warm haven of the cottage, Maggie and Logan drank ale and ate a supper of oatcakes and salted beef. Maggie, sitting on the plaid he'd laid before the fire, cocked her head. "Perhaps it will storm through the day tomorrow."

The wistfulness in her words spiked under his skin, and Logan kept his eyes hooded so she wouldn't see how easily she fired his blood. Any indication that she wished to stay longer with him was enough. "Why?"

"A windy Christmas bodes very well for the year, according to my mother."

"Does it?"

"Aye. My mother also encouraged the old laird to burn a *cailleach* on Christmas Eve."

"A *cailleach?*"

"The men would carve a log in the shape of an old woman to represent the Queen of Winter. We would build a great bonfire in the castle courtyard, and everyone would watch the queen go up in flames. As she burned away, so did all the terrible things, like death and poverty and grief, that had occurred during the year. Once she turned to ash, the clan could begin the New Year afresh."

"Your mother was superstitious."

"She was." Maggie sighed. "I miss her."

"When did she die?"

"It's almost ten years now. But I remember her every day. Before she died . . . she told me I must keep strong. Keep to myself and remain independent until I knew I was safe." Maggie gave a small laugh. "I'd no idea what she was talking about."

"But now you do?"

"I . . ." Her voice faltered. "I'm not sure. Perhaps she spoke of a husband who would protect me. But since she died, I've always felt safer on my own than under any man's protection—even my husband's." She paused. "I feel safe with you though."

That silenced him. They gazed at the fire until she turned to him, raising a dark brow. "Don't you have any superstitions up north?"

Logan relaxed against the side of the bed, stretching his legs toward the fire. His leg wound felt better tonight than it had the night before the battle.

"On Christmas day, we eat bannocks with sowens in the morning—" Logan suppressed a grimace. He had never been fond of sowens, for the bitter taste and gelled texture of the fermented mixture of oat husks and meal had never appealed to him. "And in the afternoon, all the clansmen participate in a contest of marksmanship."

She slanted a teasing glance at him. "Do you win?"

"I've been known to win on occasion."

She chuckled. "I'm not surprised."

His gaze fastened on Maggie as a memory swept through him. Last year, he'd won the contest again, and his brother had given him his musket as a prize—the same musket he'd kept through battle and had stolen back from one of Argyll's men before he'd escaped from captivity. On Christmas day after the competition, Logan and his brother had stood in the village square admiring the new weapon, and Mrs. Sinclair, the village's oldest, tiniest, and most eccentric woman, had hobbled up to them.

"'Tis a lovely weapon, indeed," she'd said in her warbling voice when the brothers had turned to her in question. Her small, piercing black eyes looked up at Logan from her wrinkled face. "Ye'll kill with it, no doubt."

Aware of the impending uprising, Logan hadn't doubted it, either. He'd nodded gravely down at her.

She gave him a toothless smile. "Aye. And ye'd best keep it near, too. For it'll lead ye to yer one, and without it, ye'll ne'er keep 'er."

"My . . . 'one'?" Logan had asked, his brows raised in question.

"Aye." Mrs. Sinclair cackled. "Ye canna understand what I'm saying, lad, but soon ye will. Verra soon." And just like that, she'd turned and shuffled away, leaving the brothers staring after her in bemusement.

Was Maggie his "one"?

Logan shook his head as if to fling away the thought. It was nonsensical, for God's sake. His weapon hadn't led him to Maggie; her lost brooch had. He wasn't one to dwell on sentimental and superstitious fancies, much less believe in them.

"What?"

He blinked at her. "What, what?"

"What are you thinking about?"

"Nothing," he said flatly. "Tell me more about your Christmases."

Her eyes flashed, and she scooted closer to him. The curls framing her face danced about as she blew out a breath. "Our family gathers at the MacDonald seat a few days before Christmas. I suppose because it takes a few days to hang all the sweet-smelling boughs and wreaths. And, of course, to cook all the pies and bannocks."

He watched her as she continued, telling him of how her mother brought her and her cousin their sowens in bed on Christmas morning, then how they all gathered in the great hall for a morning feast.

"It hasn't changed much since Torean's father—the old laird—died. But it feels different."

"How's that?" Logan asked.

She sighed. "Torean's intentions are good, but he's very young. His da was healthy as an ox, and he died unexpectedly of an apoplexy a year ago. I don't think Torean was fully prepared for the duties he was forced to take on."

Logan understood. He didn't feel prepared at all for the responsibilities he'd face once he returned home.

"He's far younger than you," Maggie said, as if reading his mind. "He has less experience of the world. I . . . I think that's why he might have been taken in by Innes Munroe."

"They are friends?"

"Aye. They've become good friends in the past few months. I cannot imagine what it is about Innes that Torean finds so alluring."

"Perhaps he doesn't understand the man's nature. It is possible he will learn to better judge others as he grows older. Perhaps he still searches for his wisdom."

A shudder rippled over her shoulders. "I hope so."

The storm raged on, and Maggie and Logan talked long into the night, keeping the fire stacked high with the warming peat. Talking to Logan invigorated Maggie—he actually listened to her, unlike most men, who treated her more as an object than a human.

She realized that not only did she trust him, she liked him.

His smile grew easier tonight. When he smiled, his eyes crinkled at their edges, and when he looked at her with those dark eyes, he really looked. His gaze didn't gloss over her. He observed, he studied, he took her in.

And she took him in, too. The way his shirt fell over his shoulders and showed the bulge of muscle beneath. His perfectly masculine face, his dark eyes and brow, his thick, nearly black shoulder-length hair.

She wanted to rub her cheek against the rough shadow of a beard that had formed on his jaw. She wanted to trace the curve of his bottom lip with her fingertip. And then she wanted to touch him all over. Every dip of every muscle. From head to toe, he was the most beautiful man she'd ever seen. And he looked upon her as though she were the most beautiful woman.

She glanced up to see him focused intently on her.

She shuddered again, and those thick brows snapped together. He glanced from her to the fire and back again. "Are you cold?"

"No."

He cocked his head. "Will you . . . May I?" He reached out cautiously, as if he were frightened she might scurry away at the gesture. But she wasn't afraid anymore. She craved his touch—she had ever since they'd walked out in the snow together. Though she truly wasn't cold, she gratefully snuggled into the crook of his arm.

The contact jerked through Maggie, jolting her all the way to her toes. Simultaneously both of them stiffened and then pulled back.

She stared at him. Had he felt it too?

He gazed back at her, his brows arched in surprise. And then, before she knew what was happening, he cupped her head in his hands and tugged her toward him. He didn't hesitate—his lips descended on hers.

A sharp, piercing need spiraled through Maggie. She wrapped her arms around his neck, sifted her fingers through his soft hair, and pulled him closer. His lips were warm and smooth, but he kissed like a starved man tasting ambrosia. His mouth took hers, possessed it, left her gasping as his erotic touch traveled through her veins and ignited every inch of her skin.

He nipped her lower lip, then soothed it with tender kisses that moved to the corner of her mouth and across her jaw. His lips traveled to her earlobe in a whisper of sensation that made Maggie groan.

Finally he pulled away, grinding his teeth. A muscle quivered in his jaw, and she could almost see him clinging to the taut thread of his control.

He did this for her. Because she'd pulled away from him so often, he wasn't certain of her response. His hesitance served as yet another sign that he was an honorable man.

This was the moment. She swallowed. The wafts of peat smoke drifting through the rafters seemed to pause in suspense. Even the flames of the fire stopped flickering.

If she said no, he'd respect that. He'd stop. But if she said yes, if she asked him to continue . . .

She'd been celibate for five years.

She wanted Logan Douglas. In a way, beyond the original pain and distrust and trauma of her experience with Innes Munroe, she'd wanted Logan from the moment she'd seen him.

Staring at him, she released a slow breath. With deliberate motions, she moved her hands to the pin that closed her plaid. She tossed the pin aside and let the plaid slide down her body to puddle at her bottom. Logan watched her every move with rapt attention.

She rose onto her knees on the mattress and pulled off her shift, revealing her body to him. His dark eyes raked over her, similar and yet different from the first time she'd stood naked before him. The hunger in them made her shiver.

Never breaking his gaze from hers, he rose and stripped off his plaid and shirt in seconds, exposing his magnificent body, marred only by the linen bandage wrapped around his thigh. The flames of the fire cast flickering gold tones over his skin. She'd never seen anyone so well muscled. So broad. And his cock jutted out proudly, spectacularly, in proportion with the rest of him.

"Lord, you are beautiful," she whispered.

He lifted her to her feet and drew her against him, connecting their bodies from head to foot. She pressed her cheek to the hard muscles of his chest. His shaft felt like a brand against her belly. Hard and ready.

He lowered her onto the bed, and then he moved over her to kiss her again, his arms trapping her body. Heat twined around their bodies, wrapping them in a cocoon of warmth. Reaching up, she pressed her hand over his heart. It beat wildly beneath her palm.

He pulled away and stared down at her, wildness flaring in his eyes.

"Logan," she breathed, "why are you shaking?"

He blinked hard, as if trying to return to himself, to restrain himself from allowing instinct to take over and doing what his body—and hers—craved. "I don't want to hurt you."

"Nonsense." Wickedly, she thought she wouldn't mind a bit of pain to heighten the pleasure. She bit her lip, though, too shy to tell him that.

"You are so small."

She swallowed a sigh. "Stop."

He trailed a finger down her cheek. "So delicate."

"No. I'm a strong woman."

"So perfect," he rasped.

She sensed his withdrawal and knew she must stop it. Running her palms over the curve of his masculine chest, she pinched his nipple gently. He clenched his teeth.

"I think you are afraid of me, Logan Douglas."

"No," he growled.

She applied pressure on his arm until he rolled off her, and she quickly rose to her knees, straddling him and pressing her center over his hardness. Her slick folds collided with his burning heat, and they both gasped.

"What is it, Logan? Why do you hesitate?" Emboldened, she leaned down to flick her tongue over his ear. "I'm not going to break." She nipped his lobe.

Beneath her, he shuddered. She glanced down to see he'd clutched the bedcovers in his fists. She wanted those hands gripping her, not the blankets.

She slid her body erotically up and down over him, allowing her breath to whistle out in pleasure. "Yesss," she murmured into his ear. "I want you. All of you. Don't you want me?"

"Maggie," he said, his voice so low she could scarcely hear. "You don't . . . I can't . . . you're a lady . . . too fragile."

She ground her teeth in frustration. She wanted him inside her so badly. Wanted to reach down and place him at her entrance, then lower herself over him. Even more desperately, though, she wanted him to be the one to initiate their coming together. She wanted him to lose himself. Wanted to see that feral light of lust smoldering in his black eyes as he took her.

"Maggie—"

Her lips descended on his, cutting his words short. His lips were so soft, so perfect. She couldn't get enough of him. He was heaven. She slid her tongue over his lower lip, kissed his chin, and traveled downward over his neck, tasting him. He tasted like the Highlands would taste if they were transformed into a man, like heather and peat and fire and snow. She closed her teeth over his flat nipple, and a low growl rumbled up from his throat. But she didn't linger there. She kissed along the light trail of hair leading from his belly button to his groin, and then she pressed her cheek against the long length of him.

"You're so hard," she whispered. "Maybe you do want me, after all."

She blew lightly on his shaft. He held himself rigid, fists clenched in the bedcovers, and she smiled. *Almost.* But not yet. Gently, reverently, she feathered tiny kisses down his silky length. His heat scorched her lips, but it was a heat she gloried in.

She touched him lightly with her fingertips, allowed her tongue to flick over him for a tiny taste. Still he didn't move, but she sensed him unraveling. Traveling to the tip of his cock, she continued peppering kisses over him. Ever so gently, she wrapped her fingers around him and stroked up and down. Just lightly enough to drive him to distraction.

She couldn't keep still. Each time her breasts touched him, she bit back a groan. A fire had built between her legs and there was only one way to douse it.

"Mmm," she hummed over him.

She heard him growl, and satisfaction flooded through her. Before she could kiss him again, strong arms hauled her upward, flipped her onto her back, and pinned her to the bed.

His face was drawn, his lips thinned, and his eyes narrowed. He used his knee to press her legs apart and, without preamble, thrust into her.

Sensation exploded through Maggie. Sweet pleasure with just a hint of pain as her body adjusted to accommodate his size.

Maggie clenched her teeth and contained the scream just in time, for she retained the bit of sense that told her he would instantly pull away thinking he'd harmed her. Somehow she warped the scream of pleasure into a whimper, and she arched up into him, wrapping her arms around him.

He didn't seem to hear her. His nostrils flared as he lowered himself to her, pulled out, and thrust into her again with such force, her body shifted higher on the bed.

"Oh," she groaned, closing her eyes. She needed this. Needed him.

He braced his arms above her shoulders so she wouldn't slide upward, and he surged into her yet again.

Flames whispered in the fireplace, and the cocoon of heat squeezed tightly over them as Logan began a rhythm of hard thrusts, moving in and out of her body with excruciatingly pleasurable force. Within moments, the heat curled through her skin, coalescing to tingle between her legs, constricting her muscles in a tremor that she was certain she wouldn't survive.

She gasped, the air rushing out of her body as he completed every thrust. If she didn't hold on to him, she'd fly apart. So she gripped his bulging shoulders and squeezed her eyes shut as the warmth wrapped around her muscles, coiling tighter. And then it happened. The tense bands of heat snapped, and pleasure exploded within her. Maggie arched against him. Her muscles tensed even more and then shuddered and released, rippling over Logan's cock.

She cried out, clutching Logan even tighter. He was her anchor, the only thing keeping her safely attached to the earth. On the edge of her consciousness, she felt him go hard over her, and he froze, a solid mass of muscle wedged against her womb, as pleasure consumed them both.

Chapter Five

Ages later—or maybe only a few minutes had passed—Logan pulled out of her and slumped beside her. Shame consumed him. Not only had he lost all control and taken her like a heathen, he'd come inside her, risking his seed taking root in her belly. He'd never done that with a woman before. He'd never been so thoughtless.

He ground his teeth and stared up at the rafters. "I'm sorry."

She shifted in the bed, turning to face him. "Why?"

He dragged his gaze to focus on her. There was no reason to beat about the bush. They both knew what he'd done. "I hurt you. I spilled my seed inside you."

She went very still, a frown frozen on her face. She was silent for a long moment. Finally she said, in a lethally quiet voice, "I really want to hit you right now, Logan Douglas."

He stared at her in shock, and then he understood. "Of course you do."

He forced his languid muscles to rise to a seated position at the edge of the bed. He found his shirt on the floor and picked it up. "If there is a child . . ." He sucked in a breath. "I will do whatever you wish, Maggie." Angrily, he brushed the back of his hand over his brow. "Forgive me."

"Stop it!" Rising onto her knees behind him, she slid her arms around him, and it was his turn to freeze. "You silly, foolish man. Stop apologizing."

She slid around his torso to settle on his lap, wrapping her legs around him, and he couldn't avert the surge of arousal her touch elicited. She framed his face in her hands and pulled it down to hers. She kissed him on the lips. "That was exactly what I wanted. What I needed."

"I hurt you," he said stubbornly.

She kissed his nose. "No, Logan." She brushed her lips over his eyebrows. "No. You gave me pleasure." She pressed her mouth against his forehead. "So much pleasure."

"I came inside you," he said, unable to keep the self-condemnation from his voice.

She touched her forehead to his. "I know," she whispered. "I'm sorry for that."

"It's my fault."

"No, it's mine. I pushed you. If I am with child, it is my own doing. It's not your fault."

"I will stay with you until we know."

"That's not necessary. I know you are in a hurry to get home. If there is a child, I can care for it. My clan will help. No one would turn me or the babe away."

"Nevertheless, I will remain until we know. And if there is a child, I will take you north with me."

She pressed her lips to his jaw. "Let's not think about it anymore. There's no point agonizing over a remote possibility."

He pushed his fingers against his temples. Her words hit him like slaps in the chest. Of course she didn't want to discuss leaving her clan to come home with him. The truth shouldn't surprise him. She was a MacDonald, and these mountains were her home, not the flat wildlands of the northernmost part of Scotland. It was ludicrous to expect her to leave everything she'd ever known for a mere stranger she'd been trapped with in an abandoned cottage.

Further, she was the MacDonald laird's cousin, and he doubted that MacDonald would sacrifice his kinswoman to a man from so far who possessed comparatively little. A match between Logan and Maggie would do nothing for her clan.

Groaning to himself, he wrapped his arms around her and crushed her against him, burying his face in her hair. "I'm a brute."

"Aye." She pressed her cheek against his chest. "And that's just how I want you to be. If you were any other way, I wouldn't—" She broke off abruptly, and he cocked his head in question. Glancing up at him, she gave him a half smile. "I wouldn't like you nearly as much as I do. I feel utterly secure with you."

Confused as hell, he frowned. She made no sense. "How could you say you feel secure with me when I treated you no better than that Munroe bastard?"

She went stiff in his arms, and fire flared in her blue eyes. "You're nothing like Innes Munroe. Nothing!"

"I was rough with you, as he was. And worse, I took it further."

"No, Logan!" She pounded a little fist against his chest, and he looked down at it in surprise. "You were rough, but it was . . . it was . . . exquisite roughness. It was perfect." She made a grating noise of aggravation. Her hands flew upward, and she took hold of his shoulders and tried to shake him. "Listen to me."

He stared at her, perplexed. She was so . . . He didn't know. He just knew he'd never met a woman like her. Never met a woman who made him *feel*.

"I have never really desired roughness . . . but just now, with you, I wanted it. And I was right. . . . It felt . . . well, I've never felt anything like it. I've never gone . . . felt . . . that explosion . . . that peak . . ." Her voice dwindled, and she looked away, frustrated, her lips so taut they turned pale.

He widened his eyes in amazement. She'd never experienced an orgasm before. He couldn't prevent the male satisfaction that flooded through him at that admission. He gathered her tight against him, fighting the prideful grin doing its best to split his face.

"It's never felt so . . . *good*," she finally said on a sigh. She reached up to touch his face. "Now do you understand?"

"Aye." He pressed his lips into her hair. "But it still doesn't change the fact that I might have given you a child."

She leaned against him, her cheek against his chest, and they sat in comfortable silence for a while. Logan ran his hands up and down her spine, allowing the odd feeling of contentment to flow through him.

Finally, she took a deep breath. "When I was married to Duneghall, I prayed for a babe."

"Did you?" he murmured.

"In our fifth month of marriage, I discovered I was with child."

Logan fought the stiffening of his muscles as some emotion he couldn't decipher clawed at his chest.

"But," she continued, "I lost the babe a few weeks later. And then, before the midwife said I was healthy enough to try again, Duneghall was killed."

A sudden, hot burst of possessiveness nearly overwhelmed him. He wished she'd never been married. He hated that another man had her first. If he'd known her then, he never would have allowed it.

He slammed the lid on those roiling emotions as quickly as they'd flared within him. Those were thoughts he shouldn't be having. He and Maggie were from different clans from different regions. They led separate lives. He couldn't let his feelings for her stand in the way of the responsibility that had been his sole focus since he watched his brother die.

He wasn't even certain she felt anything but a temporary carnal attraction toward him.

He laid her on the bed and tucked the covers around her. Vulnerability softened her oval face and his heart tightened. Leaning over her slight form, he stroked her cheek with the back of his finger. "I'm sorry you lost a child."

She gazed up at him with shining eyes. "I still feel sad sometimes, but it was long ago."

He glanced back at the hearth, remembering it was Christmas Eve. "I should stoke the fire."

"Aye." She smiled. "We must keep the elves away."

As he stacked another block of peat on the dwindling flames, she asked, "Why haven't you married?"

He shrugged. "I never felt compelled to. My brother was the heir, and he married young."

"Does he have sons?"

"No. Three daughters."

"So you were his heir, and his holdings are now yours."

He nodded. Logan had always coveted his independence. He'd never wished for his brother's many responsibilities, but now that they were his, he wouldn't shirk them.

He turned back to Maggie. There was a chance that she could be carrying *his* heir. Yet another newfound responsibility, but not one he wished away, he realized with no small measure of surprise.

He wanted her beside him. He never felt so *right* as he did with Maggie MacDonald.

He hesitated, staring at her flushed cheeks, the contrast of her black hair against her pale skin. She roused him in every way. He wanted to lie beside her, and yet . . .

"Come to bed," she said quietly.

"You don't wish me to sleep on the floor tonight?"

"No."

He moved onto the bed and turned on his back, staring at the ceiling with his hands clasped behind his head.

"You were so cold that first night after you awoke," he murmured.

"Aye, I was."

"After you fell asleep . . ."

She lay very still, waiting for him to continue.

"I lay beside you for a while. I couldn't let you suffer," he said. "Not even in sleep." He turned to her, and when he saw the understanding in her expression, relief washed through him.

"I needed your warmth, but I was too proud and too afraid to admit to it."

He turned back to face the ceiling beams, staring up at the wisps of smoke gathering in the thatch.

"I dreamed about it, you know," she murmured.

"Did you?"

"Aye. I dreamed that someone was near, keeping me safe and warm. It felt so right, in my dreams. In life, though . . . well, I spurn such closeness, even from people I know. I'm accustomed to being on my own, you see."

"As am I."

"Nevertheless . . ." Her voice dwindled and she tried again. "I find I like the feeling of you lying beside me. It's . . . comfortable."

"Aye," he agreed.

"It feels safe." She made a small noise of confusion. "It's an odd feeling."

He gazed up at the ceiling in complete understanding. "Aye."

They lapsed into a companionable silence, comfortable and warm, the lengths of their bodies touching lightly as they lay side by side.

"Did you love your husband?"

Logan frowned, wondering where the hell that question had come from, and why he'd asked it. He didn't even want to know the damned answer. He gave himself a mental smack on the forehead and spoke in a tight voice. "Forgive me. You don't have to respond."

"It's all right," she said. "I did love him, but I was very young. I think of love differently now."

"How old were you?"

"Nineteen when he died. Eighteen when we married."

"Ah." That made her about twenty-four. Five years younger than he was.

"I've changed since then, I suppose." She laughed softly. "I never imagined I could enjoy roughness in a man . . . but you're rough all over, and I like it in you."

He cut a sidelong glance at her. "Is that so?"

"Duneghall was very kind and tender with me, always . . . But perhaps that's why I never . . ."

Her flush flared crimson in the firelight, and it was beautiful. He pressed his lips to where the red slashed over her cheekbone.

"Bonny Maggie," he said against her skin.

Something—a hint of mischief, perhaps—flickered in her eyes, and she turned the conversation around abruptly. "What about you? Have you taken many lovers?"

"Er . . ." He pulled back. "That is not something most women wish to know."

"I do."

"Not so many, and none . . . none I would have married."

She turned to face him, her brows drawn together in confusion. "Why not?"

Because they weren't you. Banishing that thought, he shrugged. "They didn't want commitment from me, nor did I wish for it from them. They were lasses to warm a man on a cold night . . . not to spend a lifetime with."

"I see." She looked thoughtful.

It was difficult to keep from touching her. Whenever she was close, his fingers itched to feel her skin against his own.

"You make me feel so . . . different."

He cocked his head. "What do you mean?"

"Different from how anyone has ever made me feel." She paused. "Special."

She was special. The most special, precious thing he'd ever seen. Raising his hand, he fingered one of her soft curls, then brought it to his lips and kissed it. He pulled it straight and released it, fascinated by how it bounced back. She watched him, her lips tilted in a soft smile.

Tenderly, he touched her plump bottom lip with his fingertip. He trailed his hand across her red-splashed cheekbone and down her nose, marveling at how it turned up slightly at the end. Then he gently traced her bruised eye and her arched, dark eyebrows. Finally he pressed his lips to the freckle between her brows.

She lay passively, studying him, the expression in her blue eyes unfathomable. He continued his exploration with his lips, moving around her hairline to her rounded jaw and then over the soft, silky skin of her neck. As he slid his lips over her collarbones, brushing over the scab between them, her hand tangled in his hair.

He moved on, allowing his eyes to drift closed, glorying in the taste and scent of her. She smelled fresh, like the forest after a rain, and she tasted like sweet cream. His lips drifted lower, and he opened his eyes as his mouth grazed the side of her breast. The pale round globes flushed wherever he touched them, and he touched them all over. Kissed them and loved them before closing his mouth over the taut berry of one of her nipples.

Gasping and shuddering beneath him, she whispered, "Logan, oh . . ."

He nipped gently, grazing his teeth over the peak, and she squealed. Suddenly tense all over, Logan raised his head to look at her. "Did I hurt—?"

Growling at him, she yanked his head back to her breast. "More," she demanded.

He gave her more. He worshipped her breasts, licked them, teased, nipped, and suckled until she writhed beneath him, groaning his name over and over.

He slid his hand between her legs and was gratified to feel her slick and ready.

"Turn over," he said hoarsely.

She flipped onto her belly, and his breath caught at the sight of her backside. Her spine dipped just above her curved pale buttocks, its top marked by two deep dimples. Her legs were slender, shapely, perfect. He ran his hands down her back, over her rounded arse, down the backs of her thighs, reveling in the smooth, supple texture of her skin. And then he followed his movements with his lips.

She trembled everywhere he touched her, as though the sensitivity of her skin had heightened a thousandfold.

He couldn't get enough of her. He could touch her like this forever. But his cock had grander ideas. It was stiff as steel, and at its base, a tumultuous ache had begun to boil up from his balls.

"On your knees," he rasped.

Again, she obeyed him immediately, rising on legs that shook like a newborn foal's, her pale skin flushed all over, as pink and soft as a peach. He bent over her, moved aside her hair, and kissed her neck as he thrust home.

Sweet heat wrapped around his cock, squeezing him so tightly, he had to grind his teeth and curl his fists into the blankets to keep from coming as soon as he was fully seated inside her.

"Ah, Maggie," he ground out. In response she arched her back and wiggled, driving him even deeper.

Instinct took over. He took her, deep and hard. Heat traveled through his extremities, deep, boiling through him, exerting a pressure so intense he had to close his eyes. Rearing up, he wrapped his hands around her waist and yanked her against him with every thrust. She helped him, slamming her weight back so they joined so intimately he couldn't tell where she ended and he began.

"Logan," she cried. Her back arched, and after the next drive he made into her, she stilled and then began to shake. A sobbing noise emerged from her, but her shake transferred to him in gut-wrenching spasms that made him shudder all over. His entire being centered in the pulsing pole between his legs and then exploded, flooding her with his soul, with his life.

When it finally began to subside, they both went boneless. She slid to her stomach, and he fell over her, only at the last second shifting as some part of him remembered not to crush her with his weight.

Sometime later, Maggie sighed and wiggled her bottom.

"Uncomfortable?" Logan sounded nearly unconscious.

"No," she murmured. "Just wanted to look at you a while."

He shifted to allow her to move, and she turned to her side to gaze at him in the flickering firelight. Outside the cottage, the wind made something flap against the stone exterior of the cottage, making a rattling noise.

"When do you think the storm will end?"

"Can't storm all winter. A day or two longer most likely."

"Then what?" she whispered. Emotion thinned her voice, and she realized she didn't want to leave this place. She didn't want to leave him. She didn't want him to leave her.

He paused for a long moment. Finally he answered, in a voice as low and thin as her own, "Then I will take you home."

Chapter Six

They delayed longer than they should have, Maggie knew. It had been a full twenty-four hours since the last snowfall. They'd been at Innes Munroe's cottage for nearly a week now—the last four days spent almost solely in bed talking and making love until both of them were sore and languid, drunk with pleasure.

Two days before Hogmanay, the sun shone high and bright in the sky. Maggie stood in the doorway, staring out at the springlike scene. Melting snow dripped from the eaves, each drop twinkling like a gem in the glare of the sun.

Logan came up behind her and rested his hands on her shoulders. She glanced back at him.

"We must go down the mountain today," he said quietly. "Your family will be worried for you. They'll be searching."

She raised her hand to cover one of his. "I don't want to go."

"Nor do I. But we have families. We have duties. Both of us."

"Aye," she agreed. Yet his duties far outweighed her own.

Logan had said he'd take her north with him, but that was only out of duty should she be carrying his child. That was no longer a possibility, for her lack of pregnancy had been confirmed this morning by the onset of her flux.

Not once had Logan suggested she travel north with him because he wanted her. It was foolish to hope that he would ask her to go with him. He had a family to care for and lands to govern. Maggie knew he liked her, but perhaps he saw her as a distraction from his new responsibilities. Nevertheless, a large part of her craved to hear him say he wanted her at his side.

He was an honorable man, a just man, and he simply intended to see her home safe before leaving to shoulder the burden of his new duties. She couldn't fault him for that, and she had no right to demand anything of him.

She was the laird's cousin, but she belonged to no one, and she hadn't wanted to . . . until now. Her friends and neighbors had called Maggie daft for preferring to be alone over marrying again. But she'd been repulsed by the idea, for she knew no one who struck her as remotely marriageable, so she had stretched her mourning for Duneghall for as long as she could.

She traced her fingers over Logan's thick, long ones. The thought of separating from him forever terrified her, but he did need to return to his sister-in-law, his nieces, and his tenants. And because she wasn't carrying his child, he *would* leave her. Soon.

Sighing, she shut the door, turned, and wrapped her arms around him.

They set out late in the morning. The sun hung in the sky as if suspended from strings, bathing the pristine white slopes in a golden wash. They paused to search the spot where she'd lost her brooch for another hour, to no avail; then they descended the mountain, walking into the late afternoon.

The sun brushed against the treetops when they glimpsed the

shimmering walls of the MacDonald castle through the leafless tree limbs in a deep-cut ravine below. The Christmas storm had reached the lower altitudes, and the roofs of the cottages surrounding the castle appeared sugar-coated and homey, with puffs of smoke curling from their chimneys.

They'd been silent for the better part of an hour. Logan had walked away from the happiest week of his life and now steamed with regret that they'd had to leave the cottage. If only they could have remained there forever.

Dreams never lasted, though. Duty called both of them home, and neither he nor Maggie would shirk their responsibilities to their respective clans.

Logan studied the MacDonald seat as they approached. It was a six-storied multiturreted castle built in the last century, compact and tall in comparison to its crumbling ancient counterparts. Sunlight reflected off its granite walls and sparkled on its steep slate roofs, sending glimmering light cascading over the more mundane thatched structures scattered nearby.

As Logan and Maggie strode along the shoveled path leading down the final stretch of mountain, a rider appeared in the distance. Two other men on horseback followed not far behind. Logan's fingers tightened on the barrel of his musket, but within moments, the lead man's angular features came into focus, and Maggie gasped.

"It's Torean," she whispered.

"Maggie!" the man shouted, recognizing her. He spoke to his horse, urging it to a canter. Logan gazed warily at the men as they approached. Reining short, Torean MacDonald smoothly dismounted. The other two held back, remaining seated on their stomping, impatient mounts.

"Maggie!" the man cried again. He gripped her shoulders and

gave her a small shake as if to test whether she was an apparition. His eyes grazed over her partially undressed form and the too-large leather boots. "My God, Maggie. I thought you were dead."

"Is that what Innes said?" she asked dryly.

"Aye. Well, he returned just two days ago, saying he'd been searching for you . . ." His voice trailed off, and his blue eyes skittered away, coming to an abrupt stop as they fixed on Logan.

"This is Logan Douglas," Maggie said. "He . . . saved me. Took me in near frozen from the snow. Logan, this is my cousin, Torean MacDonald."

Logan inclined his head at the laird but didn't speak. He could see the family resemblance to Maggie in the dark hair, blue eyes and shape of the jaw, but Torean MacDonald was tall where Maggie was slight, with stick-straight hair and an overlong face in the shape of an exaggerated oval. He had an awkward, gangling look about him, as if he hadn't quite finished growing into his adult features.

"Where are you from?" MacDonald asked.

"Near Wick," Logan returned easily enough. "I'm on my way home from Sheriffmuir."

The young man continued to assess him, his head tilted slightly. "You were captured at Sheriffmuir?"

"Aye."

"And you escaped from the governmentals?"

"I did."

"Well done!" MacDonald gave him a sharp nod and glanced at Maggie as if suddenly remembering her presence. "And I thank you for caring for my cousin. I should be honored if you would join us for a night before you continue on your journey home."

"Thank you," Logan said, though he would have stayed whether invited or not. He had no intention of leaving Maggie before he confronted the Munroe bastard.

Clapping his gloved hands, Torean returned his attention to Maggie. "Come, cousin. I'll take you home."

He held his hand out to her, but she merely stared at it, hesitating. "Torean"—she looked up at his face, a deep frown furrowing her brow—"did you sanction what Innes did? Did he take me from my cottage on . . . on your suggestion?" Her voice wavered, but she held firm, and Logan gazed at MacDonald to assess his reaction.

Torean's blue eyes darted to Logan, then fixed on his cousin. "This isn't the time to discuss it, Maggie. Come. Why, you're half naked, and those boots—"

Maggie's fists clenched at her sides. "We will discuss it now. I'll not be moving until we do."

The man released a sigh. "Very well. Aye, I told him he should take you, but—"

"You bastard!" She flew at him, her little fists pummeling at his chest. Logan crossed his arms and watched, prepared to cut in to protect her should this fool make a move to hurt her.

He didn't. MacDonald merely plucked her away from his body and held her at arm's length as she kicked at his shins. "You foolish, stupid idiot!" She stomped on his booted foot. "This is your fault! He tried to rape me—do you know that, Torean? How could you encourage such a brute? He . . . he hurt me."

"Oh, come now," MacDonald soothed. "He can't be so very bad. Surely you're exagger—"

"He's a despicable worm," Maggie spat.

"He was distressed when he lost you. He's been roaming the countryside for days searching for you—"

"Nonsense! He was in a warm bed tupping whores at Malmuirie's."

Torean frowned in apparent confusion. "He has been so distraught, Maggie. He'll be so happy—"

"Happy?" Maggie gasped. "It is because of him I was in danger to begin with."

Torean stiffened, and his voice hardened. "He's my friend and my tacksman. And he's a perfect match for you."

"He's a loathsome brute, and I will die before I allow him to touch me again!"

Torean released a breath through pursed lips. He glanced at Logan, clearly discomfited by the personal nature of this conversation in the presence of a stranger, and then returned his gaze to his cousin, lowering his voice. "We need this match, Maggie. We need to keep the clans tightly connected, especially with—"

Logan took a step toward them. "Did you hear what she said?" he snarled. "The man hurt her."

Torean's gaze shot back to Logan. "This is a family matter. Surely none of your—"

"I saw what he did to her," Logan said icily. "Look at her eye, for Christ's sake. There is also a dagger wound to her chest, and her leg was so badly bruised she could scarcely walk."

Torean's lip curled. "My cousin can be rather feisty. I daresay it's likely Innes's actions were more a result of self-defense than violence."

Maggie gasped. Her eyes gleamed, but her face went utterly pale. She smacked Torean so hard on the shoulder that he stepped backward, frowning, and raised his hand to rub the area.

"How could you say that?" she asked in a low, hurt-filled voice.

"I won't let it happen again," Logan said, his voice quiet and grim. "I'll see the man dead before I allow him to hurt her."

Torean turned his assessing gaze on him once again. "Who are you, exactly?"

"Logan Douglas."

"He's a laird of several thousand acres granted to his ancestors by King James II," Maggie provided.

Logan fought a flinch. It was unsettling to hear her proclaim his status in order for her cousin to treat him with a measure of respect when less than two months ago he'd owned nothing. Yet it was the way of the world. A man's worth was measured by the land he owned and the number of cattle he kept.

Logan narrowed his eyes at Torean MacDonald, who possessed far more than he did, but thus far had done nothing to earn his respect.

"Is that so?" Torean fingered his smooth chin thoughtfully, as if to pretend it was as bearded as a wise old man's. "And you'll cause bloodshed on my lands to keep my man from marrying my cousin, even though I have already signed the betrothal documents?"

Maggie groaned. "Oh, Torean. You haven't!"

"I have." Again the young laird fixed his gaze on Logan. "Well?"

"I will do whatever is necessary to protect your cousin." He'd kill Innes Munroe without a shred of guilt or regret, if that kept him from hurting Maggie.

"Hmm." Torean tapped his chin, and then his expression slowly transformed until excitement flared in his eyes. "Hogmanay is in two nights. The clan has gathered. I daresay everyone would enjoy a little sport."

"What are you suggesting?" Suspicion clouded Maggie's face.

Torean shrugged. "Well, if this stranger chooses bloodshed, I must at least ascertain it is honorable, controlled bloodshed."

"Torean—"

"A duel," the laird pronounced. He turned to Logan. "What say you?"

Logan shrugged. "I'm prepared to do what's necessary to keep Maggie safe."

"Looks like you have a champion, cousin."

Maggie looked from one man to the other in exasperation. "For heaven's sake, no. Absolutely not. Hell will freeze over before I'll allow Innes Munroe to touch me again, so not only is this an absurd idea—it is a meaningless one, too."

Logan disagreed. In fact, he thought it the ideal solution. He could stop Munroe honorably, without rousing the enmity of either the MacDonalds or the Munroes. The MacDonald clan was a powerful one, one that he'd rather keep on his good side.

"Logan . . ." She'd correctly gathered that he was serious, and a hint of panic edged her voice. "What are you thinking?"

"I'm thinking of your safety."

She blew out a breath through pursed lips. "What of yours?"

"What of it?"

"He could hurt you, you fool! Kill you!"

He raised a brow. "Do you think so?"

"Ugh!" She stomped her booted foot in the wet snow. "You are utterly arrogant."

Torean chuckled. "It'll be wonderful sport, Maggie. Just think of it—everyone will be there to watch. We need the extra inspiration, you know that, after the failure of the rebellion. It'll be a fine distraction."

She crossed her arms over her chest. Steam puffed from her mouth with each breath. "Your 'friend' could be killed, too, Torean, and all you think of is sport and distraction. Men! I shall never understand any of you."

She pulled her plaid tight and stomped off down the path, forcing the two waiting men to move their mounts aside as she barreled through them, kicking up flurries of wet snow in her wake.

Logan exchanged a glance with Torean and then made to follow her, but Torean clasped his arm and pulled him back. "Let her go, man. She's in a fit of righteous rage, something every man should avoid at all costs."

Logan stared after her. Hell. He didn't want her to go. Would he ever see her again? Hold her again?

Yes. Damn it, yes.

Torean grabbed his horse's reins and then turned back to Logan, chuckling. "You look like a man in need of a pint. Come, I'll walk to the tavern with you. We've good ale here."

Chapter Seven

The morning of Hogmanay dawned clear and bright. A warm sun had melted the snow, swelling the river that curved behind the castle and turning it into a brown tempest. Dampness gleamed on the barren stalks of trees and shrubs, and churned mud covered the common areas between the castle and its outbuildings. The castle women had woven rectangular wicker flats, and the men had laid them over the deepest, wettest areas so people could walk in the courtyard without sinking to their shins in mud.

Maggie had awakened early in the guest chamber she always used when visiting Torean; it was a small, cold, stone-walled room high atop one of the turrets. Deep red-and-brown tapestries draped the walls, and a similarly colored thick carpet covered the floor from one rounded wall to the other. The bed was wider and softer than her bed at home, and the window, though narrow, was nearly as tall as she. It looked over the courtyard below, which had filled early with workers erecting the stage where Innes and Logan would duel.

A servant woman patiently worked through the tangles in Maggie's wild hair while she stared out the window, gazing down at the arena upon which her future would be determined.

Freedom or slavery. She wished she had the power to make that choice for herself. Or, if not that, she wished she were strong enough to duel Innes herself.

Maggie flattened her hand over the narrow pane of glass. Despite her misgivings about the entire affair, she thanked God for Logan. If not for him, she'd have no hope at all. Torean and Innes would have already forced her to submit to their will.

The duel would take place before the noonday meal. Once the bloodshed was over, the MacDonalds would tumble back into the castle to eat and drink and be merry. No matter the outcome, they'd continue to celebrate long into the night, and they'd awake to a New Year with rolling stomachs and pale complexions.

Maggie didn't fear Logan would lose. He was a pillar of strength compared to Innes Munroe. Taller, more muscular, and certainly he possessed more experience in battle. Yet last night at dinner, Innes didn't look the least bit nervous. In fact, he'd boasted of his imminent victory. Did that mean he possessed a skill with swords Maggie didn't know about? His confidence made her feel uncomfortable and edgy, as though she might jump out of her own skin.

A knock sounded on the thick planks of her door, and Maggie looked up in surprise. People didn't often venture up this far. The reason she'd chosen this room so long ago was for its comparative privacy in the bustling environs of the castle.

As she turned from the window, the servant bustled to answer the door. When she swung it open, Logan's body instantly overwhelmed the tiny space.

Frightened by his towering presence, the woman stepped aside, her eyes wide. Logan didn't seem to see her at all. His eyes met Maggie's and his low, rumbling voice washed over her. "Good morning."

She couldn't prevent the flush of heat that washed through her from being in such proximity to him. "Logan . . ." *I missed you.* But they'd only spent two nights apart, hadn't they? It seemed like an eternity. "Why are you here?"

"I wished to see you."

"Ah." Glancing at the woman, Maggie gave her the signal to go. Logan stepped inside, and the servant slipped past him and disappeared. Logan shut the door behind her.

The heat curling through Maggie intensified, prickling her skin and tightening her cheeks. She looked down to her bare toes, curling them into the thick strands of the carpet.

"You look beautiful."

She glanced at her dress—a red tartan borrowed from a castle resident. "Half the population of the Highlands will soon know you were in my room," she murmured.

"It doesn't matter." His rugged palm cupped her cheek, tugging her gaze upward.

The words she'd kept bottled up for the past two days rushed out of her. "Why, Logan? Why are you doing this? I—I don't want you to do this for me. I don't want you to fight."

"Do you fear my death? Munroe cannot kill me, Maggie."

"It's not that . . ."

"And I have agreed not to kill him, either. We have decided that it won't be a battle to the death. I will win, and as a condition of the duel, Innes Munroe will swear to keep his distance from you forever."

"It's not that, either! I still don't want you to fight for me."

The smile slipped from his lips to be replaced by a confused frown. "Why?"

"It is not your duty to protect me."

"Munroe cannot be allowed to hurt you again."

Before she could stop it, a frustrated groan emerged from her throat.

"Why are you angry with me?"

Her hands flew upward. "I'm not angry with you!"

"What, then?" His thumb brushed over her cheekbone, sending a thousand tiny shivers down to her toes.

"I want . . . I wish I could defend my own honor."

"You're a woman—"

"It's not right that I should have to depend upon you—a near stranger—to defend what ought to belong to me and me alone."

He dropped his hand, and his eyes darkened as his gaze bore into her, seeming to seek her very soul. "Is that what I am to you, Maggie? A stranger?"

She stared at him for a long moment. The intensity of his expression sucked the air from her lungs. "No," she admitted finally. "Though it has been such a short time, just over a week . . . I feel . . . I know you." She cocked her head and stared at him, trying to decipher her own emotions. "I feel—" Her voice cracked midsentence and, clutching his sleeve, she tried again. "I feel so strongly for you, Logan. How is that possible?"

In a way, she understood, even though a part of her continued to be perplexed by the strength of her feelings. She'd been shut up with Logan every minute, every hour, every day for the last week. Never during her years with Duneghall had she spent so much concentrated time with him, nor had either of them really desired to. They lived their own lives apart from each other. Even at home when they were physically close, there had existed a nearly tangible separation between them. She realized now that she'd never truly given him her trust. Or her heart.

With plenty of food and little else to do, she and Logan had shared their most intimate secrets, body and soul. She'd never been happier.

Logan's big arms wrapped around her, and his lips descended on hers, warm and soft as ever. His fingers slid up her spine and then down again to rest at the small of her back. She reached up, plunged her hands into his soft black hair, and pulled him to her.

Maggie had kissed a man or two in her life. But nobody's kiss was as soft and gentle as this, bestowed on her by the most forbidding warrior she'd ever laid her eyes on.

"I want to be responsible for you," he whispered against her lips. "I want to be the one to defend your honor, Maggie. To keep you safe." His lips traveled to her ear and brushed over the lobe. "You're mine, Maggie MacDonald. Mine to love. Mine to protect."

Something sweet but dangerous buzzed through her like a honey-covered bee. Did he wish to care for her now? Just temporarily, until he'd done away with the threat Innes Munroe posed? Or did he mean forever?

Lord, how she wished it could be forever.

She slid her fingers from the back of his head, over his jaw and down to his chest. His heart beat furiously against her fingertips.

His palms moved down her sleeves until he gathered her hands in his own. He gazed intently down at her. "Being apart from you for just two days has been torture. I want you beside me, Maggie. Forever. After the duel is over, come home with me."

She stared at him, wide-eyed. The comprehension of what he'd just asked slammed into her with such force that her knees wobbled. And with it came the accompanying knowledge that beyond anything she had ever desired in her life, she wanted to follow him north. She wanted to leave the MacDonalds behind. Logan's home was far away, but it didn't matter. Anywhere with Logan would be home to her.

There was nothing left to keep her connected to the clan she'd been born into—not anymore. Everyone she'd loved was gone. Well, except for Torean, who'd so easily offered her to Innes Munroe without a thought to her happiness.

Still, a tight little band of resistance remained, squeezing at her heart.

"But if you lose, Torean will—"

"I won't lose."

"Tell me," she pressed. "What if you lose? What will happen then?"

"If I were to lose—and I *won't*—I would be forced to leave without you."

She studied his sparkling, narrowed eyes. And at that moment, she knew the truth, and her resistance snapped. "You'd abandon me to Innes."

She didn't mean it as an accusation, but as a statement of fact. No matter what, Logan would be true to his word. If he won, he'd happily take her as his trophy, but if he lost, he'd walk away as he'd promised. Having suffered the attentions of Innes—the most dishonorable man she'd ever known, a man who'd lie, cheat, and steal if it served his goals—this proof of Logan's nature solidified her respect for him.

He, however, took her words as accusation. His features stilled, turned hard as the castle's granite walls. "I am *not* going to lose."

Of course, he was right. He wouldn't lose a duel with Innes Munroe. He couldn't. He was so much more than Innes, inside and out.

He would win, and when he did, he wanted her with him. Beside him.

"Aye," she whispered, looking into his eyes. "Take me home with you, Logan. I want to be with you forever."

Innes and Logan faced each other on the quickly erected stage, their seconds standing a few paces behind them. The population of the castle crowded the courtyard, pressing in against the ropes delineating the edges of the fighting area. Maggie stood beside her cousin at the center of one of the ropes. Extended family members and clansmen pressed in on them on all sides. The atmosphere was raucous, most of the onlookers already half drunk and ready for a bit of fine entertainment.

As Logan's second, Donald MacDonald, stepped forward to finish strapping on his scabbard, Logan made a final once-over of his enemy. He had no inclination to waste time. He didn't doubt that he could overcome the pasty-faced, pockmarked, flabby man in rapid fashion. This assessment had nothing to do with boastfulness and everything to do with the truth of the situation. Logan and Munroe were completely mismatched.

He would finish the duel quickly. Then he and Maggie would leave this place. The thought of returning home with her by his side fortified him, made him more impatient than ever to go.

In the spring, they'd be husband and wife. Maggie would be the lady of his house. And by spring, Maggie might be carrying his child. His son.

Before he'd met this woman, he'd avoided any and all thoughts of marriage. His brother had teased him that he'd be a bachelor for life, a state that sounded perfectly agreeable to Logan. Not only had the female sex generally discomfited him, but he had no responsibility to his clan to marry or procreate.

Now as their laird, he was responsible for producing an heir, but that didn't factor into his decision either. Even if he didn't possess a single head of cattle, even if he possessed a hundred older brothers waiting in line for the lairdship, Maggie would have been the woman who made him want to end his bachelorhood. He wanted her.

Torean MacDonald shouted for silence, and when the noise of the crowd died down, he held up his hands. Logan kept his gaze fixed on his opponent, though he saw that MacDonald had raised a small tartan square in his hand.

"And . . . begin!" MacDonald shouted, throwing down the cloth. Logan and Munroe drew their swords from their leather scabbards with a whoosh, and a cacophony of cheers and shouts erupted from the crowd.

With a low battle cry, Logan lunged forward, his gaze focused, narrowed. This duel was to first blood rather than to the death. Earlier, Torean had drawn Logan aside and explained that he desired Munroe alive for political reasons. Logan had easily acquiesced to Torean's plea for mercy. Whether Munroe lived or died, Logan was going to take Maggie away to safety. Ultimately, the bastard's death wasn't a necessity.

In the end, both parties had sworn that the victor would give quarter as soon as the loser asked. And the loser would ask for quarter as soon as first blood was drawn.

With those rules in mind, Logan chose a spot on Munroe's cheek. He'd score him there, scar the bastard for life as a reminder to all of what he was.

Munroe was slower than Logan. He'd scarcely raised his sword before Logan lunged halfway across the ring, his sword held at head level. Awkwardly, Munroe blocked Logan's feint to the left side of his face.

Applause and shouts roared at him from all angles, but Logan kept his gaze firmly focused on his enemy. He whipped his broadsword around, raising the tip to the spot he'd chosen just below Munroe's eye.

Munroe's free hand flew up, flinging a cloud of dirt at Logan. Grimacing, Logan blinked and stepped back to shake it off and rub the back of his arm over his grit-filled eyes. He growled with rage. What was the bastard doing? Delaying the inevitable? Trying to distract him with dirt?

When Logan opened his eyes again, a curtain of gray covered the world. He couldn't see a damn thing.

He was blind.

Maggie clenched her fists at her sides. Her heart beat wildly against her breastbone. Sweat beaded over her brow, though the day was far from warm. She stood beside Torean, close to the marked edge of the ring in which the men fought. Bodies pressed in on them from all sides, and the air reeked of sweat and grime mixed with oiled leather and the damp wool of clothing.

After his first aggressive attack, which she was certain would bring Innes down, Logan retreated a step, shaking his head like a dog tossed into the loch might try to fling away water. It was as though Innes's flailing, awkward motions had confused Logan. And then Logan froze, his sword held upright, his expression bewildered. For a moment that seemed to drag on forever, he hesitated.

A feeling of wrongness exploded like molten metal within Maggie. "Logan?"

With a sneer pasted on his face, Innes strode forward, his

weapon aimed at Logan's chest. Instead of stabbing Logan, however, he whacked at his upraised sword. Logan recovered quickly, lifting his weapon and swiping it before him as if to protect his face. It made a whizzing noise as it sliced through the air.

Again he froze, holding the sword upright, making no attempt to attack. The panic lodged in Maggie's gut cooled into a steel block lodged in her stomach, dragging her down. She remained rooted to the muddy ground, unable to move.

"Logan!" Maggie's fists clenched and unclenched spasmodically at her sides. "Go!" Torean's hand curled over her shoulder, but she didn't pay any attention to him. "Attack him, Logan!"

But Logan didn't move, didn't attack. Innes came forward again, and with a flourish of his sword, swiped it in a downward angle across Logan's shirt.

Logan sucked in a breath. Maggie moaned softly. Red spilled over his chest, pasting his sliced shirt to his skin. He brought his fingers up to touch his bloody chest, blinking hard as if trying to focus his vision. His sword arm dropped to his side, and Maggie took a sobbing breath.

"Do you yield, Douglas?" Innes asked loudly.

Logan clenched his teeth.

"Do . . . you . . . yield?" Innes screamed.

A muscle twitched in Logan's jaw.

"No!" What was happening? Acidic tears pricked at the back of Maggie's eyes. "Don't yield! Don't give up. Attack!"

Torean's hand squeezed her shoulder. "He cannot, Maggie."

"What?" she breathed.

"They vowed beforehand to grant quarter after first blood."

Maggie's breath froze in her throat. She stared at the two men on the stage. The ruckus of the screaming onlookers around her dimmed to a background hum.

Logan had lost. Even if he wished to fight Innes to the death, even if he could kill him right now with one well-placed blow, honor wouldn't permit him to renege on a vow.

Innes raised his sword and swiped it down the opposite direction on Logan's chest, creating a bloody X.

"Do you yield?" Innes shouted. He was all but jumping up and down with victorious glee. "Do you? Do you?"

Logan fully turned his sword away from Innes, pointing it behind him. "Aye," he growled. "I yield."

The crowd groaned, unhappy that its entertainment had been cut so short. Maggie blinked through cloudy eyes as Innes raised his hands, bowed, and beamed in triumph.

"I'm going home," she said harshly.

Maggie stood in front of the long head table in the great hall, her hands on her hips, facing Torean and his closest advisors. Including Innes Munroe, who sat two seats away from her cousin. The bastards had promised her that Logan was all right, that he'd survive his wounds, but they hadn't allowed her to go to him. Because, of course, she was Innes's chattel now.

Logan had been taken straight from the duel to the castle healer. After the doctor dressed his wounds, he would continue on his journey north as agreed.

Logan had somehow lost. She didn't understand it—he seemed to have simply given up. When she confronted Torean with the oddness of Logan's behavior in the duel, her cousin just gave her a strange look, then turned away to continue the discussion of the fight with his men.

None of it made sense.

In the end, though, Logan's behavior during the duel didn't matter. All that mattered was that he'd lost. Her heart had shattered. Logan was leaving. Innes intended to rape her into submission, and Torean intended to permit it.

A shudder twisted down her spine as she met Innes's gaze. His intent was obvious in the way he eyed her over his roasted goose leg.

Over her dead body, she thought dispassionately, staring at him through narrowed eyes as he leered back at her. Goose grease smeared his thick lips and dripped from his chin, and meat chunks were wedged between his yellowed teeth.

From the beginning she'd known it was folly to place her life in the hands of men. Logan's intentions had been honorable, but in her heart she'd known it wasn't his responsibility to save her.

It was up to her to free herself from Innes Munroe. But how? Hopelessness swelled in her chest.

"I think you should stay, cousin," Torean said pleasantly. "We've marvelous entertainments planned this night. My bard—"

She grimaced at him. "No. I want to go home."

Torean's gaze flitted from her to Innes and back. "Very well."

Innes smacked his hand down on the table. "What?" he roared. "You promised I could take 'er after the duel!"

"Today?" Maggie croaked in panic. Torean had promised the brute he could marry her *today*?

Torean made a placating gesture with his hands and smiled at Innes. "My lady cousin is a touch upset and still exhausted from her ordeal in the mountains. Perhaps it would be best to give her a few days, allow her to prepare in both body and soul for her upcoming nuptials."

Maggie fought to keep herself from spitting at his feet, but the look she gave Torean made very clear her intentions when it came to marrying Innes Munroe.

"And it's for the best, don't you see?" Torean continued on, his voice soothing. "Marry her in a week's time, I say."

He lifted his glass of ale, took a long swallow, and then thumped it onto the table. He wiped the back of his hand over his mouth. "We'll have another celebration!" he exclaimed. "If you marry today, the merriment of the event will be overshadowed by Hogmanay." He narrowed his eyes at Innes. "I'll have my distillers bottle the new batch of whisky for the occasion."

Innes took a big bite of goose thigh, his pale eyes thoughtful. "Hmm . . ." he said through a full mouth. The offer of whisky had tempted him.

Torean slid a glance from Maggie to Innes. "Come now, Innes. Give her a few days, eh? I'll . . ." He paused to think; then he smiled. "You've been making eyes at Mary Steward. Why don't you take her tonight?"

Maggie bit back a gasp. Mary was one of the local loose women. To think Torean would offer her so blatantly, in Maggie's presence, stole her voice. Torean intended to allow Innes the use of his whore a few days before he intended to marry Maggie to him? The gall!

For the first time in her life, she hated her own cousin.

But then, something in his eyes caught her attention. A subtle glint, as if he were plotting a scheme. Again his gaze flitted to her and then back to Innes.

Perhaps . . .

Innes's eyebrows shot toward his hairline, and his eyes sparkled with interest. "Well, now, she's a fair piece, isn't she?"

"Oh, aye. A fair piece indeed." Torean turned fully to Maggie and offered her a gentle smile. "Godspeed, cousin. Go home and rest. In one week, your intended will come for you."

Perhaps he was buying her time.

Shaking with a fierce kind of rage he'd only felt once before, in the throes of battle at Sheriffmuir, Logan strode out the door of the doctor's cottage. His vision was clear and crisp now, almost back to normal except for the red fury swirling on its fringes. Whatever Munroe had thrown at him only had a temporary effect. Nor had the bastard cut him too deep. The scratches on his chest burned like fire, but they weren't life-threatening—a small consolation for what had to be the most anger-inducing day of Logan's life. Since he'd left the arena, he had fought with every breath to school himself from violence. The only thoughts that kept him sane were of his family, his duties, and Maggie.

He needed to get off MacDonald land. He was too angry to think rationally here. Too angry to think beyond the compulsion to draw his sword and cut everyone down who stood between him and Innes Munroe, and then stabbing the blackguard through the heart.

Munroe had cheated, but none of the MacDonalds seemed to possess any inclination to do a damned thing about it. Yet did that truly matter? Logan had made an agreement, and to break his word now would sink him to Munroe's level. Despite what the cheating, slimy, devious bastard had done, Logan would not— could not—compromise his honor.

Just outside in the courtyard of the small cluster of castle out-buildings, Torean MacDonald leaned against a wall, his arms crossed over his chest. When the laird saw Logan, he pushed himself from the stones and strode toward him.

Logan stopped in his tracks, standing stiffly as he waited for the laird to approach.

"Are you going, then?" MacDonald asked.

"Aye."

"I'd hoped you'd stay for the Hogmanay celebrations and perhaps depart in the morning."

Logan shook his head. "No. That's not what was agreed." He'd sworn to leave immediately if he lost the duel. The rub of it was, he hadn't entertained the possibility that he'd be the loser. The notion of having to leave Maggie had only crossed his mind once—when she had brought it up. At that moment, the idea of him losing the duel had been out of the question. An impossibility.

What a fool he'd been.

"Very well." MacDonald's chest expanded as he took a deep breath. "I've a horse for you."

"Why?"

"A man in your position shouldn't be walking across the Highlands." Logan didn't answer, and the laird's eyes flicked away. "What happened, man? I expected you would defeat him."

Logan's lip curled, and he rounded on the laird, furious all over again. "You suggested a duel thinking I would win, even when you'd offered your cousin to my opponent to strengthen the bond between your clans?"

"I did." MacDonald sighed. "You see, at first I thought they'd make a good match. Both of them are high-spirited, after all, and I thought Maggie's quick wit might compensate for Munroe's lackluster one. But once she explained to me what happened . . . No." He shook his head firmly. "I am fond of Maggie. I don't wish to see her hurt. Earlier, I couldn't believe that Munroe would do such a thing to her—I thought his interest in her was genuine. Now . . . Well, my cousin was in the right and I . . ." He swallowed. "I was wrong."

"You were."

The laird studied him. "You would take care of her, wouldn't you?"

"Your question comes too late. I have promised to leave this place. To give Maggie to Munroe."

The words tasted like poison on his tongue. He couldn't allow Maggie to fall into Munroe's hands. Yet how could he prevent their marriage and still keep the vows he'd made and retain his honor?

Hell if he knew. He needed time. Time he didn't have, for he had no doubt Munroe would claim Maggie soon.

MacDonald released his breath. "Aye, Munroe has won her. Though . . . I wonder if the fight was fair."

"No." Logan snarled out the word. "It wasn't fair."

"What happened?"

"He threw something—a fine dust—into my eyes. Blinded me temporarily."

MacDonald frowned. A long silence descended. Finally, the laird said, "Yet you must still leave."

"I swore that I would."

It had been stupid of him to assume Munroe would follow any code of honor for dueling. Nothing of this duel, from its inception to its end, had followed that code. He shouldn't be surprised. And now, because he'd misplaced his trust, he couldn't legally accuse Munroe of wrongdoing. It was simple: Fair or not, Logan had lost, and therefore honor demanded he must abide by his side of the bargain. He must leave this place.

"Yet you never promised not to return," the laird said suggestively.

Logan stared at him. MacDonald was right. Logan had promised to leave MacDonald land straightaway, but he'd never made any promises to stay away. He could return. It was allowed, approved by the laird, and he'd never agreed not to.

But if he came back here, what then?

"Again, I ask you to stay. Just for Hogmanay. Your agreement to the conditions of the duel can be delayed until tomorrow."

Logan shook his head. "No."

MacDonald nodded, but regret darkened his blue eyes. "Very well, then. Your mount is saddled and awaits you in the stables."

The horse MacDonald had given him was a chestnut mare, a fine English horse, not one of the diminutive creatures usually seen in this part of the world. Logan rode back up the mountain, retracing the path they had taken from the cottage.

The landscape had changed from its appearance a few days ago. Now the steep slope was a cold wasteland. Most of the snow had melted, and everything looked frozen, forbidding, dead, and damp. In spring, the land would be reborn, but now the mountain was lifeless and dull.

As the horse climbed, the air grew colder and the snow more widespread. With each outtake of breath, the animal released a cloud of steam. When her chest began to heave with exertion, Logan turned the horse toward a distant dripping noise, which he assumed must be a stream. He'd water her and give her a brief rest before deciding what to do next.

The stream was situated in a small ravine. Obviously it wasn't a permanent body of water, rather a temporary collection of recently melted snow. The water trickled down the shallow banks in rivulets, then collected into a trickling pool between walls of dirty snow.

He dismounted, took the animal's reins, and led her to the water, the X-shaped wound across his chest stinging with the movement of dismounting. Gratefully, she bent her head and began to drink.

Logan raised his gaze to take in his surroundings. Just ahead, past a row of bushes, was a small half circle of a granite rock face. The familiarity of the place slammed into him. He hadn't recognized it at first. But it was where he'd found her, lying facedown in the snow, nearly dead from the cold.

Innes Munroe had put her in that position. He'd have no qualms doing it again.

Logan stood still, reins gripped in his hand.

He loved her, damn it. He possessed a powerful compulsion to care for her, protect her. From the first moment he'd laid eyes on her, his love for her had grown. Now it was a force within him, something that couldn't be denied.

Out of the corner of his eye, he saw something gleaming in the waning light. He swung his gaze toward the shining object on the ground.

There it was.

His jaw dropped. She was wrong. That dragon wasn't standing on an agate. It was standing on the damned largest diamond he'd ever seen. The stone was crystal clear, its facets luminous. Perhaps it was made of paste, he conceded, but if so, he'd never seen a counterfeit gem more brilliant or beautiful.

He released the horse's reins, and in two long strides, he stood before Maggie's lost pin. He crouched before it and gathered the heavy silver object into his hand. His fist curled around the cold metal. Even through his fingers, the sun glinted off the facets of the diamond, casting sparkling beams of light onto the lifeless terrain.

Honor be damned. Maggie MacDonald was his. Innes Munroe would never lay his filthy hands on her again.

Chapter Eight

At dusk, most of the castle occupants were sotted, and covering himself with a plaid, Logan thought he might slip through the great hall without garnering any attention. But then Donald MacDonald, the man who'd served as his second, spotted him.

Pushing himself through a group of revelers, the old man strode up to him and clapped him on the back. "Douglas! The laird said he'd welcomed ye to the Hogmanay festivities, but ye'd decided to leave us regardless."

"Aye," Logan said. "But I changed my mind."

Donald smiled. "Well, then. Come join me in a dram."

"Not tonight." Logan's gaze roamed the torch-lit interior of the grand hall. He didn't see Innes Munroe or Maggie, though Torean MacDonald sat at the opposite end of the room, his cheeks flushed. The busty woman sitting beside him offered him her cup, and he drank heartily from it.

"Och," Donald said soothingly. "Yer looking for Munroe, aren't ye? The bastard." He spat at his feet. "Well, ye needn't worry 'bout him, for he's locked himself up in his bedchamber with his wench. I doubt anybody'll lay eyes on him till—"

But Logan had already pushed past him and was heading for the stairs at a near run.

His wench? Maggie?

He didn't give a damn if anyone saw him now. Good God, was he already too late? Had Munroe taken Maggie upstairs? Had he been raping her as Logan had delayed, locked in his misguided attempt to retain his honor?

Logan barreled up three stories to Innes's bedchamber. When he reached the man's door, he turned the handle and found it locked. Of course.

Maggie could be in there. If she was, he'd never forgive himself.

Without hesitation, he rammed his shoulder into the door until it splintered. Then he reached through the gaping hole in the planks, released the latch, and pushed the remains of the door open.

A woman with sleek black hair sprang up from the bed, clutching a dun-colored blanket to her naked chest.

Thank God, it wasn't Maggie. Nevertheless, Logan took one look at her face, at the tears streaking her pale cheeks, and renewed fury exploded through him.

"What's this?" Munroe heaved his body upward and the blanket slid down, revealing the mass of white flesh that was his torso.

Logan stepped inside to reveal himself, kicking the remains of the door shut behind him. He stood tall, his hand on his musket.

Munroe sneered, but not before Logan saw the quick flash of fear in his eyes. "Our duel is over. What are you, an idiot?"

"You cheated." Logan's voice was low. Deadly.

Munroe released a sputtering breath. "There is no cheating in battle. You do whatever it takes to win, you damned fool. We don't follow those foolish lowland rules of dueling. You should know that. We fight in our way. The Highlander way. Whatever it takes to win."

"The Highlander way?" Logan asked with a sneer of his own. "You believe the Highlander way is the way of the underhanded and devious?"

Munroe's lips spread into a grin. "It worked, didn't it? I am the victor, and rest assured, I will claim Maggie MacDonald for my own."

Logan turned to the woman cowering in the corner. One side of her face was mottled and swollen where someone—most definitely Munroe—had struck her. "Go, lass," he urged her in a low voice. "Go find some help."

She rose and scurried away, fumbling as she tried to work the broken door. Watching Munroe, who glowered at him from the bed, Logan thrust open the door for her. She scuttled down the passageway. Logan backed over the threshold, keeping his eyes on the man in the bed. When he was out of Munroe's sight, he turned to follow the girl toward the stairs.

Munroe wasn't worth talking to, much less arguing with. Logan needed to find Maggie. Perhaps she was in her room in the tower. He'd search there next.

Just as he raised his foot to step from the landing onto the stairway, a floorboard creaked in the corridor behind him. Tightening his grip on his musket, Logan spun around.

Munroe stood not ten paces away, naked, flushed, and sweating. He yanked his hand out from behind him. The barrel of a pistol shimmered at Logan in the dim flickering torchlight.

Munroe's finger tensed on the trigger.

As in the duel, Logan was faster than his enemy. In a fraction of a second, he raised his musket and aimed at the center of Innes Munroe's chest. And fired.

Deafeningly loud, the boom of the shot echoed in the confines of the enclosed space. Munroe lurched backward with the force of the ball entering his chest, and then he collapsed flat on his back, his head cracking against the wooden floor. Blood gushed from the hole torn in his breast.

Logan stared down at him. A year ago, Mrs. Sinclair had told Logan to keep his musket close, that it would lead him to his "one." He hadn't suspected there was any credence in her words. He'd kept the weapon near because it was the last gift he'd received from his brother. Now he realized he had followed behind the barrel of his gun when he'd first found Maggie's brooch, and then Maggie herself.

The truth struck him like a hammer. Innes Munroe had to die. He would never have let go of his desire to possess Maggie Mac-Donald. Logan had to kill the man in order to keep Maggie safe.

As the footsteps of scores of people pounded up the stairs behind him, Logan slowly lowered his gun.

Curled into her only upholstered chair, Maggie sat staring at the lazy, low flames of her fire, blinking back tears. She'd convinced her servants to leave earlier, to enjoy the Hogmanay bonfire and then join the ongoing festivities at Naughton's mother's house.

Logan had lost the duel, had left her forever. Honor had compelled him to leave her to Innes Munroe.

Hogmanay had always been her favorite holiday. When Maggie was a child, she and her mother would join the other women in the castle kitchens in the days leading up to Hogmanay, helping to prepare the feast. On Hogmanay day, Maggie would play with the other children; then in the evening, after a heavy supper, she would sit in awe as she listened to the castle bard tell glorious tales of the MacDonalds.

Late at night, with their bellies full and their eyelids heavy, Maggie and Torean would follow her mother upstairs to the nursery. Speaking in low tones so as not to wake the other children, her mother would rub their backs and tell them about the legends of New Year's Eve.

She said that when they grew older, they would stay up until the New Year dawned. She warned them to be wary of strangers on Hogmanay. If a light-skinned, light-haired man knocked at the door after midnight, it was very bad luck indeed and boded poorly for the future. If a dark-skinned, dark-haired man came bearing gifts of salt and coals, it would mean good luck for the coming year.

In later years, Maggie participated in the ritual with glee. She'd laughed behind her hand as she watched the older women ply dark young men with packs of salt and coals and then send them to make rounds, ensuring that the person making the first footing of the year into each home was a dark-haired man bearing the requisite gifts.

Maggie glanced at the clock. It was past midnight already, she realized. It had been a long, painful day. It was the New Year, and Innes Munroe planned to come for her soon.

How would she endure it? How could she survive a life without Logan?

"*Keep to yourself,*" her mother had said. "*Be independent and self-sufficient until you know you are safe.*"

Maggie rose and slowly turned in a circle, surveying the interior of her cottage. In the years after Duneghall's death, she'd felt safe here. But now that Innes Munroe had invaded this space and stolen her away, it was no longer secure.

She'd only be safe if she were with Logan. She knew that now. She must leave this place. Run. She was no brawny man like

Logan, but she was no fool. If she prepared herself well enough, she'd survive the elements.

Rapidly, she calculated what she needed to do. She must gather what she needed and slip away a few hours before dawn, early in the morning when all the people were still sleeping off the effects of Hogmanay. She'd bundle up and carry the barest supplies necessary for a weeklong walk. By the time everyone awoke, she'd be long gone. And if they came searching for her . . . well, there was an abundance of places to hide in the mountains.

Excitement welled in her chest. She was going to follow Logan home. To hell with Torean and Innes, and their duels and promises. They weren't worth her trouble.

When Innes came for her, he wouldn't find her. She'd be long gone by then. She'd be with Logan.

Was that what her cousin had intended for her to do? Was that why he'd given Innes a whore? To distract him from pursuing her? To give her a head start?

As Maggie hurried to her shelf of clothing, her heart expanded with forgiveness for her cousin. She took a plaid from the shelf and spread it across her bed; then she picked the lightest but most nourishing foodstuffs from her pantry and tossed them to the center of the plaid.

A sharp knock sounded on her mended door, and clutching a packet of dried fish in her hand, Maggie stiffened.

Innes Munroe's image flitted through her mind. Innes was fair, light-haired, and light-skinned. Would he be the pale stranger bringing bad luck to her doorstep? Would he come for her so soon?

Yes. Knowing Innes, he would. He'd be drunk and violent. He'd hurt her.

Another knock. More urgent.

She looked around wildly for something to use as a weapon. Finally her gaze alighted on the iron fireplace tongs.

She lurched forward, dropped the packet of fish on the bed, and grabbed the tongs. This time when he broke down the door, she'd be waiting to wallop him over the head.

"Maggie, it's me."

At the sound of the voice, the fear drained out of Maggie in such a powerful rush, she was left gasping for air. Her knees nearly buckled. The fireplace tongs fell to the floor with a clatter.

"Logan?"

"Open the door, Maggie."

She jumped forward, yanked the door open, and threw herself into his waiting arms. Just as quickly, she retreated, horrified. "Your wounds! Oh, did I hurt you?"

"No," he said gruffly, stepping inside and shutting the door behind them. "Come here." He tugged her back into his embrace.

For long moments, they stood holding each other at her threshold. Maggie closed her eyes, letting the questions simmer, but when they began to well, she pushed them aside. Later. For now she just wanted to touch him, to revel in his closeness.

She burrowed her head into his shoulder, breathing in his essence of heather and peat, and taking in his ever-present warmth. He pulled her closer, held her body flush against his, from head to toe.

"Why did you come back?" she whispered.

"Did you not wish me to?"

Her breath left her in a harsh exhalation. "I wanted it more than anything! I was planning . . ." She glanced at the bundle she'd began to gather on the bed. "I was going to slip away. To . . ." She took a deep breath. "To follow you."

"I'm glad you would have come to me." His arms tightened

around her, and his lips pressed into her hair. "Even when I was the one to have failed you."

Satisfaction flooded through her. There were no admonitions that it was a foolish plan, that she was too weak, that she would have perished in the mountains. Instead, he trusted her. He respected her enough to know she would have found him.

"You didn't fail me, Logan."

Turning from the bed to her, he slid a knuckle down her cheek. "I brought you something."

He dug into the folds of his plaid and brought something out. She gasped. Was that her mother's brooch?

"What have you done to it?" She gazed wide-eyed at the enormous clear gem that had replaced the agate. "Is that a diamond?"

"I'm fairly certain it is," he said. "And this is exactly how it appeared when I first saw you."

"You went back to that place?"

He nodded. "I don't know how—I wasn't intending to go there. But when I stopped the horse, there I was. Your brooch was on the ground. Partially buried in water and mud, but the gem sparkled and caught my eye."

"*That* gem?" she questioned, still not quite believing it.

He frowned at her. "Aye." He turned the brooch over in his hand so they could study it from different angles. "You cannot believe this is an agate."

She released a breath. "It was an agate last I saw it. It was . . . an amber color." Now it was crystal clear, with the barest hint of gold that glimmered when the firelight washed over it.

And then it struck her. "Oh. Heavenly Lord . . ."

"What is it?"

She blinked at her brooch. "My mother. She said . . ." How could she voice it without sounding mad? "She said this brooch would tell me when I met my soul mate. The man I'm supposed to spend my life with. I . . . I think it's telling me now."

Logan's frown deepened. "How can that be?"

"The agate has transformed into a diamond."

For long moments, they both stared at the enormous gem, scarcely breathing. It merely sat on Logan's hand, the dragon's talons wrapped protectively over it, glittering in the light of the fire.

"Come home with me, Maggie."

Her gaze snapped up to the harsh lines of his face. His wide forehead, thick brows, strong nose, and his dark eyes. He was the most beautiful man she'd ever seen. The most masculine.

She reached up to touch his rugged cheek. "I've never wanted to be taken care of," she murmured. "But when you are near me, Logan, I want you to care for me. I want your protection, the safety that I know you can offer me. I want to go home with you." She swallowed, almost afraid to reveal her heart. "But I wish to care for you as well. Protect you as well. I wish to be your partner. In all ways."

Logan smiled. "Of course. I wouldn't expect anything less." He paused, then swiped the pad of his thumb over the plump part of her lower lip. "I want to marry you, stand beside you, sleep with you. I want you to bear my children. I want to grow old with you."

"But . . ." She took a deep, sobbing breath. "But what of Torean and Innes? They'll come after you."

"Munroe is dead, Maggie."

"What?" she gasped.

"I killed him."

"What . . . what happened?"

Setting the brooch on the arm of the chair, he once again drew her close. "I found Munroe abusing a woman named Mary Steward."

"Poor Mary," Maggie breathed. "Did Torean see what happened to her?"

Logan nodded.

Maggie pushed out a breath. "He finally understands what a brute Innes is."

"Aye. After the duel, he asked me to stay at the castle for Hogmanay. I think, even before I told him about Munroe blinding me, he suspected the man had cheated—"

"Is that what Innes did to you?" she breathed. "Blinded you? I didn't know. I was certain something horrible had happened." She touched a fingertip to the corner of his eye.

"Aye."

"But you can see now?"

He nodded. "The effect was temporary."

"So Torean understood and regretted his promises to Innes, but was trying to work out how he could honorably repudiate those promises without gaining the enmity of the Munroes?" she asked.

"Exactly. He is still cautious and unsure of his leadership, and I think he was taking his time to work out his final decision on the matter. He was trying to be wise. Yet when he heard the gunshot and saw Mary Steward so ill used—well, he regretted Munroe's fate no more than I did."

She looked up at Logan in wonder, stroking her hand along his cheek. A late-night dark bristle had broken out over his jaw, and it scraped against her fingertips. "You've saved me after all. Twice."

"He'll never bother you again. And he'll never hurt another woman."

She shuddered. "I . . . I'm glad."

"I brought you something else." Logan dug into the folds of his plaid and brought out two small packets. He handed them to her. "Open them."

She complied, grinning when she saw what they contained. "Salt. And coals."

"Your cousin asked me to give them to you. He said you'd understand."

She looked up at him. "Does this mean . . . ?"

"Aye, Maggie. He's given us his blessing. Munroe is dead, so there is no more lure of a political alliance with his clan, though he assured me that the politics no longer matter to him. The laird has approved our union."

Emotion surged through Maggie, so sweet and so strong she could scarcely breathe.

Logan Douglas was her destiny. The look of love in his eyes obliterated any lingering doubts she might have held on to. He was hers. The agate in her mother's brooch had transformed into a diamond, confirming it.

"I love you," he said. "I've loved you from the moment I saw you, and when you awoke and opened your mouth to challenge me I loved you more. When we made love the first time, my love for you grew, and then it grew more in the days afterward as we lay together, sharing ourselves with each other. I love you as I've never loved another soul. Will you be mine, Maggie MacDonald?"

"Aye, Logan Douglas. If you will be mine in return."

He touched a callused fingertip to her lips. "Aye, my love. I will be yours."

Sweet happiness swelled in Maggie's chest. She pushed her fingers into Logan's silky black hair and drew his head close.

"I love you, Logan Douglas," she whispered, gazing into the shining depths of his eyes. Then she leaned forward and claimed the soft, masculine lips that would belong to her forevermore.

Yuletide Enchantment

SOPHIE RENWICK

Chapter One

Isobel had been six the first time she had seen him. It had been midsummer's day, and the Scottish air had been warm and scented with wildflowers and heather. He was drinking the cool, clear waters from a loch and didn't notice her watching him. She had stood still for long minutes, mesmerized by the magical aura she sensed around him. The next time was when she was thirteen, the day of her mother's funeral. He had stood atop the hill and watched them through the thick mist that hovered over the church graveyard. She had shielded her eyes in order to see him better. Despite the distance separating them, she somehow felt that they were connected in a strange, otherworldly way. She had felt solace then, during that dark hour. Her heart was less heavy, her pain more tolerable.

The next time, she was sixteen, racing along on her new mount, her hair whipping wildly behind her as she ran the mare through the grouse and heather while reveling in her newfound freedom. He had followed her path, and when the mare's hoof had stumbled over a rock and thrown her to the ground, she had opened her eyes to see his fuzzy outline towering above her.

It had been five years since that day she'd been tossed from her horse and struck her head on an old stone cairn. Years since she had seen him. Yet she hadn't wondered if he still resided near Mac-

115

Donald Hall, for she knew he did. She'd felt him still, that mystical connection that was so strange, yet familiar.

Today he was standing on a hilltop, the mist combining with snow as it fell from the clouds, blanketing the Highlands. He was big, broad, a majestic lord looking over his lands. The power and grace he exuded mesmerized her.

The scraping of wood against leather drew her gaze away from the rugged hilltop, and the male that stood atop it. "What are you doing, Ewan?" she demanded of her brother as he pulled the bow from his leather holder.

"Shh, Isobel, dona make a sound," he murmured as he deftly maneuvered his gelding to the left. "What a prize he'll be mounted above the hearth, and just in time for Christmas, too."

"You'll do no such thing," she snapped, struggling to pull the bag of arrows from her brother's shoulder.

"Leave off," he grumbled. "I want him for Father. And I want him with a big tartan bow."

Panic suddenly seized her, and she struggled harder to grip the arrows from her brother. "You canna kill him," she cried, nearly climbing atop her brother's horse. "Ewan, you can't."

"'Tis a sign," Alistair Douglas said as he reined his mount in beside her. "The White Hart doesna' just appear to all for nae reason."

"Look at the arrogance of him," Ewan said, awe in his voice. "Just standing there looking down on us as if he were lord of these lands, and not Father."

Alistair's gloved hand rested over the bow, his gaze boring into Ewan. "You know the story of the beast, laddie—the White Hart is sacred in these parts. He's a sign that the Otherworld is close by. 'Tis an omen we see. Leave it be, Master MacDonald, and find sport elsewhere."

"You've gone daft." Ewan glanced at the old gamekeeper as if he were a lunatic escaped from an asylum. "You might believe in those ancient tales of Annwyn and its creatures, but I no longer believe in faeries."

"Bite yer tongue, laddie," Alistair hissed, his blue eyes widening in alarm as he looked sharply around them. "The woods 'ave eyes an ears, and the Sidhe will nae have qualms about provin' ye wrong."

"That white stag is going to be stuffed and mounted at MacDonald Hall regardless of faeries and Sidhe and whatever other creatures may come to stop me. Let them come," Ewan said with a smile. "It'll make the hunt that much more interesting. Look at him, he's all but challenging me to come after him."

"It's Christmas," Isobel reminded him. "Must you take delight in bloodshed?"

"It's not Christmas for another five days, Isobel," her brother reminded her. "Just enough time for old MacKenzie to get him mounted."

"We're supposed to be gathering greenery and searching for the Yule log, not hunting. Put your bow and arrows away."

"By all means continue searching for the greenery to decorate the hearth, and the log to warm our fire, but let me worry about the hart."

"Why do you wish to kill him?" Isobel asked, exasperated with her brother. "Why canna you let him live a long and hearty life?"

"Because he is the ultimate prize. A White Hart is more than a stag, Isobel. He is a creature of power and magic. A rarity. A true hunter cannot resist such a beast. And this one, with his proud bearing, will be immensely satisfying to run to ground."

"You trespass on hallowed ground, Master MacDonald. This is Sidhe ground. The stag is a warning to ye."

"Warning acknowledged," Ewan said with a smile. "Now it is time to hunt."

"You're not looking to go after that, are you?" the Earl of St. Clair shouted as he came riding up beside them. "At least not with arrows."

Ewan glanced at the earl who had appeared so suddenly. By the look of his lordship's horse, he had ridden fast and hard. "What brings you to these parts, my lord?" Ewan asked suspiciously.

"Not to poach on MacDonald lands, I assure you," the earl replied with characteristic dryness. His gaze then turned to her. "Good day, Miss MacDonald. You are looking very lovely this afternoon. The Scottish air becomes you."

Isobel felt herself bristling under the earl's blatant stare and the little jab she perceived. She had spent the better part of the year in England with her father and brothers knowing the earl never left his family seat in the Highlands. She had effectively avoided him, until now. "Good day to you, my lord."

"It is good to have you and your family back at MacDonald Hall."

"Indeed, but for how long it will be I canna say. I have grown rather fond of London, and I daresay I would be leaving behind a good many friends."

His gray gaze narrowed. "I am sure, Miss MacDonald, that here you might find any number of friends to replace those in London."

He was too far from home to be out on a casual jaunt, Isobel thought as she watched a muscle work in his jaw. She could well imagine what sort of business had made the reclusive earl leave his manor, which was on the far side of the hill and a treacherous ride in this weather.

"Ah, St. Clair." Her eldest brother, Stuart, greeted the earl as he rode up. "Father said you had arrived to welcome us back to the district. I thought, or rather hoped, that I might find you here."

St. Clair regarded her brother with a hooded gaze. "It appears that I have arrived just in time. Your brother has an eye for this hart and is bent on seeing it stuffed and mounted."

"I've hunted this beast since I was sixteen, and he has always evaded me," Ewan said with more than a bit of petulance. "This time he won't."

Isobel tried once more to tug on the leather strap, but Ewan nudged his horse forward, and out of her grasp. "Go on with Alistair," Ewan told her. "Take the sleigh and load it with greenery. I'll meet you back at the hall for a cup of wassail."

With a nudge of his boots, Ewan sent his mount racing toward the hill where the stag stood motionless. Stuart and St. Clair went racing after him, but it wasn't clear to Isobel if the earl was actually helping or hindering her brother.

"What now?" she asked the old retainer as she watched Ewan and Stuart maneuver their mounts among the stone remnants of what had once been a glorious medieval castle.

"We leave."

Alistair turned his huge bay around and cantered to the sleigh where Isobel's sister-in-law, Fiona, and her lady's companion awaited them.

"Isobel," Fiona called, waving her over. "It is a man's pastime, the hunt. Pay it no heed. Come, you can ride with me, and Mr. Douglas can bring your horse back."

No heed, indeed. Glancing over her shoulder, she watched the stag. Defiantly he stood his ground at the summit awaiting her brothers and the earl.

"Run it to ground!" she heard Stuart call to Ewan. "It's in your sights, man!"

Ewan pulled his bay to a stop and reached behind his back for an arrow. The stag charged, running down the steep incline, the damp earth and freshly fallen snow flying up behind its hooves. Instead of fleeing and running for the safety of the forest, it charged, antlers down, straight for Ewan.

Isobel knew that whether with guns or bow he was considered a crack shot. Her brother would not miss, despite the swiftness of the stag.

"No!" she cried, racing ahead. Her horse huffed with the burst of speed, and the thunder of her mare's hooves on the soft ground momentarily disturbed Ewan's concentration.

"For God's sake, Isobel," Ewan thundered. "Would you for once act like a lady?"

"I'll not let you kill it just so you can mount its head on a plaque," she yelled, circling her horse around them, then pulling up short before her brother. The arrow was now pointed straight at her heart. "I'll not sit at the table and have it staring at me as I eat."

"The point is moot, as you'll soon be wed to the Earl of St. Clair and dining at *his* table."

Her stomach fell to her toes as her head snapped in the direction of the earl. He was seated atop his huge horse, his gloved hands resting on his thigh. Their gazes collided across the distance where the infuriating man held it, watching her reaction.

When had such a thing been decided? And why was it Ewan had learned of her betrothal before she had?

Because Father knew she would fight it with every ounce of her being. Father had more than likely sought to coerce her twin into forcing her to come to her senses in regards to the earl. Yet here he was, looking at her, challenging her to deny him to his face. She didn't like the earl, and she didn't like the way he looked at her, either.

The straining sound of wood drew her gaze. Shaking off the thought of the marriage she would not agree to, Isobel turned once more to her stag.

"Ewan, please," she begged as she glanced over her shoulder, checking the position of the hart, who was still running towards them. "For me. For Christmas. Please don't kill it."

But it was too late. She saw Ewan's leather-clad finger lift from the string, watched helplessly as the arrow left the bow and soared over her shoulder.

"No!"

Turning in her saddle, she saw the arrow pierce the white hide, saw the black eyes go round, turn wild, as the beast continued to charge, its enormous rack poised for fight.

"Get out of here, Isobel," Ewan commanded as he took her mare's bridle in hand and forced her mount forward. "For the love of—" He stopped short, stunned as the stag ran past her and straight at the earl. St. Clair's mount bucked, startled, tossing him hard onto the ground. The stag, now in a murderous rage, charged the fallen man. But it suddenly stopped and looked at her. For the barest of seconds, their gazes collided. She saw something in those black eyes. A plea? But for what?

And then it was gone, running into the woods, and she and Ewan were on the ground, helping St. Clair.

"Come along, miss," Alistair said impatiently as he gave her his hand. "It's time to hie back to the hall."

The retainer was nervous. She saw the trembling in his hand, the way his gaze continually strayed to the forest where the hart had disappeared.

"Come," he barked irritably. "'Tis not wise to tarry. They will be out for sure now, now that their king has been wounded. You dona want to be here when they do."

"Who?" she asked, accepting Alistair's help in regaining her mount.

"The Sidhe," he murmured in a voice that trembled. "Now let us be off before they discover us."

With the slap of a glove against its flank, Alistair sent her mount cantering off toward the large Jacobean-style country house that loomed ahead. But she stopped halfway and glanced back over her shoulder at the woods that were outlined through the snow. Alistair tugged the reins from her hands, forcing her mare to follow in the wake of his gelding.

"Be warned, miss: Those who go into the woods at night don't come out."

Chapter Two

The change from stag to man was swift but painful, stealing the air from his lungs as his body twisted into limbs and torso. Breathing heavily, Daegan stumbled over the exposed roots of an oak tree. The falling snow made the mossy, damp earth slippery and he fell to his knees, clutching his ribs as the iron tip of the arrow spread its poison into his blood.

"You were foolish this day to allow the mortals to taunt you into attacking."

In agonizing pain, he looked up through the long strands of black hair that hung in wet tendrils over his eyes. Not that he needed sight to know who stood before him: Cailleach, the supreme goddess, and she was madder than a chained hellhound who had been starved for days.

Falling onto his backside, Daegan used the old, weathered tree trunk for support. Fighting for what was left of his honor, he schooled his breathing and buried the pain. He did not want the goddess to know how much he suffered. Pride. It was all he had left.

"I thought you more intelligent than this," she snapped, dropping to her knees. Her emerald green cloak, edged in white rabbit fur, flared out around them, narrowly missing the small patch of blood that streamed from his wound. "You are Prince of the Sidhe, the male ruler of Annwyn, *my consort*," she hissed as her pale fingers pulled at his hand, revealing the arrow shaft, which had broken in two. "You would unbalance our world, would allow chaos to enter, and for what? A girl? A *mortal?*"

"She is no longer a girl, but a woman," he hissed, as the arrow tip tore free of his flesh. Cailleach seared him with a look of disgust as she tossed the metal tip onto the snow-covered ground.

"Why did you do it? I saw you standing on the hilltop, challenging that human male to a hunt."

Daegan closed his eyes, refusing to think of the reasons. But they came nonetheless. There were only two reasons why mortals were able to see him in his altered form. The first was a sign that the Celtic Otherworld was near and that the humans were venturing too close to Annwyn's sacred lands. His appearance was a warning to superstitious mortals to keep away from the woods that led to his world. The other was a sign that a great trespass had occurred. This had been the reason why he had appeared to the hunters, to show them that he took the betrothal of Isobel to another man as a grave insult, and a mistake, one he would soon rectify. Those humans had taken something that was his and given her to another. Mine, he had wanted to shout from the hillside. *Mine.*

"Must I remind you yet again that she is not one of us? She cannot be yours."

"So you have told me," he panted as he slumped lower to the ground, the pain once more an agony he was afraid he could not endure. "Leave it," he groaned as she tore at his clothes, exposing the ragged flesh to the cold and snow.

"Quiet. You are not the sole ruler in this wood, my prince. You will submit to me now and do my bidding."

Her fingers, remarkably warm considering the weather, probed and prodded the skin around the gaping hole in his side. With every pump of his heart he could feel the poison from the iron mixing in his blood, burning in his veins. His magic, though considerable, was no match for the iron poisoning that would claim him. To be brought so low, and by a mortal arrow at that.

"We haven't much time," she muttered, shoving aside the silk of his waistcoat. Bending forward, she murmured an incantation, words he would have known save for the poison spreading to his mind. Then there was a flash of white before his eyes, and he felt the blazing heat of Cailleach's mouth against his skin, sucking the poison from his body.

His mind fractured, and he slumped to the ground, eyes closed as the white swirled around him. Her lips and mouth worked swiftly, yet gently, and he felt his nipple harden as her fingertip grazed it. Pain gave way to euphoria, the kind that opium or alcohol gave to mortals. The deeper she sucked, the greater the exhilaration that heated his blood. Soon he did not see Cailleach's silvery blond hair, but Isobel's red curls. He saw her head moving against him, her body curling over his as she hungrily moved her lips and tongue over his skin. He was no longer aware of his wound, just the enticing feel of her tongue circling his nipple. In his mind, he saw her mouth on him not as a necessity to heal, but as a prelude to lovemaking. He saw Isobel, not as healer, but lover.

With a hiss, Cailleach straightened away from him, her green eyes filled with contempt. "It is her you envision and not I?"

It was true he was Cailleach's consort, but in name only. Together, they ruled Annwyn, as had each Sidhe king and each goddess for thousands of years. They were together, their lives intertwined, but not as a male and female. That physical, mystical bond was not there. It had never been. It never would be. They were not lovers, but partners.

He did not look away in shame for thinking of a mortal while Cailleach sucked the poison from his blood. There was nothing to be ashamed of, this desire he had for Isobel MacDonald. In the beginning he had tried to resist, but after years of failing he now allowed himself visions of marking her for his own.

"You will not do something so foolish ever again. You once saved her life, and she has saved yours today. There is no further debt to be paid. No reason to ever see her again."

Cailleach stood, her cloak looking just as unrumpled and majestic as it had when she first appeared. She was immaculate, stunningly beautiful, and utterly untouchable.

"Your eyes betray the Unseelie in you," she said, watching him with her clear gaze that saw to the depths of his soul. "I have always known it lurked there, but never have I seen it more than I do now."

He saw aversion in Cailleach's eyes. His grandmother, the eldest of the Seelie king's three daughters, had scandalized the court by marrying an Unseelie warrior more mercenary than knight. That was, until it became apparent that the king was dying and there was no one to take his throne, for their sons were the only male issue amongst the king's grandchildren. Only then was the mixed blood of Daegan's father and uncles acceptable at court.

"You knew when the time came that I would be next in line to rule, despite my grandfather's Unseelie blood," he reminded her.

"You are not king yet, Daegan," she reminded him.

He laughed, despite the fatigue and pain that lingered in his body. The Seelie Court of the Sidhe were not warriors; they were thinkers and poets who lived in light and beauty. But the Unseelie, the Unholy ones of their race, were mighty warriors who lived in darkness and violence. Their powers were cunning and brute strength. They were dangerous enemies, but as Cailleach had discovered during her centuries as his consort, they could make for loyal and trustworthy allies.

Was it the Seelie blood, or the mysterious and dangerous Unseelie blood that lured Cailleach to his side? And which side was it, he wondered, that made him lust after his beautiful mortal?

"When my father dies, I will be king. In fact I have been king for many centuries now, acting in my father's stead as he wastes away from grief over my mother's death. You need me, Cailleach. Regardless of my mixed Seelie blood, I am a pure Sidhe. And a full-blooded Sidhe is what Annwyn needs. Who else has the pedigree of a full Sidhe? The strength to protect Annwyn from the mortals?"

"There is another."

A raven hovered over the tops of the trees, dipping and lifting, and Daegan laughed, his eyes closing once more. "You think *my* Unseelie blood is difficult to control? I dare you to try issuing orders to *him*. His blood is full Unseelie. You will have no consort in Bran."

Cailleach lifted her delicate chin in defiance. "This day you have brought danger not only to Annwyn but to yourself. It will be the last, Daegan. Leave the mortal to her kind, or I shall see to the matter myself. I doubt you will care for my methods."

"Touch her, Cailleach, and you will know the wrath of my black blood."

They sat that way, his violet eyes holding her green ones as each of them searched for the other's weakness.

"Do not make the mistake of thinking you are the only one who feels, who wants," she said, her resolve softening. "But our path is fated, not chosen. We cannot change who we are. There is no room in your life, or in Annwyn, for a mortal."

She faded into the snow and mist that was spreading through the forest, yet he still felt her presence hovering like a shroud above him. It smothered him, suffocating him until he felt he could not breathe.

An image of Isobel, walking in the forest—in Annwyn—suddenly came to him, calming him, slowing his hurried breaths. She looked at home in his world, walking among the towering oaks and pines. As she strolled through the woods, her hood slipped back, revealing her auburn hair and pale, unmarred skin. Her lips were red, parted in wonder as she strolled deeper into the enchanted woods. He knew he would never see anything lovelier than Isobel smiling, carrying a wreath of holly and ivy in her hands. Did she know the meaning of what she held in her hands? Did she realize how sacred they were to his people?

No, how could she? This was his vision. His dream of transformation and pleasure. She was not here, nor would she ever be. Mortals did not venture into the woods at twilight. He would be safe here, to rest upon the snow-covered ground and indulge his fantasy of Isobel lying naked upon a stone altar. It was a fitting dream for the Sidhe who would be king, to take his queen atop the altar where his people worshipped.

His dreams were still his own. Even if his life was not.

Chapter Three

I t had not taken much to escape the festivities. For the first time ever, Isobel had feigned a headache. Believing her overwrought by the afternoon's events, her family had excused her from tea. Climbing the stairs to her chambers, she had disappeared out of her father and brother's sight. Instead of turning to walk down the wing of her family apartments, she turned right and down the servants' staircase. When she found herself outside, she ran to the stable, relieved that the stable boy was at the back brushing one of the horses.

She'd saddled her mare quickly, retrieved the bag she kept hidden for her secret moonlit rides, and threw on a cloak and scarf, which she secured with her clan pin. Then she charged the short distance to the woods where she tethered her mare to a tree.

Whatever Alistair had said about people going into the woods, never to be seen again, she didn't care. She needed to find her stag and make sure he had survived the hit from Ewan's arrow. The hart had consumed her thoughts. The memory of his eyes haunted her. There was an almost human quality to them, and that look he had given her before running off? She didn't understand it, but it compelled her to find him, to make certain he was still alive.

She didn't think she had been gone long from the house, but when she looked up and saw the darkening skies over the barren treetops, she knew she had tarried too long in the forest. But her senses, the same ones that told her to flee, were certain that the white hart was close by.

Carefully she stepped between the exposed roots of the giant oaks, holding on to their trunks for support. The caw of a bird startled her, and she looked up to see an enormous raven lift off the branch of a tall Scotch pine. It circled above her, dipping low, flying between the trees, then circling back. Despite the waning light and the dim moonbeams which could not penetrate through the thick canopy of pines, Isobel saw, or rather felt, the bird's predatory gaze boring into her.

I only want to see my hart, and then I shall leave this place.

Stumbling over the roots and the thick underbrush of hawthorn, Isobel walked deeper into the woods, conscious of a sense of foreboding that worked its way down her spine.

The raven, she saw, continued to follow her, but he no longer circled her like a hawk circling a mouse. Now he flew from branch to branch, following her progression into the forest, his head cocking with what could only be described as curiosity.

Curiosity had killed the cat. She hoped tonight she was not the feline in question.

Rounding a group of rowan trees, Isobel stopped abruptly. In a shaft of moonlight, beneath the leafless canopy of an old oak, lay her hart. He was asleep on the ground, hind legs buried beneath his great, muscular hide. His forelegs curled like that of a dog. His head, with the enormous rack, was pillowed on the snow that glistened with crimson drops of blood.

Its eyes flew open, and for seconds, the animal didn't move. Its hide did not even flicker in agitation. There was nothing to show her that the animal was startled. No evidence that he would run from her.

Creeping forward, she extended a hand, whispering softly, "I won't hurt you."

He watched her, his large black eyes following her every move until she was a few steps from him. Then he lunged to his feet. His head dipped low, and she reached out to touch him, running her fingers down the slope of his muzzle. The stag allowed the touch, and she saw his eyes close as if he savored the feel of her fingers on him.

He was incredibly soft, his pelt like silk, the color unlike anything she had seen before. In the daylight he had been white, but in the moonlight he glowed almost silver, an incandescent color that was beautiful and otherworldly. It was as if his pelt absorbed the moonbeams and turned them into glistening crystals.

She studied the rack that Ewan had wanted as a trophy. It was wide and heavy. Awe-inspiring. Capable of impaling her and shredding her to bits. She trembled at the thought of feeling the thrust of his antlers through her chest, and she shrieked when she felt the warm wetness on her hand. When she looked down, she half expected to see her own blood on her palm, but there was nothing there save the stag's mouth gently nuzzling her hand. Then the flat of his head was in her palm, and he was brushing against her like a kitten. His eyes were closed, nostrils flared, taking in her scent as he pressed closer to her, encouraging her to touch him.

"You are the most beautiful beast I have ever seen," she whispered as she stroked one of the curling antlers. His hide flickered, shivering, and he lowered his head farther, encouraging another touch. "Such strength and power," she murmured, "yet grace and gentleness, too."

His head lifted, and he looked down at her. Standing beside her, his chest broad and lean, he dwarfed her with his size. He was any hunter's prize kill, yet the thought of this magnificent animal slaughtered and stuffed made her feel ill. This regal stag was made to run free.

"He did hurt you," she whispered as she saw the angry red mark on the animal's side. She brushed her fingers over the wound, which looked superficial. While no doubt painful, it would not prove deadly. The stag sidestepped her touch, prancing just far enough away to evade her fingers, yet he kept close to her, circling her. She felt him at her side, her back. The ends of her hair tangled in his antlers, and she thought she heard him inhale deeply of the heather-scented soap she had used that morning.

You are mine, she heard whispered on the winter wind that made its low howl through the leafless branches.

Suddenly she felt warm, her legs weak, her belly fluttering with the sudden release of butterflies. It was a man's voice. Dark. Sensual. Compelling.

Stay with me.

She trembled once more as the stag pressed closer, his muzzle now bent to her neck. Puffs of gray vapor rose between them and she closed her eyes, disconcerted by feelings that swam in her.

Stay forever.

Something touched her, a hand on her shoulder, the press of lips against the bounding pulse of her throat. She felt the harsh exhalation of a held breath, followed by the movement of her hair over her shoulder.

The raven cawed loudly and swooped down between them, drawing the stag's attention. Confused and frightened, Isobel bolted and ran over the uneven ground, falling to her knees over large, distended tree roots. Branches tore at her hair and the tartan scarf she had wrapped around her neck. Pulling the wool, she continued running, never once looking back until she broke free of the branches that seemed to have tried to keep her within the forest.

When she at last turned back, she saw the white stag standing on the edge of the forest watching her, his great chest heaving. His black eyes compelling her back to him.

She walked away, unable to stop looking back over her shoulder. The stag was still there, still watching her.

Next time, she heard through the night sky. *Next time you will not run from me.*

"The female is fearless, I'll give her that. Braver than most males of her kind."

Daegan watched as the raven fell from the tree limb, landing before him as a man—a naked one.

"If Cailleach catches you in that state, you'll be banned."

Bran smiled, a twinkle in his distinctive mismatched eyes— one pewter, one gold. "The goddess is a prude," he said, even as he used his magic to clothe his naked body. "I don't know how you stand her, Uncle."

"You are a warrior, not a ruler. I do not expect you to understand my allegiance to our goddess."

"Then it is fortunate that you were the eldest and not my father, for I would not want to inherit the throne. I much prefer killing our enemies to negotiating with them."

"You never did understand duty," Daegan said, watching the fading shadow of Isobel vanishing into the twilight.

"Duty is what brings me here."

Daegan glanced at Bran. "What duty is this you speak of?"

"Carden is missing."

"I have heard." Three weeks and still the raven had not found him. To Daegan's eyes, Bran was steaming with anger and fear. A weakness, that. It was not like Bran to show vulnerability.

"You know I must find him."

Daegan nodded. "I will help if I can."

"I believe Morgan has cursed him."

Daegan glanced sharply at Bran. "A dangerous claim against a powerful goddess. What proof have you?"

"None but my instincts. Carden is innocent. He had no part in my squabble with Morgan, but she has punished him to punish me."

"You ask much if you're asking me to go up against Morgan. I have no allegiance to your half brother, Raven. He is not of my blood."

"I know. But as a Sidhe, you have a duty to me, and I to you."

"There is nothing to be done now if Morgan has cast her spell."

"'Tis not only Carden that brings me to you, but something else."

"Oh?" he asked, intrigued. Bran thought of nothing but his search for his half brother. To say the hunt for Carden had become an obsession was putting it mildly. "You have not seen to any duty these past weeks other than searching for the Gargoyle. What brings you out of the hunt now?"

Bran glared at him. "I think you know."

"I do not," Daegan replied.

"What do you mean by pursuing that mortal?"

Daegan shrugged his shoulders. His hair, the same inky black as Bran's, whipped about his face as the wind rose up and howled between the naked branches. "Why should you care what I do?"

"Because I am next in line of succession, and I do not like what I see."

"Then you wish me to leave Annwyn for you to rule more wisely, my nephew?"

Bran growled. "I have no patience for ruling, or desire for the throne, you know that. I care about finding Carden, nothing else, and your actions are interfering. You are upsetting the order of our entire world. Now tell me, what makes you pursue this woman and not a female of Annwyn?"

"What drives you to search fruitlessly for your brother?"

Bran scowled fiercely. "It's not the same, and you know it."

"What is different? We follow where our souls would lead us. I want the woman. I have for many years. I believe she is my destiny. Is it so wrong to want a human?"

"At the cost of our home, our world? Yes."

"You have never loved. You don't know what it's like."

"And I would never be so stupid as to give my heart to a human. They're treacherous, conniving creatures. She would betray you and slit your throat without a second thought. She will expose us to her kind."

"She won't."

Bran snorted. "You're blinded by mortal beauty. The feeling will pass. Let it go."

"She ran from me," Daegan murmured, acknowledging the pain he felt in his heart.

"You frightened her. She saw you as a beast."

"In my mind, I was a man."

Bran gazed at him, his eerie, mismatched eyes penetrating through the darkness. "You would betray us all, Uncle."

Shaking his head, Daegan refused the truth behind Bran's words. "Follow her as the raven and make sure she arrives safely."

"Why? When it would be to all of Annwyn's benefit if she did not?"

With a roar, he reached for Bran's throat and shoved him against a solid oak. "If you do not see to the task, I will, and I might never return. You know what that would mean."

Bran's eyes flared wide. "That is what the humans call blackmail."

"I wish only to have her safe."

Bran flashed into his raven's form, but the glare from his eyes told Daegan he was less than pleased to do his bidding.

"And what am I to expect in return for seeing the mortal safe?" Bran asked.

Daegan met his gaze. "I will convince Cailleach to banish Morgan. Morgan will not like the Wastelands. She'll break the spell rather than be banished." Daegan looked up at the raven circling him. "Is it a deal, then? My woman for your brother?"

"This bargain will no doubt come back to haunt us both, but I have no choice but to accept. No one has more sway with Cailleach than you, and no one other than the supreme goddess can talk sense into that witch Morgan."

"We have a deal, then?"

"We have."

As Bran flew off, leaving Annwyn, Daegan raised his hand, palm up, to the moonlight. A silver pin in the shape of a dirk glistened on the forest floor in front of him. The MacDonald clan pin. Isobel would be back for it. And he would be waiting.

Chapter Four

Isobel sang the opening strains of the "Coventry Carol," and Fiona joined in as they wound strands of ivy and cedar, mixed with pine boughs, to decorate the mantel of the fireplace.

"Are you sure you should be reaching like this?" Isobel asked, breaking off the carol as she saw Fiona stand on tiptoe to stuff a bunch of holly into the bough.

"I'm with child, not an invalid."

"Still, Stuart would have my hide if anything happened to you, especially since it was my idea to decorate the parlor for tonight's reading."

"As the eldest brother, Stuart is used to getting what he wants. You and your family might indulge him, but I do not."

And that's why Isobel utterly adored her sister-in-law.

Fiona winked at her and passed her a ball of mistletoe. "Put this somewhere special."

"And where would that be?"

"Where the man of your dreams can find it."

Isobel glowered. "How about the rubbish bin, then? I'm sure St. Clair would never dare look in the rubbish."

"You heard." Fiona scrunched up her nose. "How long have you known?"

"Ewan blurted out the news yesterday afternoon when we were gathering the pine and holly. I don't think he meant to let the cat out of the bag, but he did, and I've been stewing about it half the night." The other part of the night she'd spent having strange dreams of a violet-eyed, dark-haired stranger. She didn't know what concerned her more, her marriage to the mysterious Earl of St. Clair or the feelings her dream man had stirred within her.

She had tried hard not to think of that dream or the feelings of arousal it had given her. A woman of good breeding did not think of such things. *Should not know of such things.* Yet, the images had been there, haunting her all day. The silhouette of a man outlined in shadow and moonlight, standing at the foot of her bed. The way he stood watching her, the virility she felt coming off him in waves. She had not been scared to see him there. It was as if she had always been waiting for his midnight visit.

"Who are you?" she had asked as he walked slowly around the bed.

"Daegan, a prince of the woods. A lover come to you in a dream."

She had fallen back on her pillows, utterly entranced by the deep timbre of his voice.

"Lover," she had repeated, letting the word roll from her tongue.

"Yes, lover." His eyes, which were a strange violet hue, met hers, as his hand pulled the sheet back, revealing her body in the night rail that had ridden up high on her thighs. "Would you like that, Isobel? Me loving you?"

She couldn't breathe, let alone speak. He had seduced her with his voice. Bewitched her with his eyes, and forced her with little more than a fluttering sweep of his fingertips up her thigh.

She didn't freeze or fight when he leaned over her, pressing into her, on top of her. She didn't turn her head away when his lips brushed hers. No, she sank farther into the down pillow and opened her mouth to him, allowed him to teach her how to kiss, his tongue tangling with hers. When her hands entwined through his long silky hair, he took it as an invitation to explore her body. He fondled her breasts, traced her curves as he lifted the gown slowly up her legs, past her hips. She moaned into his mouth, and he deepened the kiss, circled her hard, pulsing nipple with the pad of his thumb.

Knowing it was only a dream, she let him take what he wanted.

"Just a feel of you," he whispered. "A small taste."

His hand skimmed along her belly, down to her curls. Her own hand wrapped around his wrist—not to stop, but to ensure that he would continue. When she felt the first brush of his blunt finger parting her, her eyes closed and she arched, wanting more than just that soft brush.

His strokes were slow, thorough. She could hardly bear it, the pressure deep within her, the ache to be filled with his fingers.

And then his mouth had kissed her *there*, and he had whispered darkly, *Open to me.*

"Issy? Issy?" Fiona called.

Isobel struggled back from her dream and into reality. How she wanted to relive that part, when her dream lover had slid along the length of her body and insinuated himself between her thighs, kissing and touching her for hours. He had made her cry out, tear at her sheets, beg for something she didn't know how to name.

"I'm sorry?" Isobel asked, trying to hide the huskiness in her voice. "You were saying?"

"Not me. You were the one speaking. Then you just stopped."

Isobel flushed. "Oh yes. I was wondering how long *you* have known about the earl?" she asked, refusing to think of how she had awakened that morning, thoroughly aroused. Her nipples had been hard little points against her nightgown, and her thighs had been wet. In the dream, her stranger had kissed and touched her until she had shook and wetness had leaked from her. He had liked it. Had told her so. Those hours had awakened a pleasure and passion she didn't realize could exist between man and woman.

Just a dream, she told herself. She'd only had it because she was angry at her father and Stuart for drawing up a contract with St. Clair. There would be no love, no warmth with the earl. There certainly would not be the intimacy she'd known in her dream. She could not imagine the earl caressing her so tenderly, putting his fingers against her most intimate place, lapping at her and whispering to her as her stranger had.

"Issy?" Isobel shuddered, realizing Fiona was looking at her strangely. "Are you all right? You're positively flushed!"

"Fine," she muttered, and resolved to put the dream out of her mind. Reaching for a strand of shimmering gold braiding, she wove it in and out of the bough. "The gas lamps will add a nice effect to this braiding, don't you think?"

"I think you're avoiding my question."

Isobel sighed and dropped onto the brocade settee. Boxes of Christmas decorations were strewn beside her. Even now, one of the downstairs maids was up in the attic searching for more.

Normally, decorating MacDonald Hall for the annual Christmas ball was the highlight of the season, but this year, her heart wasn't in it. She half wondered if St. Clair celebrated the holidays. He'd certainly never put much effort into making merry on the occasions that he had traveled to the hall for Christmas.

Isobel couldn't imagine being married to such a boring man.

Handsome or not, the Earl of St. Clair was not who she would have picked for her lifelong partner.

"And who would you have picked?" Fiona asked.

Isobel groaned. "I hadn't realized I said the words aloud," she muttered. Lord, she really was out of sorts today.

"Well?" Fiona asked again as she placed some candles among the greenery. "What sort of man would you wish for?"

"One who loves me," Isobel muttered in a huff. "I don't think that's asking too much."

"And what else?"

Isobel emptied a box of red and gold balls onto a velvet cushion. Without looking at Fiona, she replied, "Passion seems the sort of thing one might ask for in a marriage."

"Indeed," Fiona said, smiling, "passion is a must."

Fiona and Stuart had that in spades. Every time Isobel turned around, Fiona was in Stuart's arms, their lips pressed together. And each time Isobel saw them like that, she longed for the same with a man of her own.

"What makes you think that you will not have passion with the Earl?"

Isobel shrugged. "I don't think the Earl feels strongly about anything other than his lands and his money. A wife, I think, would come in a distant third, possibly even fourth, after his favorite hound."

Standing, Isobel kicked the train of her dark emerald green gown behind her and straightened her bustle. She then proceeded to the giant pine tree that stood in the corner of the parlor. With little hooks, she placed a few of the red balls on the branches before standing back to see where more balls and ornaments might be placed. After the decorations were all on, the candles and garland would come next. That task had always been left for Stuart and Ewan, who were, of course, nowhere to be found.

Behind her, Fiona came up and hugged her tight. "Have an open mind, Issy, you might find you're wrong about the Earl."

"Not bloody likely," she snorted. The proper Earl of St. Clair would probably swoon if he heard her unladylike talk. But then, Isobel doubted very much it was her good manners the earl was interested in. Her dowry, more likely.

"Well, now," came the sound of Stuart's voice. "You're supposed to be resting."

Fiona ignored her husband's pointed gaze. "And you're supposed to be helping trim the tree."

Stuart sauntered into the room and placed a kiss on his wife's lips. "What about a sleigh ride?" he asked. "I've asked the groom to have the horses readied."

Isobel hoped she could prevail upon Stuart to stop at the forest. She'd lost her clan pin yesterday, and she had a feeling it was in the woods where her scarf had gotten tangled in the low branches.

Her clan pin was a MacDonald heirloom. Handed down through the female line, she'd been eighteen when her grandmother MacDonald had given it to her. She couldn't allow it to be lost. Not when she'd dreamed of giving it to her daughter someday.

"A sleigh ride is a lovely idea, Stuart. I shall tell cook to prepare a crock of wassail, and we can sip it along the way."

"Perhaps, then, Miss MacDonald, you would be so kind as to accompany me."

Isobel whirled around. In the doorway was the Earl of St. Clair, looking sullen and not at all interested in a brisk ride in the cold. "Good day, my lord," she replied while curtsying. "What brings you to the hall yet again today?" Lord, was this to be a daily penance? she wondered. Could she expect the earl to arrive on her doorstep every afternoon?

A strange look passed between the earl and her brother. His mouth moved, but no sound came out. Then he pierced her with his gray eyes. "Your brother has been so kind as to invite me to be a guest of your family for Christmas."

"Has he?" she asked sweetly, while casting Stuart a venomous glance. "How thoughtful he is. Will you be staying through to twelfth night?" She almost feared his answer. When he nodded, she gritted her teeth. Two weeks with the earl. She'd rather have a tooth pulled.

"Well?" St. Clair drawled, offering his arm. "Shall we? I would be honored if you would enjoy the ride with me."

"Of course, my lord. I shall change and be with you directly. Stuart, you will be chaperoning, of course."

"Of course."

Of course. Everything was arranged. She was to be married off to the earl. She would be a countess, a true lady. She would have estates in England and Scotland. Her future husband was handsome and rich. And she was most likely the most miserable woman in Scotland.

Thank goodness Fiona and Stuart were sharing the sleigh with them. Isobel was not yet ready to be alone with the man. Lord, she didn't even know his Christian name. Or his favorite color, or . . . or any of the other meaningless things couples learn about each other during a courtship.

Worse, she didn't think the earl was the sort of man who knew the first thing about courting. He seemed most uncomfortable sitting beside her. Whenever their shoulders or knees would touch, he stiffened as though a brisk gust of air had blown down his collar. And sharing a lap fur with him was far too intimate for Isobel.

Across the sleigh, Stuart blew on his hands to warm them, and Fiona reached for them, drawing them inside her rabbit fur muff. Isobel arched her brows and looked out at the beautiful hills that passed them by. If the earl hoped she might bestow the same sort of kindness, he was hoping in vain.

"Shall we sing a carol?" Fiona asked. Stuart groaned and the earl positively glowered.

"Oh, let's!" Isobel agreed, relishing the look of pain on the earl's face. "I love singing, though I croak like a frog." She laughed, watching as his expression of pain deepened. "Don't you love singing, my lord?"

"I . . . I . . ." He moved his head, stretching his neck as though his tie was strangling him. "I do not sing myself, but would like nothing more than to hear your voice. I've always thought you sing like an angel."

Drat. She had sung every year at the ball, and St. Clair had heard her. There went her idea for sending him packing by singing like a fishwife.

"I only know the words to 'God Rest Ye Merry, Gentlemen,'" Stuart replied irritably. "If you would sing, it'll have to be that one."

"Well, then, shall we begin?"

As they sang the opening bars of the carol, St. Clair maneuvered the reins to turn the sleigh in the direction of the forest. Despite her attempts to be sulky, Isobel found herself enjoying the ride and the fresh, crisp air of the afternoon. She loved Christmas. The food, the carols, the presents. But most of all she loved spending time at MacDonald Hall. For most of the year, her family was in London. Stuart and her father owned a steel factory that supplied the railroads. It was only during Christmas that Isobel came back to the country of her birth, and the home they had shared when her mother was alive.

"Shall we stop and take a stroll?" the earl asked.

"I'd love a walk," Isobel agreed. "And I'd like to find some more holly for the centerpieces."

"Then we are agreed." The earl pulled the dapple-grays to a stop right before the forest. "This seems as good a place as any to stop."

Isobel froze as she remembered being in the forest and emerging from the exact spot where the sleigh now stood. She recalled the stag. The raven. The voice she had heard whispered on the breeze. She was certain it was those memories that provoked her into dreaming of that strange man. A man who was vastly different from the Earl of St. Clair.

"Shall we?" St. Clair offered her his hand. "I believe we will find lots of holly in the woods."

Isobel followed beside him while Fiona and Stuart contented themselves with picking pine cones from the trees at the edge of the wood.

"Are you not afraid of venturing into the wood?"

"Of course not, my brother is only footsteps away," she replied.

The earl chuckled. "I do not refer to myself, Miss MacDonald, but the other creatures who reside there."

"Rabbit and deer, do you mean, my lord? Hardly imposing creatures," she laughed, deftly stepping over a thick tree root.

"I meant the Otherworld folk."

Isobel stopped short. "Do you mean to tell me that you believe in faeries and trolls and unicorns?"

"Not trolls and unicorns, but faeries, aye. I believe in the Sidhe."

"You're superstitious."

"Do you not believe in the stories of our ancestors?"

She had once. It seemed like such a long time ago when her mother and grandmother had spoken of the faeries and their enchanted forests. Of course, they meant to frighten her away from venturing into the woods. Only the stories hadn't frightened her, but enticed her.

She'd been enticed into the woods yesterday, as well.

"Have you ever been in the woods, Miss MacDonald, and heard something strange? Have you ever felt as though there were eyes upon you, watching you from the cover of trees and moss?"

Isobel shivered. "I . . . I don't know what you mean, my lord."

He smiled. "I think you're every bit as superstitious as me."

"Does that surprise you?"

"Aye. And it pleases me as well. We'll have something to talk about once we are wed." Isobel gritted her teeth at the smugness she heard.

"You presume much," she said haughtily, letting her hand drop from his arm. She walked away from him, ignoring his sharp intake of breath. He reached for her arm and pulled her to a stop.

"You cannot feign ignorance, Miss MacDonald. I made my intentions quite clear to you this past summer, before you turned tail and ran off to London. Your father has agreed. I will have you for a wife."

"Why?" she asked. "There are many women who would have you in a trice. Why pick me?"

"Your father and I—" The earl stopped and looked up at the swaying trees. "Did you hear that? Someone called my name."

She hadn't, but Isobel was eager for a reprieve, no matter how short. "Stuart, I think. I'll wait while you see what he wants."

St. Clair looked skeptical, but then his eyes narrowed and his head cocked to the side as if he were listening. "Do not go any farther. I will return in a minute."

Isobel scowled at the command and lifted the hem of her long cloak. She would do what she pleased. Besides, she had her clan pin to find. She had a feeling it would be where she had seen her stag. She remembered her scarf getting tangled in the branches and knew that was what happened to her pin. And she would get it, despite what St. Clair, the stuffed shirt, had to say about going deeper into the woods alone.

Rounding the clearing of trees and roots, Isobel stepped over a few of the branches that had fallen to the ground. She was certain this was the spot. Falling to her knees, she searched through the thin layer of snow, pine needles and dried leaves for the silver pin.

"'Tis a shame to ruin such a charming view, but I would hardly be a gentleman if I left you on that cold ground."

With a squeak, Isobel jumped up and whirled around.

"Is this, by chance, what you're looking for?"

A figure of a man came out from between the trunks of two trees. He was tall, his legs muscular and fit in his snug-fitting buckskins and black shining boots. Around his waist he wore a belt with an intricately carved sword that sported a jeweled hilt. On the belt was a leather pouch decorated with a Celtic triscale.

As he emerged from the darkness into the daylight, she saw he was wearing a long black cloak and a richly embroidered waistcoat. His throat was bare, despite the cold, and his skin was bronzed as if it were summer, not the first day of winter.

As he stepped slowly out of the shadows, Isobel felt herself moving back until her shoulders brushed against the oak. She watched with a mixture of fear and curiosity as the man's face was revealed.

The sight robbed Isobel of breath. The shoulder-length black hair that blew freely around his broad shoulders, the aquiline nose and the high cheekbones, the mesmerizing violet eyes all came back to her in a blurry image. It was the man from her dream.

Holding his hand out to her, he uncurled his fingers and allowed her to see what he held in his palm. Their gazes collided and he took a step closer to her. "I have been waiting for you, Isobel MacDonald."

Chapter Five

She was the loveliest woman he had ever seen. Despite the fact that her glorious red hair was covered by the hood of her velvet mantle. Even with the shadows that concealed her pale skin and wide blue eyes, Daegan knew it as the truth. Isobel MacDonald was stunningly beautiful.

He had seen that beauty last night, when he had come to her in a dream. He had tasted her sweetness as her lips parted beneath his. He had felt her passion as he pressed her back on the bed and touched her.

Even now, he could still feel the tentative touch of her fingertips against his cheeks, his shoulders. She was innocent, but beneath her purity, there was a passion that burned hot.

Her gloved hands came up to her hood and she shoved it back, revealing a cascade of auburn ringlets that fell artfully from her coiffure. Her eyes were just as wide and clear as last night, yet he saw something different in them—awareness. That she was aware of him, that the memories of them together were flooding her consciousness made his blood hot. The animal in him wanted to press her back against the tree and mate with her. The Sidhe in him wanted her thoroughly enchanted before he claimed her and made her his. A quick rut was not what his Sidhe half desired. Only a full night exploring her body would satisfy him.

"How did you come by my pin, sir?" she asked breathlessly.

He could tell she recalled the dream and what she had allowed him to do. It was there in her eyes, the way her body seemed to grow lax. The perfume of her arousal that seemed to cloak him.

It was fortunate he had found the clan pin, for with his magic he had used it to enter her dreams. Once she had the pin back in her possession, the spell would cause her to return to him night after night in the groves of Annwyn.

"Sir?" she asked warily. "How did you come by my pin, and how did you know it belonged to me?"

"Are you not Isobel MacDonald of MacDonald Hall?"

She lifted her chin. "Yes."

"Then this is yours. I found it while wandering the woods on my morning walk."

"You have me at a disadvantage, sir," she said, her gaze taking him in from head to toe. "I don't believe we've met."

He smiled as he stepped closer to her. "Is that true, Isobel?"

She sucked in a breath as he came to stand directly before her. "I . . . I do not recall being introduced, sir."

"I am Daegan, prince of these woods. Perhaps now you recall our acquaintance?"

Her eyes flared and her breathing grew harsh. "I am quite sure you are not known to me."

He reached out and she flinched. He soothed her with a whisper as he attached the pin to her cloak. "I know you well, Isobel. And I intend for you to know me just as intimately."

Isobel could hardly breathe. How could he be here standing before her. The man from her dream. *Daegan.* She remembered his name, that he had claimed to be a prince. She had thought it a bit of fancy, a remnant from a young woman's childish fantasies of being a princess swept off her feet by a handsome prince. She hadn't truly believed that the man was real, nor could she have imagined him being even more handsome and virile in person.

"Ah, I think the lady doth remember," he murmured as his knuckles raked along her cheek. "Is it all coming back now, *muirnín?*"

"I . . . I dreamed of you," she said. Blushing, she immediately looked away, but he lifted her chin to have her look upon him.

"More than that. Last night, I came to you in your sleep."

His thumb, warm and soft, caressed her chin, then slid upwards toward the corner of her mouth, eliciting a warmth that rushed through her veins. "And . . . and . . ." Isobel swallowed hard, unable to finish or concentrate on anything other than Daegan's thumb stroking her.

"And we kissed. Touched."

She licked her dry lips, remembering how, and *where* he had touched her. "Am I dreaming now? I must be, for how can any of this be possible?"

"No. You are not dreaming. 'Tis real, this meeting. 'Tis fate."

The sound of twigs and branches snapping beneath heavy footfalls shattered the tension that had grown between them. Daegan narrowed his eyes and growled at the disturbance.

"I cannot see you again," she said, glancing at the open space where any second the earl might happen upon them.

"But you will, Isobel. You will. Tonight is the winter solstice, and when the moon is full, you will come to me, and I will tell you all you wish to know, and I will make you mine."

"There you are," the earl snapped as he shouldered his way through two pine trees. "I told you not to go haring off. Took me forever to find you."

Daegan was gone, as if he had evaporated into thin air. Perhaps he was an apparition, something her mind had conjured up to save her from worrying about her upcoming marriage. But the lingering warmth of Daegan's fingers on her chin, his knuckles on her cheek were real enough. How could she believe she had actually met this man in a dream? It was impossible.

"Well, shall we return? Mrs. MacDonald is tired and cold."

Fiona. She had all but forgotten about her brother and his wife. She'd been lost in Daegan's hypnotic violet gaze, and the sensual aura that seemed to hold her spellbound. She musn't think about him anymore. Her fingers sought the pin, and she was relieved to find it secured against her cloak. As she felt its familiar outline, Isobel couldn't help thinking of Daegan, wondering what *muirnín* meant.

Beloved. The word seemed to be whispered through the forest. *Mo Muirnín. My Beloved.*

She mustn't believe. Must not get her hopes her up. This could not be real. Perhaps she was tired from her restless sleep the night before, perhaps knowing the earl was to be her husband had driven her mad, for how could a man enter another's dream?

No, she must not believe she would ever see her stranger again.

Tonight, Isobel. You will return to me.

Stuart placed the prized thick oak log onto the iron stand. "A fine piece of wood for the Yule log," he announced as he lit a match. "May it burn bright and hot these next days, and may everyone's dream come true. Ready?" he asked, casting his gaze about the parlor. "Has everyone their wish in mind?"

Isobel tried to be practical and wish for good health for herself and her loved ones, but a pair of violet eyes and a sinfully seductive mouth came to mind. She shoved the thoughts away, but Daegan's image reappeared and refused to let go.

With a whoosh, the match lit the old dried log and it burst into flame, the orange flames flickering and crackling, the black smoke curling up the flue. To her despair, Isobel realized she had been wishing for just one more night with Daegan as her brother lit the traditional Yule log.

Just another silly superstition, Isobel told herself. Wishes upon the Yule log did not come true, any more than being kissed by a stranger beneath the mistletoe meant you were kissing your soul mate.

Silly, silly folktales that no longer had a place in these modern times.

"You've done such a lovely job decorating the parlor, Isobel," her father said quietly as he sat beside her on the settee. "You've got your mother's eye."

Isobel scanned the greenery on the hearth and the flickering candles on the tree. The parlor did look spectacularly festive. Even the presence of the Earl of St. Clair seated in a chair beside her could not mar this moment.

"You will make St. Clair this festive next year," the earl said in a confident, deep rumble.

Now the moment was officially ruined.

"Will you not sing for us?" her father asked as he gazed into the flames that flickered and waved. "I would hear you sing the Wexford Carol. It was your mama's favorite."

St. Clair sat back in his chair and watched her from the veil of his long, dark lashes. It unnerved her the way he watched her.

"Papa, I don't think—"

"Come, lass. 'Tis not much to ask, is it?"

No, it wasn't. Except that she didn't want to get up and sing for the earl. But she knew she had no choice. Smoothing her hands down her crimson-colored gown, she sashayed to the tree, her satin train and bustle crinkling with her steps. Her hands trembled and she purposely stood partially turned away from the earl and focused her gaze on Fiona, who was smiling in encouragement.

Her voice wasn't in perfect pitch at first, beginning in too high a key; then it steadied as her nerves calmed and she allowed herself to think not of the earl but of her mother.

The song ended, and everyone in the room clapped and begged for another. By the time she had finished the third carol, Isobel was parched.

"Ah, the maid is here with the tea things, or sherry if you prefer. It is, after all, the festive season, and there is nothing like a good sherry to warm the body and lift the spirits," her father announced. "Then I thought I might read some Dickens. Or perhaps Stuart might wish to take over the task this year."

"It would not be Christmas, Father, without hearing you read *A Christmas Carol*."

Her father inclined his head and lifted the red leather book to his lap. "I shall begin after Isobel finishes pouring."

Isobel made the rounds, pouring the tea and ensuring that everyone received a piece of currant cake. The earl made certain their fingers brushed when she passed him his cup, and Isobel gritted her teeth, trying to hide her frustration. Perhaps, had she not had that dream or met the mysterious Daegan, she would be pleased by the earl's attentions. However, she had dreamed about Daegan, and now everything seemed to come back to that, to him. She had thought of nothing else since their meeting in the woods that afternoon. She wanted to see him again, wanted to ask a hundred questions, wanted to feel what she had in her dream.

"Thank you, Miss MacDonald," the earl murmured as he accepted a second cup. "Perhaps you will sit with me while your father reads from Dickens's tale."

There really was no polite way to refuse, so Isobel took the empty chair beside the earl. They were sitting far too close in her opinion, but no one seemed to pay them any heed, not even when her gown, which was full and puffy from the layers of petticoats and bustle, spilled out over the chair in a mountain of brilliant red silk. She couldn't help but notice how some of it cascaded over the earl's knee. The earl noticed, too, for when he looked up at her, it was with an expression of heat that made her shiver. There was no mistaking what she saw in those gray eyes.

Her father chose that moment to begin reading, and Isobel fixed her attention on the sad story of Tiny Tim and the ruthless Ebenezer Scrooge. While her attention was focused on her father, the earl's, she knew, was focused on her.

Snow fell outside the large window, and Isobel felt her mind begin to wander as the warmth of the fire and the sherry she was sipping lulled her into lassitude. It was some time before her father closed the book and announced that the hour had grown late and that he was headed to bed.

"A moment of your time, Miss MacDonald," St. Clair asked before she could leave.

"I will wait for you in the hall," Fiona announced as her gaze volleyed between Isobel and the earl. "And then we can go upstairs together and leave the gentlemen to their port and cigars."

"We won't be but a minute," the earl replied, watching Fiona leave the room. Then he turned to her. "Miss MacDonald," he began. "I realize that while we have been acquainted for some time, you have not really had the opportunity to get to know me. I wish it had been different before the marriage contract was drawn up, but the past cannot be changed. I would have you know, however, that I do intend to court you properly."

Isobel felt at a loss for words. When the earl picked up her hand and held it in his, she didn't know what to do, or where to look. She did not want this with him. As strange as it was to admit, what she wanted was the enigmatic Daegan. A man she knew even less about than the earl. Yet he had captivated her thoughts like no other had ever done. He had seduced her with his kiss and artful caress. *That* was the man she wanted. Daegan.

"I think you and I will get on well together, Isobel," St. Clair murmured, using her Christian name for the first time. And then he kissed her, a quick brush of his lips against hers. "Good night," he said, releasing her.

As she walked up the stairs, Isobel couldn't help but think that the earl's kiss was nothing like Daegan's.

Chapter Six

In an ancient grove of oaks, the moonlight shimmered through the naked tree branches. The air was warm and soft, much too warm for a winter's night. It should have been cold and biting, yet as it passed through the thin material of Isobel's lace nightgown and wrapper the faint breeze was a welcome caress.

Surrounding the grove were megaliths, tall standing stones that formed a circle around the wood, lending it a pagan air that suited the eve of the winter solstice. This was not where she had first seen her stag, yet there was something familiar about it too that pulled at her memory. It was as if she had been here before, a long, long time ago.

She walked in silence, the pearls sewn into her white gown glinting in the moonlight. It was pure magic, this grove, like something out of a fairy tale. At the end of the path was a stone slab that had been made into some sort of altar. Covering it was a beautiful blue velvet cloth embroidered with a gold triscale like the one embossed on the pouch Daegan had worn. There was also a tall pewter cup that resembled a chalice, and a dirk that was curved and imprinted with strange markings. Mindlessly she traced her fingers over the scrolling etched on the blade. Everything felt mystical and otherworldly. *So strange yet so enticing,* she thought as she walked around the altar, her fingers brushing the velvet of the cloth.

Her heart beat faster with every step. Why was she here? Was she dreaming?

Suddenly the stag appeared in the circle, his hide glistening in a shaft of moonlight. He made not a sound, but turned and walked away. She followed it into a darker part of the wood, where it disappeared between two oaks. When she stepped between the trees, she found herself back in the grove, only this time Daegan was leaning against the altar, his legs crossed at the ankle, his arms crossed over his chest. He was watching her intently, his gaze straying over her body as the thin gown and wrapper molded against her breasts and thighs.

"Good eve, Isobel," he said, his voice husky and enthralling. She felt herself go liquid at the sound of his deep voice. "I have been waiting for the moon to rise so that you could come to me. And now, you are here, looking lovely by the silver light."

"You were not here a moment ago," she said, looking around the grove for a glimpse of the stag.

"Aye, I was here, watching you."

She shivered, not liking the feeling of being studied unawares. "Am I sleeping? I must be, for there is snow on the ground, and the branches creak and move as though the wind is blowing between them, but I feel none of it."

He came toward her and reached for her hand, pulling her deeper into the circle. He stood close to her, his fingers tracing the outline of her cheek. "Do you believe in the Otherworld, Isobel? That alongside your world, another exists?"

She looked around wonderingly. There was no denying that it was different from her world. But this was a dream. In sleep, magic could prevail. In reality, it didn't exist.

"You are in Annwyn, the Celtic Otherworld. It is separated from the mortal realm by the thinnest of veils. This sacred grove is the gate to our world. It is called the Cave of Cruachan, or the entrance to the Otherworld."

She stared at him in disbelief. "None of this can be real. It must be some fantastical dream." She smiled as she thought of her father reading to them. "Perhaps, like Scrooge, I've gone to bed and now I'm having dreams caused by indigestion. The clock has struck midnight and the ghosts will descend. I suppose that would make you the spirit of Christmas Past, wouldn't it?"

"I'm not a spirit, Isobel. Nor is this a dream," he murmured, lowering his mouth to hers.

His lips, soft and warm, brushed against hers. She gasped as she felt her own mouth tremble in response. Another brush, then another that was deeper, more hypnotic. Her body responded to his kiss, the way his arms wrapped around her, gathering her close to his chest, which was hard against her soft breasts. The contact of their bodies made her skin tingle with little vibrations that seemed to hum along her nerves.

When Daegan tilted his head and deepened the kiss, Isobel clutched at the edges of his black cloak, her legs weak. When his tongue touched hers, her knees threatened to buckle, but Daegan caught her in his arms, bringing her even closer to his body as he ravaged her mouth with his.

No, Daegan's kiss was not like the earl's. The way her body seemed to come alive in his arms was nothing short of magical.

"Isobel," Daegan murmured as he nuzzled the space beneath her ear. "How can I make you see that this is not a dream? That I am really here with you?"

"Kiss me again," she whispered. Her body ached for more, more than a kiss, she knew. She might be a virgin, but at one and twenty, she knew of matters between men and women. She knew what she wanted from Daegan. "Please," she begged, clutching at his shoulders. "I know what I want, and that is you."

His violet eyes seemed to darken as he once more lowered his head and captured her mouth. This time, though, the carefulness was gone, replaced by a thrilling hunger that fueled her blood.

Daegan was ravenous in his kiss, his lips commanding hers, his tongue dueling with her own. And his hands . . . Good lord, he left no place on her untouched. The edges of her breasts, her hips, her buttocks. She moaned into his mouth when he cupped her bottom in his hands and deepened his kiss, plunging his tongue into her mouth.

She mewled against him, accepting whatever he would give her. When he broke the kiss and pressed his lips against her bounding pulse, she sighed and closed her eyes, allowing herself to indulge in the forbidden pleasure.

"You know not how long I have waited for you," he groaned as his lips brushed her throat. "In Annwyn time moves much slower than in your world. An hour spent here is but a minute in your world. Imagine the torture I have endured waiting."

She heard what he was saying, but could not focus on the words or make sense of them. She only wanted more, more kisses, more touches. And she wanted those caresses to be on her bare skin.

"Please," she whispered into his silky hair. "You know what I want, Daegan."

"Yes. I know what you want, *muirnín*. And I will give it to you."

Daegan's lips and tongue tasted the sweet skin of Isobel's throat and the swells of her breasts. Her hands were fisted in his hair, clutching and tugging, begging him without words for more. The way she said his name did strange things to his brain, making him think of nothing other than hearing her shout it as he slid inside her. She whimpered when he pulled at the satin tie of her wrapper. He pulled the garment from her and let it fall to the ground. Then he reached for the sleeve of her night rail, tugging until he revealed one perfect coral-tipped breast.

"You are so beautiful, Isobel," he said with reverence ringing in his voice. "You were made to be savored in the moonlight."

Her passion-glazed eyes met his and she smiled. "Will you savor me, then, Daegan?"

"Aye. Forever."

He circled her erect nipple with his tongue, making her moan. Her body was warm, flaring to life beneath his hands. In the circle of the grove, his magic spell hovered, keeping out the winter chill and wind. She would be warm in this grove. Protected. She would be his.

Pulling away, he met her gaze. "I must have you, Isobel." He didn't wait for her reply, but took her lips hungrily, kissing her with all the need and desire that was swimming in his veins. She felt so soft against him, so right. Her breasts were full and high, and made for his mouth and hands. And her thighs hugged and molded his erection as if she had been designed for him. Everything about her was perfect.

Isobel felt her legs weaken as Daegan started to slide her nightgown down over her hips. His mouth followed the trail of the silk, his lips grazing her skin as he slowly exposed her. With shaking hands she clasped his head in her hands while he kneaded her belly with his mouth, the masculine scent of him wafting up to heighten her senses. Instinctively her fingers curled in his hair, clenching tightly as he nuzzled her curls through her chemise.

His mouth made her crazed. The lust she felt made her dizzy.

She wanted him, whatever he would do to her. Even though she was betrothed to St. Clair, she wanted this night with Daegan.

On his knees, he kissed her sex. Hungrily, she clutched at his shoulders. When he lifted her leg and placed it over his shoulder, exposing her, she moaned and raked her fingers through his silky hair. His tongue was hot, wet, scorching her. She should be ashamed of what she was doing, but the pleasure was so great that she shoved the guilt away and enjoyed Daegan's tongue.

Soon she was scratching her nails down his shoulders, biting her lip to keep from crying out as she began to shake. When the trembling was over, he looked up at her, his eyes dark and unreadable.

"Be with me, *muirnín*." He lifted her into his arms as if she weighed nothing more than a feather. "Let me show you what it can be like for us."

Their gazes met and held, and Isobel saw the hope and hesitation in his eyes before he set her down on a bed that was cushioned with furs. How had it suddenly appeared in the middle of the grove?

A dream, she reminded herself. A lovely, passionate, vivid dream.

"Say that tonight you'll give yourself to me, Isobel."

"Yes." And she would savor the memories of this dream for many, many nights. She wanted this, and she wanted to experience it with Daegan. No man had ever made her feel this way, so conscious of her femininity, of her own desires and needs. She felt beautiful and sensual, and tonight she was going to give in to temptation.

Kneeling, Daegan placed her legs over each of his muscled thighs. His hands, a stark contrast against her pale flesh continued to slide up her sides to cup and squeeze her breasts. "You won't ever regret this, Isobel," he vowed, trailing his tongue up her belly. His silky hair tickled the undersides of her breasts, making her skin erupt in gooseflesh.

"I could never regret anything I do with you." She sighed deeply. How could she regret something that felt this wonderful? Good lord, if she didn't know better, she would say she loved him. But he was only a dream, no matter how handsome, how powerful. A dream of a lover who was as ensnared by her as she was by him.

His head was atop her breasts, his eyes searching hers through the pale shaft of moonlight. He looked boyish and vulnerable, and infinitely lovable. "Tonight, I will show you why you were made for me."

She watched him unfasten the pewter clasp to his cloak, tossing it to the foot of the bed. Then he removed his shirt with short, vicious movements, flinging it onto the ground along with his trousers and boots before turning to rest lightly atop her. The instant his naked body made contact with hers, Isobel felt a jolt of awareness. He felt heavy and warm and very male.

"No other man shall ever have you. You're mine, Isobel. You have been since the first time I saw you."

His possessive words thrilled her and she moaned, angling her hips so that his fingers would dip lower and part her. "Please."

"Please what?" he teased, his tongue laving her nipple before he captured it between his teeth and bit gently. "Please stop?"

"No."

"Tell me, Isobel."

His mouth was pure magic, and just when she thought she couldn't stand it any longer, he turned his attention to her other breast, all the while his fingers continuing to tease the flesh of her sex.

"Make love to me," she panted, her hips arching fiercely in order to feel more of his touch.

And then his mouth was on hers, his lips and tongue demanding as his fingers parted her and stroked her. She cried out when she felt him insert one, then another finger. *"Please,"* she gasped.

Daegan had never had a woman beg for his touch before. Never had a female made him so aware of his virility. Everything about Isobel pulled and tugged at the primitive urges buried deep inside him. The desire to take her was strong, almost impossible to resist. All his senses cried out to sink himself inside her tight welcoming body and claim her for himself.

She rocked against his hand. He watched as she learned and responded to the rhythm of his touch, her hips moving seductively in time to his fingers as they pleasured her.

She was built so perfectly and lush, with full breasts and hips. The Sidhe females were tall and lean, small breasted and narrow hipped. The males of his race had to challenge each other for them, and the male who won spent the rest of the night proving his worthiness to be her mate. It was as much a battle of wills as it was pleasure. But this, with Isobel, was true magic. She was soft and feminine, yielding to his skills. Her desire and acceptance made him feel more virile and masculine than his hardest-won conquest—a conquest he could no longer remember.

As he looked down at Isobel lying beneath him, he realized that this would forever be his, this pleasure, this lazy and perfect loving. And this woman. Mortal or not, she was the only female he wanted.

Daegan reached for her hands and pinned them in his, holding them above her head. Her breasts brushed his mouth, teasing him with taut, coral nipples. His erection was riding hard between her soft thighs, driving him forward, urging him to part her. To take her in an act of raw possession.

He gave in, parting her with his shaft, allowing himself to slide along her, feeling the slickness of her desire covering him. Her tongue came out to wet her lips and he captured it with his mouth, imitating what his body would soon be doing inside her.

And then he was inside her, filling her as she continued to tremble, his strong hands fitting her thighs against his waist as he pushed farther and farther into her body.

Isobel moaned his name, unable to disguise the desire—God help her, the love in her voice.

"Say my name again, *muirnín*," he whispered.

"Daegan," she whimpered as he pushed past the last remaining barrier of her virginity.

And then he was moving atop her, the muscles of his shoulders and arms bunching and tightening with his exertion. His strokes were slow and intentional, forcing her to take all of him, and she did, took everything he had to offer and gave what she could of herself, including her budding love. She didn't know how it could happen so fast. It was impossible. But anything was possible in dreams, she reminded herself, even making love on a bed in the middle of an enchanted forest!

Wrapping her legs around his lean waist, Isobel followed him, rising up to meet his thrusts. There was no pain, only pleasure as he loved her, held her tight and kissed her cheek.

"My God, it's never been like this," he groaned into her ear. "You feel so good. So right."

Isobel felt his seed start to spill inside her. His breath came in harsh pants as he rested his head between her breasts. Isobel drank in the scent of her perfume mixed provocatively with Daegan's spicy scent. Thinking he was finished, she hugged him tight, but he rolled with her, bringing her atop him.

He smiled as she squeaked in surprise, "You didn't think I was done with you?"

She moaned, unable to say anything when his fingers circled the top of her sex. The strange vibration she felt when she touched him was magnified when he touched her there.

"Come for me, Isobel." He encouraged her in a husky whisper before he captured her breast and began to suckle. The rhythm of his finger and his mouth synched, and her hips rocked. He was still hard and filling her deep as he showed her how to move.

She clutched at his shoulders and cried out, unable to bear the sensations rushing at her, and all along he brought her higher, wouldn't let her stop or push his hand away. Then she was trembling and shaking and clutching him wildly, hoping she would never awaken from this dream.

Chapter Seven

Isobel snuggled up to Daegan and closed her eyes as he trailed his fingers along her naked shoulder. She thought her dream would have ended by now, yet here she was, still in the forest, and in bed with Daegan.

"How do you feel?" he asked, and she smiled at the concern she heard in his voice.

"Alive," she murmured, purring like a well-fed kitten.

"I fear I was too rough for your first time. I went too fast, took what I wanted before thinking of you, and what you desired."

"I got what I wanted," she said as she yawned, "you making love to me."

He gathered her close and squeezed her tight. Her hands wrapped around his waist, and she marveled at the strength in him. "What's this?" she asked as her fingertips brushed a ragged edge in his side. Pulling away, she saw the angry red mark below his nipple.

"Do you not remember the arrow?" he asked, puzzled.

"The arrow hit the stag," she murmured, drawing away from him. "In the same spot."

"Isobel," he whispered, reaching for her. "Do not be afraid."

"What are you?" she cried, kicking at him from beneath the fur blankets. She wanted to wake up—*now*.

"I am Daegan, Prince of the Sidhe. You are in Annwyn. My world."

The breath left her lungs as she grappled with what he was saying. "No," she cried, trying to wake up from this dream that was turning into a nightmare. "I don't believe—"

He caught her face in his hands. "You must believe. Look around you, Isobel. You're not at home, in your bed. You're in my world. My bed."

"This is just a dream. You're not real. The Otherworld isn't real."

"Does this not feel real?" he asked, kissing her. "Was it not real when we were making love?"

It had certainly felt real. But how was any of this possible? It wasn't logical.

"There are many things that mortals do not understand, Isobel. My kind is only one of the mysteries out there."

"You're an animal," she gasped, her gaze dropping to the scar left by the arrow.

"I am a Sidhe who can, by birth and magic, shift into the shape of a white hart."

"You're . . . you're not a man."

"No. But I feel as a man feels. I hurt as a man does when the woman he desires, the woman he has loved for so long, rejects him."

Some of her fear and disbelief left her. If his words were untrue, would she have seen the sincerity, the hurt shining in his violet eyes?

"You don't have pointy ears," she blurted out as she stared at him. "And you're not small."

He smiled and brushed her hair over her shoulder. "Pixies are small, as are brownies. They're mischief makers. I am of the Sidhe, a fairy race that looks mortal. I do not have pointy ears, or wings. But I can weave magic." He waved his hand to encompass the grove. "I used magic tonight to make it warm for you. I placed an enchantment spell on your clan pin so that you will return to me and these woods night after night."

"Why?" she asked in a breathless whisper, her heart beating madly in her chest.

"Because I have loved you for many years, Isobel, and have only been waiting until the right moment to reveal myself."

"And why is this the right time?"

"I could not bear to see you married to another. Not when I want you as my wife."

Isobel swallowed hard. He was everything she had dreamed of in a husband. He loved her, he was considerate and passionate. There would be pleasure with him. But even if she could bring herself to believe his story, what future could there be for them? He was magical. And she was a mortal without any special powers. She could never have him for her husband, not really.

He must have known what she was thinking, because he reached for her and brought her into his arms. "I have taken your virginity, Isobel. That makes you mine. That is the way of mortals, isn't it?"

"No, it is not. I am the Earl of St. Clair's. The contract is already drawn up. There is nothing that can stop it."

With a growl, he pulled away from her, his eyes black. "Do you think a mere mortal can stop me from having you? I am stronger and smarter than any human. My magic knows no bounds. Nothing could stop me from keeping you here, with me."

"No," she cried. She was well afraid now, afraid of being trapped in something she did not understand.

"You're mine," he raged, reaching for her hands. "And a Sidhe never gives up what is rightfully his."

"I am no pawn, Daegan, for either man or Sidhe."

"You're bound to me, not by magic, Isobel, but by love. Only allow yourself to admit the truth."

"It can never be, Daegan. I'm sorry!"

"Isobel!" he cried, reaching for her but clutching only thin air. She seemed to be floating away, and the last thing she saw was Daegan on his knees calling for her to come back.

With a jolt, she awakened in her own bed. The dawn was breaking, the sun an orange disc rising slowly above the white clouds.

She was awake. Alone. Dressed, she realized, in her nightgown and wrapper. The remnants of her dream came back to her, and she realized that her breasts felt swollen and her thighs were stiff, as if she had been in the saddle too long. And then she saw it. The small, circular red stain on her nightgown, and knew her night with Daegan was no dream. It had been real. She had given her virginity to an immortal who could never be hers.

She cried then, her feelings finally unguarded. What was she to do now? How would she explain her loss of virginity to St. Clair?

Even as she thought it, she knew she could not marry the earl. As strange and as impossible as it sounded, she loved Daegan. How had it happened? She barely knew him—no, that wasn't the truth. Somehow she had felt him as a presence in her life these past years.

Lying down, she snuggled her cheek into the pillow and sniffled away the last of her tears. Sunlight crept in through her bed curtains, illuminating the clan pin that lay on the empty pillow beside her. Daegan had enchanted her pin. He'd told her that the spell would bring her back to the forest—to Annwyn—night after night. The pin was the link to him, the spell that drew her.

Jumping up, Isobel snatched the pin from the pillow and shoved it to the back of a drawer in her wardrobe. She would forget about the pin. Would never touch it again. Putting it out of mind would free her from the spell, and Daegan's hold. For she needed to break the hold he had over her. They could never really be together. A mortal and a Sidhe? No, it would never work.

"I saw the white hart this morning," St. Clair announced at supper that evening.

"The beast is still alive, is it?" Ewan grumbled.

"Strange, to be sure," the earl murmured. "The animal stood his ground with me, again. I may have imagined it, but the beastie appeared to be challenging me."

"What's this about a white hart?" her father asked as he rested his utensils against his plate.

"Magnificent stag," Ewan declared. "Would look right at home with its head mounted on a plaque above our hearth."

Isobel thought of Daegan and closed her eyes. He didn't deserve to be hunted, to be killed. The thought of her brothers running after him, shooting at him, made her feel violent.

"Let us gather a hunting party for the morning," her father announced. "Fifty pounds to the man who fells this stag and brings me his head. He shall have the place of honor over the hearth."

Ewan slid his gaze to her. "What do you think of that, Issy? A bounty on your hart?"

She glared at her brother before turning her gaze to her father. "I would ask that you spare this animal, Papa. He has done nothing to harm anyone here. He does not cause mischief, or eat from the gardens. He is a beautiful creature, meant to be left alone, not hunted."

"I, for one, will not take part in such a hunt," St. Clair announced. "The white hart is a mystical creature. A sign that the Otherworld is near."

"Afraid of a few fae?" Ewan snickered. "I'm surprised, St. Clair; you seem to be such a steady bloke."

The earl cleared his throat. "I have seen one myself."

"*What?*" the entire table asked in shock.

Good lord, was St. Clair touched in the head?

"I was five, and I saw him crawl in the library window—"

"Did he have black hair and violet eyes?" Isobel asked, interrupting him.

The earl looked at her strangely. "No, he was fair, his skin as pale as a ghost's, and his eyes were black. He—he took my mother, and she was never seen again."

"What makes you think it was a Sidhe and not a man," Ewan challenged.

"No man carries this." St. Clair reached into his jacket pocket and pulled out a dirk, very similar in design to the one she had seen on the altar last night. "'Tis called an athame. It is a ritual knife used in their sacred marriage ritual. I've done extensive research into Druid religion," he said, passing the dirk to Stuart, who sat on his right. "The ancient Celtic priests carried similar objects and similarly worshipped the moon. The Sidhe, the Druids said, gave them this religion."

Her family looked at the earl as if he were mad. But Isobel knew he was sane, and more than that, correct. The Sidhe were real. So was Annwyn.

"So you see, I will not invoke the wrath of the Sidhe. I will not hunt the hart. Leave it be," the earl muttered as he began to eat his supper.

"And you expect us to just swallow that rubbish," Ewan scoffed.

"What a delightful dinner," Fiona said, with a glare at Ewan. "We are so happy to have you for Christmas, my lord. I do hope you are enjoying your stay here with us at MacDonald Hall."

Ewan grumbled and Isobel glanced away. The earl nodded and picked up his fork.

"Shall you read A *Christmas Carol* again tonight?" Fiona asked Isobel's father in what could only be a desperate attempt to get the dinner conversation back on track.

"Of course, of course," her father chuckled. "But first, I'd like to hear more about this hart. Crafty wee beastie, is he?"

"He is indeed, Father. But do not worry. I will get him for you."

Isobel glared at Alistair. So did St. Clair, she noticed.

"I would have a care, MacDonald, before you go taunting the beast," the earl warned. "Leave the hart alone."

"And why is that?" Ewan asked.

The earl sat back in his chair, his long, tapered fingers brushing against the blade of the athame that rested on the table. "Because you may very well find one of yours carried off in the night, never to be seen again."

Chapter Eight

The moonlight glittered on the snow-covered ground. From her window seat, Isobel sat and watched the snow gently falling. In her palm was the clan pin. The silver tingled in her hand, warming her palm. She felt the call of the enchantment, the whispering voice of Daegan. *Come to me, muirnín,* but she ignored it. Tried to pretend she didn't hear him in her thoughts, feel him in her heart.

He was an animal. A Sidhe. Had it all been a lie? The dream? The night in Annwyn when he had loved her so well? Could he even love a mortal?

She didn't know what to think. How to feel. How to go on. She only knew that by returning to Annwyn she would only confuse matters.

Her heart was already engaged; it had been since she was six, when she first saw her hart drinking from the loch. He had been a presence in her life since then. She could not deny it. But what he was . . .

With a sigh, she put the pin down on the windowsill as she rested her head against the window. Annwyn was before her, calling to her. She could see it through the frosted panes and the snow. Her eyelids flickered as her gaze dropped to the pin. Of their own volition, her fingers reached for it, her breathing growing harsh, her vision growing hazy with sleep.

Yes. Come to me.

No. She must not. She could not return there. Could not allow herself to be lost in a world she didn't know. A world she feared with a man who was not a man at all.

With one last look she rose from the seat and made her way to the lounge by the hearth. She would wrap gifts and forget about Daegan. She would continue on as though she had never met him, never tasted his kiss or experienced his touch.

Return to me.

No, I cannot.

You are mine, and you will come.

Her heart lurched, her body softening to the possessive sound of his voice. It was all she had ever wanted, to be loved and desired. Yet her mind warred with her body, with her need for Daegan's touch. She was tired of being a pawn of men. First her father, then St. Clair. Now, Daegan with his commands.

If you want me so much, she challenged, casting a glance at the window, *then you will have to come and take me.*

Opening the door of Isobel's chamber, Daegan found her asleep on the chaise before the fire. Surrounding her were presents wrapped in red and green and tied up with big, shining gold bows. It was Christmas for the mortals, and Yule for his kind. It was the birth of Christ the humans celebrated, and the birth of the sun god and longer days for his people. The sacred days for both celebrated birth, life, and joy. There was no difference in that, no great division between their kind. The humans worshipped the sun and prayed to their god. The Sidhe worshipped the moon and prayed to the nature gods. They were not that different. Yet how did he convince Isobel of that?

As he came closer to her, he realized that she was dressed for bed, her filmy nightgown, supposedly virginal, excited him. From somewhere deep inside, he felt the stirring of his demons. Passion, hot and scorching, rushed through his veins as his hungry gaze took in the picture of Isobel, her pale limbs outlined against the bloodred velvet while shadows cast by the fire danced across her creamy skin, rendering the silk dressing gown almost translucent.

Swallowing hard, Daegan approached the chaise, his eyes roving every inch of her, admiring her lush thighs, the roundness of her hip, the full, heavy breasts that strained against the ties of her gown.

He wanted her.

It wasn't merely a need to make love to her or to kiss her senseless. He desired her with a possessive passion that frightened him. There was so much at stake, not only for Isobel, but for himself as well. He could not leave Annwyn. He would cease to exist outside his world. But living without Isobel was not a life, but merely an existence.

She had resisted the lure of the enchantment spell tonight. He had waited and waited, pacing the grove, knowing why she resisted the call, feeling her fears, her doubts. But it angered him. He had strengthened the spell, and still she did not come to him. And then he heard her challenge. He had not thought of anything after that. The animal in him took the challenge. He was ready to mark and claim—*to mate*. The Sidhe in him was willing to sacrifice everything to prove himself worthy of her.

She had flung a challenge in the wind he could not resist or ignore.

Resting his thighs against the curved arm of the chaise, he looked down at the angelic form of the woman he would have as his wife. She had angered him as no other had ever done, rendering him nearly savage with jealousy when he thought of her with St. Clair or any other male. And yet, when he looked at her, her glorious curls in disarray, her copper lashes fanned lightly against her cheek, he could think of nothing other than waking her slowly with passion.

He could not stay angry with her for leaving him alone. It was mortal fear that ruled her, not her heart. Seeing her sprawled out provocatively, his anger completely dissipated, leaving him thinking of all the different things he wanted to do to her.

Unable to resist temptation, he leaned over the arm of the chaise and stroked the hair from her face. When his fingers trailed down her cheek, she instinctively curled into his hand. He smiled as she mumbled something unintelligible. His fingers continued to trace a path to her neck, where they shakily reached for the ties of her gown. Parting the lace ruffle to expose the pale globes of her breasts, his breath caught as he realized she was completely naked beneath.

A log crackled and sparked in the hearth, sending a flicker of light along her thighs that illuminated the curls that lay nestled between her legs. He itched to part and taste her. To awaken her with his mouth.

Forcing himself to take things slower, Daegan concentrated on removing the gown from beneath her. Once she was naked, he pulled his shirt over his head, his appreciative gaze traveling up and over her as the linen slipped from his fingers, landing on the floor. His eyes once more moved up the length of her legs. He remembered the way they had felt against his waist—soft, welcoming, infinitely feminine. He imagined his hands pressing into their softness while he plunged into her, her husky moan welcoming him, telling him she needed him as much as he needed her.

Sighing heavily, she turned onto her back, her breasts bouncing with the movement. Trailing his hands up the length of her waist, he stopped to cup them. They were full and heavy, the nipples already peeking out from between his fingers. Unable to resist, he pressed her breasts together, kissing each firm bud

Isobel moaned sleepily, arching her back and thrusting her breasts farther into his mouth. He groaned when he felt her hands steal behind his head, her fingers combing into his hair.

"I didn't think you would come."

"You should have. You're mine, and I always come for what is mine. How could you think I'd be able to stay away?" he asked against her mouth before sliding his tongue inside. She moaned, angling her hips invitingly. His hand stole down her belly where he kneaded a path to her curls. It was arousing to see his large hand stroke her possessively. She was his, and he wanted her to want him as fiercely as he wanted her.

"I have proven I want you, Isobel. Now I demand the same."

Her fingers gripped his hand, and her legs clamped tightly together when his finger slid into her. She whimpered as he parted her and slid his finger along the length of her sex, which was damp and ready for him.

"Can you not feel how much I want you?" she asked as she took his wrist in her hand and forced his finger deeper inside her. She moaned, spreading her thighs wider for him.

He could feel his demons nipping at his heels, driving him to satisfy his needs. He wanted to brand her with his passion. To leave his mark so that she would know that she belonged to him, and only him.

"So sweet. Yes. You want me. I feel it," he murmured, his finger slipping inside as his breath caressed her wet flesh. She began to pant and twist beneath his ministrations. He loved how she raked her hands through his hair.

He pulled her up to straddle his hips, his fingers sinking into her thighs as he slowly lowered her onto him. Her body arched, her long curls grazed the velvet cushion as her breasts bounced evocatively with every one of his thrusts. He loved watching her body move in time with his. Loved how her hair glistened in the firelight, the ends rubbing against the silk in time to his strokes in a rhythm that was both slow and seductive.

His finger stole into her curls, and she whimpered in appreciation. She sank farther onto him, totally impaling herself on his length. He heard her suck in her breath, and he nipped at her ear as his finger continued to tease her sensitive flesh. She tightened, then jerked in his arms, her bottom provocatively grazing his thighs. He smiled into her hair as the soft cries of her release splintered the air, and he watched as her face softened into exquisite bliss.

His seed spilled forth as he continued to rock against her, her warmth enveloping him, caressing and tightening around him.

"I won't ever let you go, Isobel," he said against her hair. "No matter what happens, you'll always belong to me."

"Do Sidhe men always wake their women so?" Isobel asked as she yawned. Daegan chuckled and wrapped his arms around her as he lifted her from the lounge and carried her across the room to the bed. "I couldn't resist. You looked so enticing."

Isobel sat up, her long hair dragged over Daegan's chest. "I'm glad."

He covered her lips with his index finger. "I cannot always come to you, Isobel. My magic . . . my essence is intertwined with Annwyn. I cannot exist for any time outside its realm. You will have to come to me."

"I'm sorry," she said, biting her lip. "I was confused. I didn't know what to do, but I always knew I wanted you."

He kissed her soundly then. "I could not bear another night without you."

Isobel lay in his arms and enjoyed the feel of his fingers lazily making circles on her back. She was content and happy like this, in Daegan's arms.

"What are we going to do?" she said with a sigh. "How will we stay together? I do not only want to have you in my sleep, Daegan. And you cannot live in my world—"

"There is a way for you to live in mine," he said, "but you will have to decide if it is the path you wish to walk."

"What is it?"

"I could offer you the rite of lanamnas."

"And that is?"

"It is a sacred ritual of my people. It is a sort of a handfasting, but for us, the lanamnas is only taken with a soul mate. It is an eternal vow, *muirnín*. You will be my wife in all ways, and I will be your husband."

"And we can be together if I agree to this rite?"

He nodded. "But there is a price for us to be together. Once we are eternally bound, you cannot leave Annwyn—ever."

Her heart sank. To never see Fiona again, or her father. To never see her soon-to-be niece or nephew . . .

When she looked up at him, it was through tears. "You speak of eternity. Are you immortal?"

He stroked her cheek. "We can be killed, by iron and black magic.

But if left in peace to live out our natural lives, it is possible for my kind to live many hundreds of years, and when it is our time, our magic dies, our inner light wanes, and we fade into Summerland."

"Would I live that long then?"

"In Annwyn you would. Once you are bound to me and my magic, I will make it so."

"Everyone I love will be long dead before I die." Biting her lip, she forced back the croak in her voice. "And in the afterlife? Where will I go? To our heaven or to your version of it?"

"I do not know." His gaze softened, and he kissed her brow, then her nose, before softly brushing his mouth against hers. "'Tis much I ask of you, Isobel. I know that. I will not press you. I will release my spell on the pin, and my hold on you. You see," he said, cupping her cheek, "I love you too much to see you unhappy. Come willingly to me, understanding all that you will give up, or come not at all and be happy and know that I will always love you."

"Daegan!" she cried as she threw her arms around his neck. "Why must it be so hard for us!"

"It is the way of star-crossed lovers, is it not?"

She grumbled, but then sobered. "I nearly forgot," she said, pulling away from him. "My father has organized a hunting party for tomorrow morning—"

"And I am to be hunted?" he asked with a grin.

"Do not make light of this," she said, slapping him lightly on his arm. "You must take care to keep hidden."

"You worry?" he asked, rather pleased.

"Of course I worry. My father wants your head mounted and hung above our fireplace, for heaven's sake."

He laughed and gathered her close. "I can take care of myself, *muirnin*. There is no need for these tears, for come the night I will be waiting for you. You will see."

She wiped the tears away with the back of her hand. "Will you stay with me tonight?"

He nodded and settled against the headboard. "I will stay with you. Forever if you will have me, *muirnín*."

In the morning he was gone. Isobel hurried and got up from bed and rang the bell for her maid.

Elizabeth arrived seconds later. "Ack, Miss," she cried, rushing over. "Donna rush. Breakfast is nae ready yet."

"My father and brothers," she grunted, twisting in order to undo the buttons of her nightgown. "Have they left yet?"

"Nay, miss. The horses are only being saddled now."

"Good, then fetch my riding habit and leather boots."

"You're gonna ride this morning, before tea?" Elizabeth asked. "That's not like you, miss."

"I know," she huffed, straightening her hair as her maid pulled the black-and-gold habit from the wardrobe.

"Why donna you sit, miss, and I'll se tae your hair."

"I'm in something of a rush, Elizabeth. I won't be fussing with it today."

She shocked her maid speechless when she pulled the wool skirt from the hanger and jumped into it without her drawers and petticoats. "Help me, Elizabeth. I can't manage the buttons by myself."

"Are you all right, miss? You 'aven't taken ill, 'ave you?"

Isobel laughed. "Perhaps taken leave of my senses, but I assure you, I'm hale and hearty in every other aspect. Now then, Elizabeth, if you will inform the groomsman to prepare my horse."

She had Daegan to save this morning.

Chapter Nine

In the end, Daegan had evaded them. Thank the Lord, she thought, glancing up at the sky. Daegan was safe. But for how long? she wondered.

Well, at least he had not come to any harm. She had been terrified for him. Every time she had seen the trees of the forest sway she had feared he would emerge, prepared to charge.

But he hadn't. She wondered what had kept him away. Instinctively she knew it wasn't fear. Daegan was fearless. Perhaps it was for her own peace of mind.

Closing her eyes, she thought of him and the night they'd shared. She also thought of his proposal, if it could be called such. A rite, he had called it, a way to bind them together forever. She only had to sacrifice her family to his.

Why could love never be easy? she wondered. As she patted her mount's muzzle, Isobel turned away. She was cold and hungry. A good meat pie and a cup of tea is what she needed.

"Don't go."

She gasped and looked up as she caught the shadow of someone emerging from her horse's stall. *St. Clair.*

"Good day, my lord."

"Good day, Isobel. I trust your ride was successful."

"The hart was not found."

St. Clair looked relieved. "But you've seen him, haven't you?"

Isobel cocked her head to the side. "Not of late, my lord."

"The hart. He is yours."

Isobel took a step back as the earl came closer. "I don't know what you mean."

"He was going to impale me, and yet, when he saw you standing there, he couldn't bring himself to do it. To murder me before you."

She laughed, a tight, high-pitched sound. "He's an animal, my lord."

"Aren't we all?" the earl murmured as he came to stand toe to toe with her. "But to return to the hart. For some reason he's marked you."

"Forgive me, my lord, but I'm really rather hungry and would like to change clothes before luncheon—"

His arm shot out, preventing her from moving. "They say the hart is really the ruler of Annwyn. And Annwyn is always ruled by the Sidhe."

Isobel swallowed hard, but held his gaze.

"Have you seen the hart in his man's form, Isobel?"

"Of course not!" she cried. "This is just rubbish!"

"I have watched you, you know. You always seem drawn to the woods. Now more than ever, I see you looking at them."

"I like nature."

He smiled, but there was little warmth in it. "Last night, at the table, did you believe me?"

"About faeries?"

"Aye."

She cast about for an answer, anything that would make him leave her alone and protect Daegan.

"I think you did," St. Clair murmured. "I saw the recognition in your eyes when I raised the athame. You've seen it before."

Isobel shook her head, but the earl quieted her protests. "I will tell you now what I couldn't say last night. The woods, Isobel, are alive, teeming with Sidhe. My mother knew that. She was seduced by their magic. By one of their males—"

Isobel tried to step to the side, but St. Clair wrapped his hands around her shoulders, caging her. "My mother began to waste away. She would sit for hours and hours, staring out the window, watching. Pining for her lover."

"My lord, really—"

"Her lover came for her; I saw him. I knew that night I would never see her again."

"And what do you mean by telling me this?" Isobel asked.

St. Clair's eyes turned molten. "I believe you are under the same spell."

Her whole body went rigid. "You are insane," she scoffed.

"You don't know, do you? Theirs is a dwindling race. They have resorted to stealing the odd human woman to . . . procreate. But in this case, I believe my mother was taken for another reason, namely her knowledge of the dark arts."

"What do you mean by dark arts?" she asked in a whisper.

"My mother was a skilled herbalist. She practiced only for the good, but she well knew the ways of the other side, the herbs and spells of dark magic, or necromancy as it is known. This is why she was stolen by the Sidhe, to act as a priestess for their dark arts."

Isobel felt goose bumps rise on her arms and neck. Daegan had said nothing about dark magic. It could not be true.

Could it?

"My lord, I beg of you, you must stop this foolishness—"

"The dark arts can be a seductive lure, Isobel. But once you're ensnared, you'll never be seen again. No mortal can save you."

"I thank you for your concern, but you needn't worry." Isobel pushed firmly on his arm and moved past him.

St. Clair raised his voice. "I saw my mother, some years later, lying at the edge of the wood."

Isobel stopped and glanced back over her shoulder.

"She was dead, her skin marked with strange symbols. Ask your gamekeeper—he'll tell you, for it was he who found her."

"Symbols?" she asked, swallowing hard.

"Dark magick."

"You seek to frighten me."

St. Clair studied her. "Are you frightened, Isobel?"

Lifting her chin, Isobel met his gaze. "Not one bit, my lord."

It was Christmas Eve, and the hall was decked out for the ball. Everywhere one looked there were garlands and mistletoe. The fires in the hearths were blazing; the chestnuts, roasting and popping.

The local merchants and their wives along with the surrounding gentry had descended upon them only minutes before.

Isobel greeted each guest at the door with her father, brothers, and Fiona, while St. Clair mingled in the ballroom. Isobel tried to smile and be gracious; after all, it was Christmas Eve. But the truth was, her heart was not in it.

Two nights had passed since she'd seen Daegan. And true to his word he had not tried to lure her into the forest. The pin had not called to her as it had in the past, and she was saddened by the thought that he had removed the enchantment spell.

St. Clair's words had ceased to bother her. She did not believe the man. She knew with complete certainty that Daegan would never hurt her. There was nothing sinister about him, nor the passion and love they shared.

It was not the earl's talk of black magick that made her stay away from Daegan, but the thought of leaving this world behind. Of never seeing her family, or holding her niece or nephew.

Would she even have a child of her own? Daegan hadn't mentioned that. Could a human and Sidhe create life? Could she have the things she longed for in life if she left her world behind to go to Daegan?

"Shall we, Miss MacDonald?" Isobel looked up to see St. Clair standing beside her, offering his arm. With a weak smile she accepted and allowed him to maneuver her onto the dance floor.

"You dance very well," he murmured as they waltzed together.

"Thank you, my lord."

"Permit me to say that you look tired, Isobel. I have noticed these past few days that you are not yourself. Are you unwell?"

"No, I'm very well, thank you." Except it was a lie. She was not well. She was sad, and that sadness seemed to be consuming her. Laughter erupted from the corner of the room, and she saw it was Ewan and his friends jesting. In another corner sat Stuart and Fiona. He was holding her hand and kissing it when no one was looking. Her father was with his cronies talking politics and finance, and she saw how he smiled and laughed. It seemed her family members were all content. Everyone was alive . . . except . . . well, it was a melodramatic thought, but she could not help it. It was as if everyone was living and she was merely existing.

"I hope I have not given you reason to be angry with me. I sought only your protection, Isobel."

She smiled at him, for the first time truly seeing him. "You are a good man, my lord. I do believe you feared for me, and for that, I thank you. But there is no need. There is nothing that will harm me in the woods."

St. Clair studied her. "You seem to be . . . resolved to something. I see it in your eyes."

She laughed for the first time in days. "I do believe I am."

When the music ended, she excused herself and left the ballroom, running through the halls and up the stairs to her room. Once there, she flung open the door and raced to the wardrobe where she had hidden the pin.

This is what she wanted. A life. A future with Daegan.

Rushing to her writing table, she took out a sheet of paper and wrote a letter to her family. She propped it up against a glass perfume bottle, knowing her maid would find it there tomorrow. And then she held the pin in her palm and closed her eyes, wishing with all her heart for one more chance with Daegan.

Daegan had almost given up hope when he heard the soft foot treads behind him. Whirling around, he saw Isobel standing there in a lovely emerald green ball gown.

"Will this do?" she asked, holding out her skirts. "I am not certain what one wears to a lanamnas."

He ran to her and swept her up in his arms and twirled her around. He kissed her soundly and hugged her tight. "Are you certain?"

She nodded. "I want a life with you."

"And your family?"

"They're all so happy and living the life they want. They'll understand. I wrote them so they wouldn't worry."

"Do you trust me, then?"

"Of course."

"Then close your eyes, *muirnín*."

She did, and when he told her to open them, they were in a candlelit chamber before an altar that was covered with the same blue velvet cloth. The dirk was there and the chalice, as well as a lit candle and long piece of white cloth.

Isobel couldn't hide her huge smile as Daegan bent down and brushed his lips against her mouth. "You take my breath away. You truly are a goddess of the moon."

For so many years she thought love would never be hers. Yet here she was, surrounded by Daegan's love and a new world waiting to be explored.

Daegan reached for her hand and placed their hands palm to palm. "Do we not need any witnesses?" she asked.

"No, this is our eternal vow. No other need bear witness to what will bind us forever. *Anam a Anam*, soul to soul. Tonight, two shall become one," he said. Picking up the dirk, he placed it tip down, inside the chalice. "The athame represents the male and the element of air, the chalice is the female and signifies the element of water. Together they symbolize the sacred union that we will enter into tonight."

He was watching her, waiting for her acceptance. " 'Tis strange for you, I know, but for my kind this is a sacred moment of the ceremony. It is known as the Great Rite, the coming together of man and woman, air and water. The athame is the phallus, and the cup, the womb. 'Tis symbolic of the union we will share."

"I think it's beautiful, Daegan."

With a smile he lifted the length of white cloth. "With this bond, I shall entwine you so that you are fated to me and I to you, for eternity. Let this bond be a symbol of our merging."

As the fabric wrapped around their hands, Isobel felt the unstoppable pull of her body to Daegan's. Their energies mingled, then slowly began to merge, becoming one.

Daegan kept his gaze focused on her face as he continued to wind the cloth around their hands. "I offer to you, Isobel, my life. My soul. I offer to shield you from anything or anyone that would harm you. I offer you my fidelity, my honor. My unending love."

The first warm tear trickled down her cheek, and Daegan caught it with his thumb. "With all that I am, I will protect you, provide for you. I will love you in the brightness of light and the cover of darkness. I will love you for eternity."

The lace was tied, their wrists held together tightly. As Daegan's words rang in her ears, Isobel felt his energy tugging at her, pulling her in so that she could truly feel his love for her. She was surrounded by his love and desire.

Closing his eyes, he pressed his mouth against her fingers, kissing them. "You're truly mine now, and nothing shall tear you away from me. *Nothing.*"

Isobel was rendered mute for several seconds by his beautiful declaration. "I don't know what to say. This is," Isobel swallowed hard. "This is new to me, Daegan. But know that . . . that I will promise to learn the ways of your world. That I will be a good wife to you and make you a comfortable home. However, I don't imagine the skills that I've been taught will work in your world. Do you hold balls for hundreds of people and dinners for three dozen here in Annwyn?"

"You worry, *muirnín.* You needn't."

"It's just that . . . I do not know what to say other than I am not happy unless I am with you, and a future without you seems bleak and lifeless. I've felt you as a presence in my life since I was six, and to no longer have that would be like starving for air. I love you!"

He hugged her close, savoring her. "You undo me with your vows," he whispered, "but while I adore what you have given me, I seek one thing more from you."

Pulling away, she stared into his eyes. "What?"

"Would you give me the vows of a human?"

"Whatever do you mean?"

"If we were in your church, in your world, what vows would you say to me?"

She smiled and curled her fingers around his. "That I would love and honor you until the day I die. That I would be a helpmate to you, and care and comfort you in sickness and health."

"And?" he prodded.

"I suppose I would have to obey you," she said, wrinkling her nose.

He laughed and kissed her fingertips. "No, the other one, something about your body."

"Oh," she whispered, pressing closer. "With my body, I thee worship."

His eyes turned the deepest shade of purple. "I have longed to hear you say those words. Will you, Isobel?"

"Yes."

Daegan's mouth skated softly down her neck, then over her cheek to her mouth. Their lips met and they kissed, bathed in a shaft of moonlight. Slowly at first, then more eagerly, their tongues touching, stroking.

"I want to make this so beautiful for you, *muirnín*."

"It already is, because it's with you."

He smiled, cupped her face in his palm, and dragged his mouth across her cheek. "Close your eyes."

She did and felt herself being lifted in his arms. "Open them."

Her lashes fluttered. Before her was an enormous bed, fit for a prince. It was draped in dark blue and scattered with plush pillows.

He put her down and she reached for him, sliding her free hand up and along his hard abdomen. Her gaze skimmed along his body, all muscled and beautiful. He was hers now. Nothing could tear them apart.

He brought their tied hands up and placed her fingers against his cheek. "Touch me, *muirnín*." he said in a voice that was little more than a broken whisper. "Touch me."

Need had replaced the masterful tone of his voice, and with shaking fingers, Isobel caressed the arch of his strong brow, down to his cheeks which were already starting to stubble with a night beard. The roughness of it grazed her fingertips, heightening her senses. She liked Daegan with an evening beard, she decided. She liked him looking hard and strong. It made her feel secure and safe in a new world where she felt so out of place.

His breathing was hard when she reached the corner of his mouth. With a gentle glide of her fingers, she brushed them over his lips, startled by the softness of them. Isobel closed her eyes when she felt him reverently kiss her fingers. The strange energy she sensed in him, formerly an even hum, spiked as she touched him.

"I need your touch—so much."

His head dropped down and he rested his forehead in the crook of her neck. She felt the tips of his fingers glide down her throat. "Don't stop," he begged. "Don't ever stop."

With her palms, she traced the sculpted contours of his shoulders. He shuddered, let out a low moan of utter pleasure. The energy increased, humming along his body, flickering along his muscles. It made her feel bold, and she pressed her body against his.

"You feel so good," she whispered, running her finger down his spine to the waistband of his pants. "So strong beneath my hands."

"You make me feel strong."

The longer she touched him, the more the energy seemed to flow between them. It was pouring off him in waves, and Isobel knew that this loving would be like nothing they had ever shared before.

She kissed his shoulder, licked his skin, tasting the salt of him. Her mouth lowered, brushing over his nipple. She flicked the tip of her tongue over it, felt it grow hard. She heard his breath catch, felt his hands comb into her hair and clutch at her curls. And still the energy ebbed and flowed. Like waves on the shore, it came in, then out, drawing them closer and closer, pulling them together so that they were bound to one another.

He moaned and pushed against her, pressing his manhood into her belly. His mouth found hers and he kissed her. Slowly, reverently. Like a tender lover he took her mouth, showing her that this night was not about lust, but love.

Over and over she brushed her fingers along his back, delighting in the shudders that wracked his body, loving the way he seemed to cling to her. Emboldened, she kissed his neck and flicked her tongue along his skin, tasting his flesh.

Daegan could barely think. Isobel's hands, so small and delicate, skated over his shoulders, building his passion, inflaming his body until he thought he might come. She drew him to her and he let himself go. Let himself be taken in by her.

Without breaking the contact of their bodies, he picked her up and placed her on the bed so that she was kneeling before him, looking up at him with her big blue eyes.

Trailing his fingers down the smooth column of her throat, he watched as they reached her breasts that were rising above the bodice of her ball gown, then down lower, to the clan pin that was cradled between her breasts.

Lowering his head, he inhaled the heady and lusty scent of her, listened to the erotic cadence of her heart beating urgently beneath her breast. The scent of her passion-infused blood was so strong it overtook all his senses. He could no longer hear, could no longer see because of the passion that was blinding him. He could only smell, and the erotic scent grew stronger and stronger until his own body was cloaked with it.

His hands, as if they had a mind of their own, reached for her bodice and pulled it down, revealing her breasts—swollen, heavy. Waiting for his touch. He lifted her, pulled the gown free from beneath, and sat her back on the bed, naked and beautiful.

Gently he pulled at the end of the cloth tying their wrists together, freeing them, then wrapped it around his wrist where he could see it.

And then she began touching him, rubbing her palms along his sensitive skin, loving him with gentle caresses.

Together they touched each other's bodies, quietly listening to the hitching of breaths and the softness of their moans. When he cupped her breast in his palm, he felt the stab of need snake through her body down to the juncture of her thighs, where she was wet and smelling sweet for him.

"You need me," he said as he nuzzled the tender spot beneath her ear. "I can feel it, that need."

Her head tipped back and her hair fell down from its pins, spilling out behind her. Daegan had never seen a more erotic or beautiful sight than his wife beneath the moonlight, her eyes closed, her lips parted in ecstasy as he gently fondled her breast.

Needing to taste her, to feel her energy inside him, he took her breast into his mouth. Loving her slowly, he watched her uninhibited response. Seeing her arch, hearing her cry of pleasure made his blood roar in his veins, made the electricity in his body arc wildly.

His erection bobbed, seeking pleasure against her lush belly. He pushed once, feeling the swollen tip of him being cushioned by her soft skin.

"You've made me your disciple, *muirnín*. I'd follow you to hell, you know."

"Make me your wife, Daegan," she asked as she rocked against him. "Make it real."

He followed her down as she slid her legs around his hips, opening herself for him—welcoming him inside her.

She was beautiful there: dark and wet, slick in the moonlight, ready for his penetration. He slid his thumb down her folds, feeling her slickness coating his skin. She writhed, widening her hips, lifting her bottom.

Her gaze found his and she smiled, opening her arms to him. "Come to me."

In a moment of sheer weakness, he fell onto her, seeking her love. It was a possession he'd never experienced before. A passion he never could have believed existed.

He slid into her, slow and easy, watching the wonder on her face as he filled her full. His hands came beneath her, cupping her bottom, angling her so that he could penetrate her deeper with each slow, measured thrust. And she took him in, her thighs clutched his hips, gripping him, pulling him farther into her.

In the quiet of his chamber, hidden away, they made love. There were no words. Only gentle caresses and the sighs of lovers whispered between them. It was magic, it was sacred, and Daegan knew, as he found completion deep inside her, that he had at last found his redemption—in his wife's arms.

As the energy crested within Daegan, Isobel felt hers rise. She clung to him, holding him in, but then it left, that beautiful energy, and became something dark and cold.

"Cailleach!"

Daegan pulled away from her and reached for the dirk that was on the altar. Covering her with the blankets, he spread his arms wide, as if he was protecting her.

"You do not intend to use that sacred knife on me, do you?"

A woman appeared then, seemingly out of a mist. She was tall and shapely, her long hair silvery blond. She was stunningly perfect, yet cold as ice.

"You have made a grievous error by bringing her. Did you think I wouldn't know? Did you think to hide her from me?"

"Daegan, who is—"

The woman turned on her. "I am Cailleach, the Supreme Goddess of Annwyn. You, mortal, do not belong here."

Isobel clutched Daegan's arm. "I am his wife."

Cailleach laughed. "He is Prince of the Sidhe. My consort. Not a human's mate."

Isobel started to retort when Cailleach held up her hand, and Isobel felt her mouth frozen. "Tell your mortal to hold her tongue, or I will cut it out."

Isobel gave a strangled whimper and Daegan whispered, "Trust me, my love."

"Now be a good girl and leave here," Cailleach ordered.

"Do not harm her," Daegan barked, "or you will do battle with me."

The goddess gave him a look of pity. "Over her?" Her gaze flickered to Isobel and back. "She is nothing. She is not even pretty. You could have any female in Annwyn."

"I want Isobel."

"Well, you can't have her." Cailleach raised her hand and sent a pulse of pain through Isobel's body. "Back to your realm, little mortal, with no memory of my prince."

"No!"

It was Daegan's voice and the last thing Isobel heard before awakening in her room.

It was Christmas Eve. The ball was under way, and she was late.

Chapter Ten

Out in the grove, beneath the moonlight, Daegan fell to his knees before the goddess. He was not afraid of what Cailleach would do to him. But the fear that Isobel would not remember him was a dagger to his heart.

"Why did you take her memories of me?" he asked, his voice hoarse.

"So she wouldn't come back."

Cailleach circled him, the athame pointed at his throat. "You have betrayed us, Daegan. All of Annwyn will now suffer because of your need to mate with this human."

"It is much more than a need to mate," he said, lowering his head. "I am certain she was fated to be my own."

"She is *fated* to marry another: a human male who will not be happy to know that his bride comes to his bed sullied by another—and a Sidhe at that."

"No!" he cried, moving to rise from his knees, but the razor-sharp point of the athame pricked his skin. "She will not wed St. Clair. *She is mine.*"

"You think so? Because you shared the sacred ritual of lanamnas with her?"

Eyes pressed shut, Daegan remembered the scene in his chamber. The binding, which he felt around his wrist. The lovemaking that had been more than magic. He had bound Isobel to him for eternity. Theirs was not a simple handfasting, but the most sacred of all unions, for lanamnas was an eternal vow taken with a soul mate. Isobel *was* his soul mate.

"Our rituals do not govern mortals," Cailleach sneered impatiently. "To her it was a night of pleasure. It was a dream. Your bonds, your vows have no hold over her."

"She will honor the ritual," Daegan growled, knowing it for the truth. "We are fated. She is my wife."

"Not in the mortal realm."

His fingers dug deep into the earth as he struggled to maintain his submissive posture. The cloak he wore surrounded him in blackness almost indistinguishable from the ground and the black cover of night. He must bow to the laws of his world and his people. He had done wrong in their eyes, yet it had felt right. It still felt right. He felt Isobel in his heart. With every beat, he felt her presence growing stronger and stronger.

"You have broken our laws. Before I pronounce sentence, what have you to say for yourself, Daegan, Prince of the Sidhe?"

"Only this: that the soul longs for its mate just as the body does. My body longed for Isobel's, but not as much as my soul did. There can be no regret in that."

There was silence. Daegan was aware of the athame wavering above him. Cailleach's hand was unsteady, as was her breathing.

"You have paid much for her. What will she pay in return?"

His eyes blazed as he looked up at Cailleach, but he kept his voice respectful. "I would ask that she be spared such payment."

"*Why?* She has taken from us our king. My consort. There is a price to pay Annwyn."

"I will pay it."

"She has blinded you with her body. Now you will suffer, and for what? One night with her?"

"Better to have one than none at all."

Swooping down, Cailleach knelt in front of him. With the tip of the athame she lifted his chin. "Do not do this, Daegan. Do not surrender yourself for her."

Their gazes collided. "Who better to sacrifice myself for than my soul mate?"

A crystal teardrop fell from her eyes and skated down her cheek.

A shred of hope rose in his breast. "Have you never loved, Cailleach? Has your soul never yearned for another?"

She looked away, but he saw the sadness in her eyes. "Yes. But I forsook him and my love. I could not be woman, lover, and goddess. My duties as ruler came first. It is the same for you."

"No."

Her gaze swung back to his. "It pains me to do this, but as Supreme Goddess, I must. You bring imbalance to Annwyn. The Dark Times will come, and I cannot allow it to happen. You know what will come next?"

"Yes. I will offer you a sacrifice."

"You will give me *adbertos*, yes, but I will choose it."

Nodding, Daegan lowered his head until it almost touched the ground. He was at Cailleach's feet, humbling himself. But it was for Isobel. For their love. It was right to offer *adbertos* to Cailleach. It was right to do this for Isobel.

"You have created chaos, upset the balance of our world. You have allowed darkness to creep into a place where only light should rule."

He accepted the truth. He had done those things, but he had been helpless. The heart and soul knew what they wanted, and his wanted Isobel.

"The consequences will be far-reaching. Annywn will never be the same. You have brought sin where there was never any. Your actions will affect another. Do you realize that? Do you care?"

I will accept his actions as my own.

Bran. Daegan looked up to see his nephew emerge from the woods. He was naked and defenseless. But his eyes, they raged. The Unseelie blood in him roiled to the surface, barely tethered. Bran had no need for weapons, not when his black blood was boiling.

"Leave us, Raven," Cailleach ordered. "This is not your fight."

"It is not yours, either, but you made it that way."

"On your knees," she spat, her eyes narrowing to angry slits. She pointed the tip of the athame to a spot on the ground. "You will pay for that insolence."

Bran fell to his knees beside Daegan. His mismatched eyes did not betray his emotions.

Cailleach glared at Bran. "You ungrateful dog. Did I not give you what you wished for? Is Morgan not banished to the Wastelands for her crimes against your brother? Did I not give you clues to discover where he has been hidden?"

"You have."

"Then why are you here instead of searching for Carden?"

"I made a pact with Daegan, and I will see it through."

"And what did you barter, Raven?"

"My brother for his woman."

"How dare you interfere in business that does not concern you?"

"He has served you well, my goddess." Bran reminded Cailleach. "Can you not forgive him this trespass?"

"Perhaps, if he would never see the girl again. But I know, I *feel* it: He will not leave her be."

"No," Daegan murmured, "I will not. Even if I agreed, I could not keep my promise. It is not within my power."

"Annwyn has no use for a king who is weakened by a mortal."

"I accept your judgment," Daegan answered. "I offer you an *adbertos*, Cailleach, and will abide by what you choose for this sacrifice."

"As will I," Bran said. "I will offer you an *adbertos* as well. With two of us offering sacrifices, you can spare the girl. Our law allows it."

Cailleach looked momentarily surprised; then she began to circle them once more.

"So be it. Daegan, Prince of the Sidhe, you are forever banned from Annwyn. You will be cursed to live as a mortal, without your magic. Your firstborn male child will be taken from your arms so that your blood might never again rule Annwyn. You will know the pain of mortals. You will mourn. You will die. You will be forever forced to recall what you gave up for your mortal. I hope she will prove worth your sacrifice. Rise."

Daegan got to his feet and stood to his full height, looking down into Cailleach's face. "Go now," she hissed, "never to return."

His gaze turned to Bran. He felt sorrow for what he had done, but still, if he had the chance to do it all again, he would not have forsaken Isobel.

"Go," Bran said through gritted teeth, "I will accept what she chooses for me. *Go.*"

Daegan hesitated and Bran glared at him. "I do this willingly. Go. Love your mortal. Have what I will not—a soul mate."

Cailleach laughed, a cruel sound that did not hide the pain she kept to herself. "No, Raven, you will not have a soul mate, but you will have something else, something you could not possibly desire."

As he walked away into the deepest part of the forest, Daegan heard Cailleach's husky voice chanting an incantation. It was followed by a brilliant flash of white light, then the agonizing roar of Bran's scream.

"The Legacy Curse is upon you now, Raven," Daegan heard. "There will be no peace for you, or within you."

Daegan closed his eyes. He would find a way to break the curse. He would repay his nephew's sacrifice if it was the last thing he ever did.

Isobel was restless. She could not dance, because she couldn't concentrate on keeping time. She had no desire to sing carols, or sip a cup of wassail by the Christmas tree. Her insides were in knots and she didn't know why.

The room was stuffy, and she was hot. Gliding over to the terrace doors, she opened them and slipped outside. The night air was cold and crisp. Snow gently fell, and the skies were black except for the moon and the bright dot that was the Christmas Star.

Inhaling deeply, Isobel brought the cold air into her lungs. It soothed her, cleared her mind, and settled her jumbled nerves. Closing her eyes, she made a silent wish for a miracle that would save her from having to marry the Earl of St. Clair.

Opening her eyes, she blinked; there was something in the distance, moving through the snow. It was not the white stag she had seen so often on these grounds, but a figure of a man walking towards her.

Rubbing her hands down her chilled arms, she watched the man's approach. He was exceptionally tall and broad. His hair was black, and he was dressed in a kilt and white cotton shirt. A thick black belt encompassed his waist, and from a loop hung a leather pouch. A triscale was embossed in the leather, and as he steadily climbed the four stairs that led to her, Isobel realized that he was the most handsome man she had ever seen.

"Isobel."

Daegan watched in horror as Isobel cocked her head to the side and studied him. She didn't remember him. How was he to explain that she was his wife? That he had once been immortal, but was now mortal?

"Isobel? *Mo muirnín?*"

"Daegan?" she asked slowly, almost disbelievingly.

He ran to her and lifted her up. "You remember."

"Shouldn't I?"

"Cailleach said she stole from you any memory of me."

"I made a wish," she said, looking up at the sky. "I asked for a miracle so I wouldn't have to marry St. Clair, and then you arrived."

"And here I am. In the flesh. Literally."

"Come with me," she commanded, taking his hand and pulling him behind her. "We can be alone in my room."

Together they slipped unseen through the servants' door at the side of the house. Quietly they climbed the stairs and entered the family's private wing without being seen.

When they reached Isobel's chamber she turned and kissed him. "You are a miracle—you know that?"

He smiled and lifted his hand to her cheek. He was still wearing the white scrap of fabric around his wrist. "Together forever," he said huskily, following her gaze. "*Anam a Anam.*"

"Soul to soul," she whispered, opening the door and pulling him inside. "I love you, Daegan. You must know how much I do."

"I am no longer a Sidhe, Isobel," he murmured as she cupped his face in her hands. "Your great white hart will never be again."

She looked at him quizzically, and Daegan hung his head, not knowing what ruled him, shame or the fear she would reject him. "I am mortal now."

She rained kisses upon his cheeks before whispering, "I don't care. It's only you I want, Daegan. The man who makes me feel whole. The man who made love to me."

He closed his eyes, love overpowering him. "I do not deserve you."

She laughed and kissed him. "I do not deserve the sacrifices you have made for me. But I am human, and I'm too selfish to wish I had never seen you or given my body to you. I wanted you, from that first moment in the woods when you smiled at me."

"I enchanted the pin so you would come back to me. I used magic to entice you."

"Do you think some spell held me enthralled?" she laughed, lying back on her bed and pulling him atop her. "It was you, Daegan. Your eyes, your voice. It wasn't the magic in the pin that had me returning to you. But you."

His expression softened. "I want nothing more than to make love to you. But I cannot, not until you know the whole truth."

"We're not married?" she asked, her voice faltering.

Daegan's eyes darkened. "Our lanamnas is binding, whether in your world or the Otherworld. We are married. But"—he trailed his fingers over her belly, his fingertip circling around her navel through her gown—"you should know that Cailleach has cursed me, and my curse will affect you."

He swallowed hard as her big blue eyes clouded with anxiety. "Our son," he murmured, glancing at her belly, "he will be taken from us so that he cannot assume the throne of the Sidhe or rule alongside the goddess in Annwyn."

Her hand flew to her belly, covering his. "Am I with child?"

He kissed her stomach, wishing it was her soft skin. "I do not know. But I would never want such a thing to happen to any child we might have. I could not bear to see you hurt, Isobel. To see my child ripped from your arms. I have enough magic left in me to perform one more thing, but you will be the one to choose."

He kissed her again and brushed his lips in her hair, inhaling her scent. The animal within him still lingered, heightening his senses. He couldn't imagine not smelling Isobel as keenly as he did now. Didn't want to imagine the day when his senses dulled and he could no longer hear her heart beating or smell her arousal blooming like a field of heather.

"Daegan?"

"Your father's contract with St. Clair. There is still a chance you will be forced to wed the earl."

She gripped his hand. "No!"

"I could, with magic, make him consent to our match, but that will use the last of my magical stores." He glanced at her stomach and brushed his hand down the silk. "Or I could cast a spell now, to protect our son and his firstborn son and all the other firstborn males of our line. He would be protected from Cailleach's curse and safe from her hands. If I do this, I cannot use magic to make your father give me your hand in marriage."

"We'll run away," she said, sitting up. "We'll go far away from my father's clutches."

"We will have to make a new home. Without his consent, we could not stay here, and I cannot go back to Annwyn."

"I don't care," she said, holding on to him. "Please, Daegan, protect our son."

"The future will be uncertain, Isobel. I will have to learn to walk in the mortal realm. I will have to learn the ways of man in order to provide for you."

"I trust you, Daegan. I have faith in you. I have faith in us."

Gently he laid her back on the bed and crawled atop her, kissing her eyelids, her nose, her chin. He made his way to her throat, then the valley of her breasts. He undid her gown and pulled it from her body. His fingers skimmed over her nipples, which hardened at his touch. When his lips caressed her bare stomach, her muscles quivered, gooseflesh spread out, and he traced the path with his thumb. Over her womb, he whispered the magical words that would save his son from Cailleach's wrath.

"It's done," he said, "the Bocan will be forever with him and his son and his son."

"What is the Bocan?" she asked as he slid up beside her.

"A shadow wraith. The Bocan will be bound to him, and when another male child is born, a new wraith will be formed to protect him."

"Oh, Daegan, you truly are my Christmas miracle."

"And you, Isobel MacDonald, are my Yuletide enchantment."

A Christmas Spirit

CINDY MILES

For all of my superfantastic and supportive readers,
who've stuck by me and all the ghosties—this one's for you.

Chapter One

"Please don't die, please don't die, *puh-leeze* don't die," crooned Paige MacDonald. Gripping the steering wheel so tightly her knuckles turned white, she stared through the swirling snow ahead and held her breath. The little standard-shift rental car sputtered, lurched, but thankfully, kept going.

Paige let out a gusty sigh. "Thank you," she whispered, and shifted into third gear. She knew she was lost. She'd missed the turnoff that led back to Inverness. But she needed to get *somewhere* fast, before the car broke down and she got stranded in this snow. She inched along, searching for any indication of a town, a house, a gas station—anything. Several more miles passed. Nothing.

All at once, she spotted a narrow path. It turned sharp left from the track she was on and then disappeared through a dense forest. A small red sign marked GORLOCH B&B stood at the base of the path. Without another thought, Paige steered the car onto the graveled lane. Maybe she could call and cancel her lodgings in Inverness and stay at Gorloch for the night? She hoped they had a vacancy. She'd worry about the car in the morning.

A few minutes passed as Paige crept her way up the snowy lane, and then her heart soared. Up ahead, a single light twinkled through the trees. A little farther and she'd be there.

Suddenly, the car coughed and lurched, and the engine died. With a heavy sigh, Paige shifted into neutral, coasted to the edge of the lane, and let the car roll to a stop. She yanked up the emergency brake and stared out into the blinding white downfall of snow. The wind whipped furiously, causing the rental car to sway. For as far as she could see, there was nothing but white. Unfolding the map she'd thrown on the passenger seat, she studied the small, threadlike marking that was supposed to be the road to her bed-and-breakfast. No signs, nothing—not even a sign for Gorloch. She frowned. Lost *and* her car had officially bit the big one. *Great.*

Glancing at her watch, she silently said a naughty word, then leaned her head back and closed her eyes.

Perhaps a self-driving tour of the North West Highlands in December hadn't been the most thought-through plan she'd ever had. But she'd been desperate to get out of the city, away from her job, her cramped apartment. So she was lost. And her car had croaked. And there was one heck of a storm outside.

At least she wasn't spending another Christmas home alone.

Grabbing her overnight pack, Paige tugged her hat down over her ears, tightened her scarf, and buttoned her wool coat. Pulling on her gloves, she gave a hefty sigh and a bit of silent encouragement, then opened the door and jumped out into the cold.

The gray wintry skies had begun to turn shadowy, and before long, night would fall. She certainly didn't want to be stranded in the woods after dark. She began to move quickly.

Trudging up the snowy lane, Paige made her way to Gorloch's. With the biting cold and wall of flurry, it seemed to take forever. Not a sound in the air except the crunch of ice beneath her boots and the wind rushing through the branches. It felt dreamlike yet calming at the same time. It looked like a true winter wonderland. The path wound around a copse of trees, and when it straightened, Paige stopped and gasped. Her breath slowly puffed out in front of her like white, billowy smoke.

The lone twinkling light hadn't come from a regular bed-and-breakfast, or from a stone cottage, or even a Highland croft.

It came from a dark, looming castle.

Paige stood still, staring. An ancient stone fortress rose from the frosty mist, uninviting and ominous. Apprehension gripped her, yet her lips were numb and snowflakes caked her eyelashes. She had no choice now but to continue on. Shifting her pack, Paige shoved her hands deep into her pockets and made for the castle doors.

As she neared the entrance, she noticed two things. One, the main castle tower was enormous. Two, unless there was a garage somewhere around back, it didn't look like a soul was home. With a deep breath, she took the remaining walk to the double doors, lifted her hand, grasped a large, tarnished brass ring, and knocked. She stepped back and waited.

No one answered.

Teeth chattering and her body shivering uncontrollably, Paige knocked again. Loudly. Seconds turned into minutes as she waited. *Oh, gosh—I'm going to freeze to death—*

"No vacancy. Go away."

Paige jumped at the sound of the deep voice and looked around. "Um, c-could I j-just use your phone to c-call a cab? My c-car's dead," she said, teeth chattering.

Moments passed, and Paige sighed and turned to leave.

"Come in, but be quick about it."

Paige looked about, but still saw no one. Should she go in? Why didn't he open the door himself? Her body quaked with uncontrolled shivers, and she stomped her feet and rubbed her arms vigorously.

"Come in before you bloody freeze to death."

With hesitancy, Paige turned the handle, pushed the massive door open, and stepped inside. The wind caught the heavy oak, pulled it from her fingers, and slammed it shut behind her. She jumped, and looked around. She saw no one. A small table and chair in the foyer contained an open ledger and a pen. A lamp burned low and cast shadows across the narrow space. Paige's gaze moved slowly and peered into the dim room beyond. "Hello?"

"Jus' sign in, lass, and sit. I'll be wi' you in a moment."

"So, you do have vacancy?" she asked, thinking she'd heard wrong the first time.

A moment passed; then that deep voice mumbled, "Aye."

"Err, great. Thanks," said Paige. The throaty brogue was so thick, she barely understood the man. Grasping the pen, she steadied her shaking hand and signed in.

In the great hall, Gabriel Munro shoved a hand through his hair and paced. He stopped, glanced at the girl, pushed his thumb and forefinger into his eye sockets, and cursed. Then he rested his hand on his hips and paced a bit more.

What, by the devil's cloven hooves, was he to do with *her*? Damn the Craigmires' arses for leaving him here alone. The old fool and his wife had sworn the weather would keep tourists away.

Gabriel glanced at the girl still shivering in the foyer. Her gaze shifted first left, then right. Then, she sat down.

It had kept all away, save *that one*. What was she doin' out in such a storm? And alone, as well?

He'd have let her leave, had she no' admitted to being stranded. He damn well couldna let her stay out in the snow and freeze. And freeze she surely would, in such a wee, thin coat and scarf. Even the hat she had pulled nearly to her eyes looked paltry. 'Twas apparent she was no' from the Highlands. Her accent had been the proof o' that.

Now he was stuck wi' her. Alone.

Christ.

He had no choice but to handle things until the girl left. With a final silent curse, Gabriel took a deep breath, readied himself, and stepped into the foyer.

The girl sprang to her feet the moment Gabriel appeared. Her eyes widened as she took in the sight of him, and he prayed mightily that he'd dressed appropriately. Still, she said nothing. She all but gaped.

"You're wantin' a room, aye?" said Gabriel.

She nodded, and her cheeks flushed. "I do."

He gave a curt nod at the desk. "Chamber thirteen. Grab your key from yon drawer and follow me."

The girl's eyes darted to the desk, and a gloved hand slowly pulled out the drawer. Finding the key, she picked it up, shouldered her pack, and looked at him. "Okay," she said quietly. Her voice, smooth and feminine, quavered just a bit. From fear or the chill, he didna know which.

Gabriel strode across the great hall toward the staircase, the light tread of the girl's boots just behind him, hurrying along. He'd settle her in for the night, then retreat to his own chamber. Hopefully by morn, the weather would clear and she'd leave.

At the staircase, Gabriel glanced over his shoulder. "This way."

"Thanks," she said quietly.

Gabriel made his way to the third floor then strode to the end of the corridor. At the last door, he stopped and inclined his head. "Thirteen."

The girl nodded, then slowly looked up to meet Gabriel's gaze. "My name is Paige MacDonald. Thank you for the room," she said. "I didn't know what else to do."

Paige MacDonald. He found himself suddenly speechless. He'd not seen the lass full-on until now. Her beauty nearly knocked the breath from him.

At least, that was what it felt like.

A wee thing, the top of her head came no higher than his chest, and her skin was the smoothest he'd ever seen. A small nose that fit her face, full lips, and he imagined her hair to be the color of straw. Only a small portion poked out from beneath her funny hat. He guessed the rest must be stuffed under it.

'Twas her eyes that caught him off guard, though. No' just the shocking color of blue, or how the width narrowed and turned up at the outer corners and gave them the most unusual of shapes. 'Twas one reason he knew her no' to be from *those* MacDonalds. The other reason? He'd killed them all before his own demise. 'Twas obvious she descended from another clan.

All of those things struck him, in truth. But 'twas the sadness Gabriel saw in the blue depths that struck him the most.

It made him mightily uncomfortable.

Just then, a growling noise interrupted his thoughts.

The girl blushed furiously, and pressed a hand against her belly. "Sorry. I haven't eaten in quite a while."

Och, damn. "Right. Err, you settle yourself in and come downstairs to the larder. I'll show you where everythin' is. Aye?"

"Okay, thanks." She turned, stuck her key in the lock, and

opened the door. Stepping inside, she glanced at him and gave the slightest of smiles. "I didn't catch your name."

He met her gaze and held it. "Munro. Gabriel Munro."

The hesitant smile on Paige's face didn't reach her eyes. "Thank you again, Gabriel Munro."

And with that she shut and locked the door.

Gabriel stood and stared. He pinched the bridge of his nose, shoved his fingers through his hair, scrubbed the back of his neck, and sighed.

What in bloody hell was he to do with a beautiful, melancholy lass? If she only knew *what* he was, she'd never have asked to stay. At least she wasna one of *those* MacDonalds. Snow or no, he wouldna have even let her through the door.

As he disappeared down the corridor, he frowned and prayed mightily that the storm would pass and Paige would leave come the morn.

Chapter Two

Paige leaned against the door, rested her head back and closed her eyes. How she loathed her silly reaction around men. Especially gorgeous men.

Men like Gabriel Munro.

Impossibly tall and broad, muscular, with long dark hair pulled back at the nape, the Gorloch bed-and-breakfast owner certainly wasn't anything she'd expected. The others had been older, warm, and friendly. Gabriel Munro, with his piercing green eyes, worn jeans, cream-colored fisherman's sweater, and brown hiking boots sort of intimidated her.

He was the most beautiful man she'd ever laid eyes on.

And quite possibly the most aloof, as well. He certainly kept his distance from her, too. Wouldn't even get the darn key for the room. *Whatever* . . .

With a sigh, Paige pushed off the door, took off her hat, gloves, and coat, and inspected her surroundings. Darkly decorated in Victorian-era reds and golds, the room contained a large, four-poster made of mahogany, with deep green drapery and plush pillows. A matching claw-foot chair sat in one corner, and a tallboy stood in the other. A fireplace sat cold and empty against the far wall. All in all, pretty gorgeous, and any other time she'd be thrilled with a place such as Gorloch. Right now, she was hungry, tired, and irritated that her car had croaked.

Across the room was an inviting alcove, and Paige hurried toward it. Kneeling on the window seat cushions, she pulled back the heavy tapestry drapes and watched the swirling snow outside. Wind groaned through the cracks and crevices of the old stone, making a low-pitched moaning sound, and Paige shivered.

It reminded her of a horror movie. And she was the brainless female victim who'd run straight into the chain-saw-wielding lunatic. Screaming.

Fantastic.

Just then, her stomach growled again, louder this time, demanding food. It'd been hours since she'd had anything to eat, and she was starved. Lunatics and grumpy proprietors be damned, she had to have sustenance. Hastily, she put her bag in the corner, freshened up, and left the room.

A cold, ancient air clung to the stone walls and passageway, sinking deep into Paige's skin. Low lamp lights emanated from tarnished wall sconces jammed into the rock, illuminating the way to the main staircase. More than once she glanced over her shoulder, a feeling of someone watching her making the hairs rise on the back of her neck. She rubbed her arms vigorously and hurried her pace.

Just as Paige stepped into the great hall, every light in the room extinguished, leaving her in pitch-black. She froze, and her heart thumped heavy beneath her rib cage as the darkness swallowed her up. She waited several moments, hoping that her host would just show up, know exactly where she was, and that she was stranded in the dark. Finally, she grew impatient, cleared her throat, and drew a deep breath. "Hello?" she said, and her voice cracked. "Err, Mr. Munro?"

Gabriel stood mere yards from the girl. He could sense her urgency, yet he found himself unable to answer her calls. 'Twas as if his bloody tongue was tied. While she couldn't see in the darkness, he could, and verra clear. While the blackness covered him, he boldly studied the quiet lass from America.

A wee thing, she came no higher than his chest. Hair the color of straw was shorn at a sharp angle and swung at her jaw. No wonder he'd no' seen it earlier, when she'd worn her hat. Wide blue eyes stood in stark comparison to her fair skin and pixielike features. White, straight teeth worried her full bottom lip, and those large eyes shifted left, then right, trying to see in the dark. She wrapped her slender arms about herself, slowly spun in a circle, and heaved a sigh.

Then, she stopped, faced him, and sucked in a startled breath. Her eyes, which appeared to be locked with his, widened to a frightening width, and she swore.

Only then did Gabriel realize the bloody lights had come back on.

She probably thought he was a lunatic.

Slowly, she began to back away from him. "Um, I was calling for you," she said, a slight quiver in her voice. Her eyes traveled the length of him, and then she glanced behind her, taking a few more hesitant steps.

"Aye, I heard," he stammered. Damnation, he hadn't meant for her to catch him looking at her so closely. He cocked his head as she continued to walk backward, seemingly toward the front entranceway.

"Why are you dressed like that?" she asked, her voice now barely above a whisper.

Gabriel frowned and glanced down at himself. The conjured image of his modern garb was gone, leaving him in his usual form of clothes: his plaid, boots, and sword.

He swore.

She turned and ran for the door.

And then everything that followed happened so bloody fast, he'd not been able to stop it.

Paige MacDonald reached the door. "I've, uh, changed my mind," she said without turning round. "No problem, seriously. I'll come for my stuff tomorrow. They're expecting me in Inverness, so I'll just go there. Um, thanks for the room." Her hand turned the door handle.

"Wait," Gabriel said. "Ms. MacDonald—"

"Bye!" And with that, she opened the door and launched herself out into the storm.

Gabriel swore under his breath and took off after her. A nighttime blizzard and she didna even have on her bloody coat! The snow had turned into a solid wall of blinding white. She'd get lost in no time. Damnation, he was going to strangle Craigmire when his skinny arse returned! Leaving him here alone was naught but trouble!

He didna get far before he saw Paige ahead of him, head down against the flurry, hurrying down the snow-covered lane. The wind blew the white flakes furiously, and Gabriel jogged right through it. Taking longer strides, he caught up with her. "Ms. MacDonald—"

The girl hollered and took off. Gabriel raced ahead of her, stopped, and crossed his arms over his chest. "Cease!" he shouted in his most commanding voice.

Just then, she tripped and pitched forward.

In the dark, Paige MacDonald's eyes widened as she fell straight *through* him.

A muffled thud sounded when she hit the ground, and Gabriel turned. The girl lay still as death in the snow, her black jumper covered in icy flakes. Kneeling beside her, Gabriel leaned close and inspected her. A small bit of red tinged the snow. The crazy girl had hit her head running from him.

With a string of foul words, he leaned over next to her ear and hollered. "Get up, lass! *Now!*"

A deep, muffled voice sounded far away in Paige's pounding head. Someone was yelling at her to get up. Where was she that she had to get up?

Then she noticed just how freezing cold her face was. Actually, the rest of her felt just as cold. Slowly, she cracked open an eye. Blinking several times, she peered through the darkness. The wind blew a flurry of white in her face. Slowly, she pushed up and sat back on her heels.

The breathtaking face of Gabriel Munro frowned irately at her. His head pulled closer. "Get up and get inside. Now."

Then it all rushed back, so fast it made her head spin. The lights had been out. They suddenly came back on. Gabriel was standing barely a foot from her, staring at her.

And he was wearing nothing but a plaid wrap, boots, and a big sword.

She'd run, she'd tripped, and she'd *fallen right through him.*

With her forehead throbbing, Paige pushed off her heels and rose. She was going to get out of this *effing* crazy place, and fast. Just her luck that she had stumbled upon Hill House, or worse: the

Bates Motel. Her brain wouldn't exactly wrap around what had happened, even though her heart sort of knew anyway.

Gabriel Munro wasn't normal. Gorgeous, yes. But normal? No, not normal at all. He wasn't *all there* . . .

"Paige!" Gabriel shouted again. He stepped forward and ducked his head to look her in the eyes. "You're goin' to get your arse back inside. You've nowhere to go, there's no one round for miles, and your lips are blue. You're bleeding! Now go!"

Paige stared at him, tried to comprehend what he was saying and what she was seeing. None of it made sense. She'd fallen *through* him, as if his body was no more than a shadow, yet he hollered at her with a fierceness that scared her. He was dressed like a *warrior*. Her insides shook just as hard as the rest of her body. Her mouth moved to speak, but nothing came out. She wasn't sure if her brain had even decided on the words.

Then, Gabriel drew closer, his face inches from her own. "Come into the hall with me, Paige MacDonald," he said, his voice deep, low, and steady. "I vow I willna hurt you."

Paige's teeth began to chatter uncontrollably, and she stared at the beauty of his features. Without much thought at all, she lifted her hand to his cheek and watched it pass straight through.

His intense green eyes never left hers.

Then, her sensible, matter-of-fact mind registered something unbelievable, unfathomable. Completely extraordinary.

Ghost.

"Please, lass. And press the bridge of your nose. 'Tis bleeding."

Her skin now ached from the cold, and the wind gusting about her made a new fit of shivers accost her body. The bridge of her nose stung like crazy. She lifted her fingers and touched the spot, and it throbbed. Drops of blood fell and landed on her jeans. She was stuck in the middle of the isolated Highlands in the fury of a blizzard, with no car, no friends, a bleeding nose, and nowhere to go.

Except inside the castle with the pleading ghost of a Scottish warrior.

Gabriel inclined his head without saying a word, and Paige decided right then she had nothing to do but give him the one thing she was most stingy with.

Her trust.

Mustering her strength, Paige gave a single nod, pressed the pad of two fingers to the bridge of her nose, and turned back up the lane, the brunt of the wind now in her face, and headed toward the castle.

At least it would be a Christmas to remember.

Chapter Three

Gabriel walked beside the girl in silence. Her steps seemed painful as she trudged toward the hall. No doubt she was scared witless. Mayhap he would be, too, were he her.

'Twas only when they reached the hall doors that Gabriel realized the lights had extinguished once again. Paige surprised him by hastening through the entrance and out of the cold. He quickly followed. Without question, she shut the door behind her. Her teeth clacked together so loudly, he thought they might crack.

"I'll show you where to find candles, but first, reach to your right and find the handle to the cloak closet." When she did, he nodded, although she couldna see. "Well done. Now reach inside and grab one of the wool coats hanging there. You're drenched to the bone from all that snow." Again, she did as he asked and wrapped Craigmire's woolly about her. It nearly swallowed her whole. "Good," he said, walking ahead of her. "Let's get a light so I can have a look at your nose. The snow has probably kept it from bleeding as badly as it should have." Not that he could do a bloody thing about it himself, but damnation. She needn't ignore it.

"Okay," she said, her voice quiet, unsure, slightly quavering. "I can't see anything."

He drew closer. "But I can, so go where I say, aye?" he commanded.

"All right."

"Good lass. Now walk slowly, straight ahead. I'll tell you when to stop."

She did, and they started together across the great hall. At the far end, Gabriel directed her. "Now stop and reach your hand out until you feel the wall."

With her free hand, she did that, too, and her slender fingers grazed the stone.

"Now turn your body left and feel your way along the wall. You'll find the archway to the larder in just a few yards," he said.

Paige started to move, and before long they were at the archway. "You can ease into the larder by turning right," he said as softly as he could.

Once in the larder, she stood still, awaiting his next command. He gave it. "Move your feet slowly forward until you find the counter with your hand," he said. She started to move, and he continued. "The second drawer down you'll find a torch."

In seconds, the girl had the flashlight in her hands. She turned it on and pointed the narrow beam at the floor.

"Lift it to your face."

She did, squinting, and he noticed a small starlike gash, just at the bridge of her wee nose. "How do you feel?"

She shrugged. "It throbs, but not too bad."

"Hmm," he said. "The bleeding has nearly ceased but you should still tend to it. You gashed it pretty fair on that root. You'll need more light than the puny torch you have clenched in your hand will allow. Follow me." He walked to the pantry, and she indeed followed. "Gather candles from there," he pointed to the pantry door.

Without a word, she did as he asked. Within moments she had a dozen or more candles, a lighter, and glass holders out and on the table. Gabriel could sense her apprehension. Her heartbeat reverberated like horses' hooves.

"I'll show you the best places to set the candles out," he said. "I, err, regret that I cannot do the task myself, lass."

"It's all right," she said. "Thank you, Mr. Munro."

"Gabriel."

She didn't answer.

Several moments later, and Paige MacDonald had the candles lit and placed in the great hall, corridor, and a few in her bedchamber. She stood there in the center of the room looking rather uncomfortable.

He didna blame her a bit.

"Now I want you to go see to that gash. Beneath the counter you'll find a first aid kit," he said, leaning against the door frame. "I'll await you here."

Lightly touching a fingertip to her nose, she winced. "Then what?"

Gabriel gave her a slow grin. "Then we shall see about curbing your growling belly's appetite, aye?"

She nodded.

Even in the shadows of candlelight, Gabriel could see Paige MacDonald's cheeks flush.

She turned to go tend to her wound, then stopped. She kept her back to him. "Are you real? Or am I dreaming all of this?"

"I am just as real as you, lass," Gabriel answered.

That seemed to be enough for Paige. She gave a single nod, then continued on. Gabriel sighed and waited.

Paige stared at her reflection in the mirror. With only a candle for
light, it was difficult to tell how deep the cut was, but she'd bet her
right hand she needed a couple of stitches. She'd hit that root hard,
nose-first. It had bled, but she bet the ghost was right that the
snow had stalled the bleeding. It throbbed and stung, and was
even beginning to swell a bit on either side of her nose. Finding
the first aid kit, she cleaned it up, pressed several thin paper stitches
over the gash, and sighed. Her nose injury seemed trivial, compared to other things.

Her host for the night had already *died*.

How could that be? Even if she'd ever toyed with the idea of
ghosts existing, she certainly hadn't thought they'd be heart-
stoppingly gorgeous or would wear medieval warrior clothes, carry
a sword, and know where the first aid kit was.

It made her head hurt even more.

He waited for her at the door . . .

Again, her stomach growled, so she took a final look in the
mirror, tucked her hair behind her ears, wondered if she'd get a
pair of black eyes, changed into some dry clothes, and set off. As
soon as she stepped into view, Gabriel's eyes were on her.

How could a ghost look so *real*?

In his kilt and sword, he was even more striking than before.
Long, dark hair hung unruly past his shoulders and a thin braid
draped from each temple. Strong, cut jaw, straight nose, and those
ghostly green eyes rimmed with coal black lashes made his features
seem all too real. Built? God Almighty, he was built, with strong,
bulging biceps that had a band of intricate symbols tattooed
around each one. His chest wide and muscular, he was bare except
the red-and-black plaid he had draped over his broad shoulders
and body. She wondered if there was one button, snap, or pin that
could be released. Would the whole thing drop to the floor? Power-

ful legs crossed at the ankles, and brown, worn boots covered his feet.

That long, sharp sword sat nestled in its scabbard over his back.

"Uh-hem."

Snatched from her perusing zone, Paige blinked and focused on Gabriel, whose grin looked more like that of a wolf than a man. *Ghost.* Man ghost.

She felt her face grow hot.

"Come, lass," he said with a knowing grin.

She then noticed he had deep dimples in each cheek. He studied her bandaging closely, but said nothing about it.

"Follow me."

Still blushing, Paige followed Gabriel Munro to the kitchen.

"You're no' scared anymore?" he asked as they crossed the great hall.

She gave a light laugh. "I wouldn't go that far." She glanced at him in the dim candlelight. "It's all very weird."

His chuckle echoed in the cavernous room. "Aye, I imagine 'tis so."

As they made their way to the kitchen, Paige noticed the scant Christmas decorations here and there, and the scent of pine filled the hall. How'd he manage that? "The pine boughs and decorations are nice," she said.

"Craigmire's doin's," he grumbled. "A waste of time, methinks. Here," he said, inclining his head toward the kitchen archway. "Help yourself to whatever you can find."

"Thanks." She felt slightly embarrassed, digging in a stranger's fridge and pantry. But she quickly found lunch meat and bread, so she made a sandwich, found a soda in the door of the refrigerator, and sat down to eat at the long, thick wooden table at the back of the kitchen.

Gabriel sat across from her.

He made her more than a bit nervous.

"Shall I leave you?" he asked.

Paige looked up from her sandwich and met his gaze. The last thing she possessed was a poker face; he could probably see the hesitancy all over her expression. Who wouldn't be hesitant? She was shacked up for the night with a dead guy. She shook her head and felt another wave of blush creep up her neck. "No. Please stay."

He nodded and continued to watch her eat.

After a moment of silence, Paige cleared her throat. "How long do you think the lights will be out?"

Gabriel shrugged, the muscles in his neck flinching. "We've no' had a storm like this in quite some time. I'd warrant a while. February is the usual heavy-snow month. Even if your car was running, there's no way you'd get through the deep drifts and ice. I fear you're stuck at Gorloch for a while."

Stuck? Well it wasn't like she had anyone waiting for her, despite what she'd said earlier. Sure, she had reservations in Inverness, but no one was awaiting her arrival. Paige swallowed a sip of soda, wiped her mouth, and studied him. She opened her mouth to ask him something, then shut it. She wanted to know more about him, but she didn't know what to ask.

He gave her a slight smile, then scrubbed his shadowed jaw with his hand. "You want to know more about me, aye?"

An arrogant ghost, she thought. "I do, yes."

"Verra well. But," he said, those green eyes locking onto hers. "When I'm finished, I want to know why a beautiful young maid like yourself is jaunting about the Highlands in a blizzard. Alone. During the holidays." He leaned forward. "Agreed?"

She nodded, embarrassed that he thought her beautiful. "Agreed."

Stretching his long, lean arms across the table, he played with a knot in the wood with a fingertip and began. "My clan's ancestral home is no' far from here," he said. "A pair of towers, an hour's ride to the north. They're derelict now and owned by Scotland's National Trust."

Paige continued to listen intently.

"I was born on the winter's solstice of the year 1115."

Paige blinked. She nearly choked. "That makes you almost nine hundred years old."

A wry smile tilted his mouth and deepened his dimples. "Aye. So it does."

Amazed, Paige shifted in her chair and leaned closer. "How did you, um, when did you—"

A frown furrowed his dark brows, and the muscles in his jaw flinched. "By the hand of a MacDonald, on the eve of my twenty-eighth birthday."

Paige gulped.

Gabriel chuckled. "No' to worry, lass. 'Tis no doubt that scoundrel wasna a relation of yours. Thankfully, that clan died out long ago. You're from America, after all."

Her hand eased to the heirloom tucked beneath her sweater and hanging from a silver chain around her neck. A clan pin, passed down from the MacDonald women before her.

Again, she gulped. *Her ancestors were from Scotland.*

And she'd heard a similar tale from her grandmother, years and years ago . . .

Chapter Four

"What's the matter, lass? You look more ghostly than I do."

Paige blinked and took another sip. She quickly decided to keep her ancestry and tale to herself. Besides. Even if it turned out she *was* one of *those MacDonalds*—and that would be a serious coincidence—she herself hadn't had anything to do with Gabriel's death. "You were murdered?" The question sounded as absurd as the situation.

"Aye. Just there." He pointed toward the raftered ceiling. "In the tower." He shook his head. "I dunna recall much—only the face of my murderer." He pushed away from the table and crossed his arms over his muscular chest. Intense green eyes pinned her to her chair. "Enough of my life's tragic ending. I've suffered it once, and that was quite enough." A smile lifted one side of his mouth. "I want to know more about you."

Paige studied Gabriel Munro. Sexy didn't accurately describe him. There was something ultimately sensual about his mannerisms, the way he stared so thoroughly at her, and she couldn't imagine what sort of impact he'd made when alive. His sexual allure all but strangled her *now*. She wasn't used to that. Not at all.

"Well?"

Paige pushed her plate away and shrugged. "There really isn't much to tell, I guess," she said. "My parents died when I was four, and my grandmother raised me after that. She died right after my second year in college." An image of Granny Corine came to mind, and tears stung her eyes. God, she missed her. "I live in a one-bedroom apartment just outside of Fredericksburg, Virginia. I commute into D.C. six days a week and work as a museum curator and researcher. I work a *lot* of hours."

Gabriel was silent for a moment; then he cocked his head. "You work at the Smithsonian?"

Paige smiled and lifted a brow. "How on earth does a ghost from the twelfth century know about the Smithsonian?"

Nonchalantly, he shrugged. "Discovery Channel. I watch Craigmire's telly oft enough. 'Tis a place I would love to visit, given another set o' circumstances."

Paige gave a soft laugh. "I see." She stood, gathered her plate, and took it to the sink.

"You're alone then?"

Paige jumped at Gabriel's closeness. He stood just behind her, so close she could have sworn her skin tingled as his words washed over her. She couldn't help it. She shivered. *An attraction reaction to a ghost? Oh, that's just precious, MacDonald . . .*

"I cannot fathom it," Gabriel continued. "You've no family left? Friends, even? No man?"

Paige turned, leaned against the counter, and met his gaze. He didn't exactly glow, but he did in fact have a sort of aura about him. She could see him just as perfectly as if she were looking at a live man. Strange, how just a couple of hours ago, she'd been running for her life. "When you say it like that it sounds awful."

"A woman like you shouldna be alone."

Paige swallowed past the lump in her throat. "Um, thanks. I think." What it actually meant, she hadn't a clue.

Just then, the wind whipped fiercely through the cracks of the stone wall, making a howling, moaning noise that left goose bumps on Paige's arms. She rubbed them. "What about you?" she asked. "Do you have anyone? Now, I mean?"

A somber expression crossed Gabriel's handsome face. "I have Craigmire and his wife, the castle owners. They're away on holiday, visiting their children in London. A fine pair, those two."

"No one else?"

"Nay," he said.

She liked the way his r's rolled and the heavy brogue of the Highlands flew off his tongue. *Seductive.* She thought he could talk to her all night long and she'd be perfectly content. Maybe she could find a book for him to read aloud.

She'd keep all that to herself.

"Why are you here?" he asked.

"Well," she said, pushing off the counter and walking to the large bay window facing the night. "I was determined not to spend one more Christmas alone. Not at the museum, not at the apartment, not walking around the park." She softly laughed and stared at her own reflection in the glass. The candlelight made the image—*her* image—surreal. "So I booked a self-driving tour of the Highlands, did *not* factor in a snowstorm, and here I am."

"Weren't you going to spend the Yuletide alone in Inverness?" he said, seemingly right next to her ear.

When she looked, only her own reflection shown in the glass. "Well, yes. I suppose I thought it'd be different somehow. Or maybe I'd horn in on the bed-and-breakfast's family Christmas." She turned and looked at him. "I guess I was wrong."

Gabriel leaned against the wall and studied her. "Mayhap no'. Here we are. Together." He smiled. "Aye?"

Heat flushed her skin. "Yes. I suppose you're right."

He leaned closer—so close, it made Paige shiver. "Then you dunna mind spending the Yuletide wi' a lonely, aged warrior?" His mouth lifted at one corner, making the dimple pit his cheek on that side. One dark brow raised in question.

Incredibly sexy.

She smiled in return. "I don't mind at all."

Of course she didn't mind. Hmm. Let's see. *Nobody* on one hand. A gorgeous, safe warrior ghost on the other. One with ripped muscles, a killer smile, sexy tattoos, and, well, just plain sexy. And fun to talk to.

She'd be a moron to accept anything else.

This Christmas—Yuletide, rather—was looking up more and more by the second.

Gabriel's gaze bore into hers for what seemed like minutes. Then that very same gaze lowered to her mouth, and even farther still, to somewhere lower than her neck, before slowly rising back to her eyes. "I couldna think of finer company, in truth."

Paige felt that infuriating blush scorch her skin. She cleared her throat and rubbed her neck with the palm of her hand. "Do you sleep?"

Gabriel's light chuckle made shivers race through her veins. It had to be one of the sexiest sounds she'd ever heard in her entire life. A total, carefree, guy laugh. And to think it came from a man who'd lost his life centuries before.

"Nay, lass, I dunna sleep. But I know you need to. You look weary, and your nose is swelling." He inclined his head toward the archway of the kitchen. "Come. I'll walk you to your bedchamber. Rest tonight, and we'll see what tomorrow brings." He gave her a deep grin, dimples and all. "You'll need your strength, no doubt. Aye?"

She thought she could hear him say *aye* forever.

Paige smiled in return and began the walk through a candlelit medieval castle with the most unexpected, gorgeous host a self-touring girl could ever wish for.

Dead or not, Gabriel Munro set her insides on fire.

She never would have guessed how happy she'd be to have her crappy rental car croak in a blizzard.

Bloody hell, he couldna keep his lecherous eyes off the lass.

As they crossed the great hall, he slipped glances down at her. So petite next to him, built slender, fragile. He'd never met a lass with shorn hair such as Paige's, but damn him, he thought it adorable the way it swung by her jaw, and how she tucked one side behind her ear. And those exquisitely shaped blue eyes and full lips made him wish even harder than ever that he had a live body.

He would have already tasted those lips by now.

Mayhap 'twas a good thing he was a bloody spirit.

"It smells great in here," she said beside him, her voice and unusual accent a pleasant, tinkling sound. "Very Christmassy. It must be the pine boughs."

"Craigmire's missus insists on decorating the place," he said. They both started up the staircase, Paige carrying a candle. "I told her no' to bother, since I'd be here alone."

"Sounds like you're not too crazy about the idea of Christmas," she said. "I suppose I understand why."

He glanced at her. "Is that so?"

"Of course," she held the candle closer to her face. "We're a lot alike, you and I. While you avoid Christmas because of your murder—"

"You avoid it because it reminds you of how alone you are."

Her crestfallen expression made him regret the words instantly. "Beg pardon, lass—"

"No, you're absolutely right," she said softly and continued the climb. Once they reached the top she started down the darkened passageway. "It doesn't matter how we *got* to lonely." She stopped at her door and looked up at him. "We both *did*. I for one am quite happy I booked a trip to the Highlands." She gently touched her bandaged nose and smiled—really smiled, and it reached her eyes. The brilliance of it nearly knocked him backward.

"It's the first Christmas Eve in years I've not spent alone. Thank you."

Those two small words, coupled with the vulnerable honesty in her voice, nearly did Gabriel in. It made him uncomfortable. It made him regret being born in another century.

It made him wish with all his ghostly might that Craigmire would never return, and that the snow would never melt, and that Paige MacDonald from Fredericksburg, Virginia, would never, ever leave.

They stood there in the shadowy passageway, he with little more than his flimsy ghostly self, and she holding a candle that cast her already beautiful features into elegant lines and planes. It all but mesmerized him, and he knew he stood there staring like a whelp of thirteen—mayhap likely drooling, too.

"Gabriel? Is there something wrong?"

Focusing his gaze, he suddenly thought nothing could be more *right*.

"Nay," he said, and cocked his head. "How do you feel?" He tapped his own nose, indicating her wound.

"Throbs," she said, not taking her eyes from his. Then she lifted a brow. "But I'll be fine. How did you change? From before? You know, your modern clothes?"

Gabriel smiled and gave a nod. "Aye. One of my perks to being a spirit. *Conjuring.* But one must concentrate on keeping the image intact." He ducked his head. "I thought I'd become rather expert at it over the centuries."

Paige shook her head and opened the door. She chuckled. "Seems like you might need a refresher course. You can't imagine how you scared me, standing so close to me wearing just," she glanced from his eyes, to his boots, then slowly back to his face, "that."

He gave her a mock frown. "Does my plaid offend?"

Her face darkened with blush. How easily he could make her do that.

"Not at all," she said quietly. Opening the door, she stepped inside and turned. "You'll be here when I wake up?"

Gabriel thought the innocence in those words would remain emblazoned in his mind forever. "Aye. Good night, Paige Mac-Donald."

She smiled. "'Night."

With that, she gently shut the door.

Gabriel stared at the solid slab of oak for several seconds, then shook his head. He lowered himself to the floor across from her door and sat.

He'd not budge an inch until the lass rose in the morn.

Resting his head back against the stone—or at least going through the motions of it, since he felt nothing behind his head at all—he let his thoughts drift back to the full, lush lips and wide blue eyes of his intriguing castle guest.

'Twas a good thing he couldna sleep.

With Paige MacDonald on his mind, he doubted heartily that slumber would have ever come.

Chapter Five

Paige lay awake for the longest time, staring at the canopy above her. She had blown out the candles except one on her bedside table and kept the flashlight nearby in case she woke up with her nose hurting. That wouldn't happen if she couldn't fall asleep in the first place . . .

Images of Gabriel flashed behind her lids, even when she did close them and try to drift off. She still couldn't believe it had all happened; *was* happening. Her brain simply couldn't accept it, and yet somehow she did. Naturally. As if she were meant to come to Scotland, to rent a car that would break down within walking distance of Gorloch B&B, and become trapped by a fierce, out-of-the-norm snowstorm.

All so she could encounter the ghost of a warrior from centuries ago.

Who was she fooling? Not only had she encountered him, but she'd become acutely attracted to him in a very short period of time. And it wasn't just his shocking good looks, either. It was everything. That *never* happened to her. Ever. With a live man, or a not-so-alive one. She just wasn't the kind of girl who attracted guys. She wasn't *unattractive*—at least she didn't think so. She just wasn't flashy, didn't stand out in a crowd. Blended right on in actually. She wore khakis and Smithsonian collared shirts to work, and during after-hour research projects at the museum, she wore jeans. Just not a guy magnet, so to speak. She lacked that certain something that other girls had.

But she'd just made a pact with a ghost that they'd spend Christmas together, so that was something. *And he'd called her beautiful . . .*

How very real Gabriel looked. Even in the shadows of a candlelit castle, he looked more alive than spirit. So tangible, in fact, she had to resist reaching a hand out to touch him. A faint, vague line of aura shone around him at times, and only that reminded her he was actually a spirit. Dead but not-so-gone for centuries and centuries upon end, he looked as though he strolled straight in from the movie set of *Highlander* or *Braveheart*—only better. More authentic, perhaps. Or maybe it was because she knew Gabriel was for real and not an actor portraying a medieval hero. No offense to Mel Gibson or Adrian Paul, of course.

But Gabriel? Good grief, he made her stomach do flip-flops anytime he came near. She'd never seen hair so long on a live man before, and it hung loose, wild and beautiful, all at once. The color of black ink, like his brows and lashes, it was a stark contrast to his fair skin and green eyes. One could take all of that in if they got past his enormous size. She figured, going by her height of five feet four inches, that Gabriel had to be at least a foot taller, maybe more. Narrow hips supported by heavily muscled thighs, and thick veins crossed the tops of his hands, snaked up his bulky arms and over his chest. It amazed her how *alive* he looked, right down to the light dusting of dark shadow on his jaw, and the minute detailing of his intricate tattoos.

In her wildest dreams could she have invoked a sexier Christmas companion? She highly doubted it.

Pulling the thick down-filled coverlet up to her chin, Paige closed her eyes and allowed the darkness to swallow her, and the howling wind screaming through the cracks in the stone finally lulled her to sleep.

By the devil's bloody horns, why wouldna the girl wake up? She must have been wearier than he'd thought. It had been nearly ten hours since he'd left her bedchamber.

Gabriel continued to pace the passageway in front of her door.

"Gabriel? Are you still out there?"

His heart jumped in its cage. Damnation, he felt like an inexperienced lad round the lass. He cleared his throat. "Aye. Are you ill?"

The door cracked open, and Paige's head appeared. She grinned. "No, I feel fine. I'll be out in just a bit."

Gabriel stared, and sucked in a breath.

"What's wrong?" she asked hesitantly.

"You've a fine pair of blackened eyes, lass," he said, and gave her a stern look. "Think you broke your nose?"

Paige shrugged. "I thought I might have. I'll be right back."

He gave a short nod. "Verra well. I shall await you here."

With her cheeks flushing, she closed the door.

How adorable he thought her to be, with her skin turning hot at the least little thing. 'Twas something he found vastly endearing about Paige MacDonald.

Among other things.

Gabriel shook his head in amazement as he continued to stare at the ancient oak door. Christ, the girl had broken her nose. Those two black eyes and slight swelling gave it away. Yet she handled it without being squeamish. Never before, in his real life or his ghost "unlife" had a woman so thoroughly captured his attention. His mind hadna left Paige alone the entire night as he recalled every word, every movement the girl had said and made. He'd been around mortals in the past, although he hadn't interacted all too much with them. Yet Paige MacDonald intrigued him, forced his lecherous mind to wander areas it hadn't wandered in centuries.

The lass was beyond fetchin', black eyes, bandaged nose and all.

He couldna understand for a second why she remained without a husband. Had he been a live man, or had she lived in his century, he wouldna have wasted a second grabbing her up and staking her for his own.

Foolish modern men.

Several more moments passed before the door opened. Paige stood before him, changed and refreshed looking.

"How did you bathe without power?" he asked.

She tucked her hair behind one ear. "There's reserved water left in the tank. I used just the bare minimum."

Dignity be damned, he allowed his gaze to wander, and thank the saints, she allowed it, although she turned a furious red. Straw-colored hair swept sharply at her jaw, a bit longer in the front, and framed her pixielike face. Two purple half-moons sat beneath each eye, and the little white bandages stretched across the bridge of her nose. The formfitting blue jumper set off those wide blue eyes, and a pair of worn jeans hugged luscious hips.

The sight made his mouth water.

A pair of scruffy brown leather boots completed her garb. He grinned at her.

"Most fetchin' company I've had in centuries," Gabriel said, and inclined toward the passageway. "Ready?"

She lifted a straw-colored brow. "For what?"

Just then, her stomach growled. Gabriel grinned.

"Apparently," he said, "another trip to the larder."

Pressing a hand to her belly, Paige chuckled. "Sorry. Bottomless pit."

"Then let us go fill it, aye?"

Together they walked the passageway to the stairs and across the great hall.

"It's still storming out," Paige said quietly. "I'm glad you're here. I don't know what I would have done without you."

Gabriel glanced down at the lass. "As am I," he answered, although he felt helpless as a babe and hadn't done much o' anything at all.

For the next half hour, he watched Paige consume quite a healthy amount of food for such a wee girl. 'Twas impressive, to be sure. Once she finished her meal of another sandwich, an apple, and several digestives from one of Craigmire's canisters, she cleaned up and grinned. "Better. Now what?" With straight white teeth, she worried her lip.

The movement fascinated Gabriel. He couldna take his bloody eyes from the girl's mouth.

Somehow, he reined in his wandering thoughts. "Now that it's a bit lighter, would you care for a castle tour?" He gave her a grin.

"You may not encounter the like given by the verra one present when the castle was constructed."

A spark jumped in the blue depths of Paige's eyes. "I would love that."

They stood close, and Gabriel resisted the urge to give her his proffered arm or stroke her soft-looking cheek with his knuckle.

Or, God help him, kiss her senseless.

Instead, he clenched his fist and smiled. "Then follow me."

Chapter Six

G abriel set off, with Paige by his side.

It stunned him how easily they got along.

'Twas a feeling he rather fancied. Mayhap overmuch.

Already his thoughts ran dark at her leaving.

For nearly two hours, they walked the halls of Gorloch. At every little thing, no matter how insignificant Gabriel thought it to be, Paige's eyes shone with blinding excitement. She claimed to love old things.

Gabriel banked that fact to memory. He had to be the oldest thing she'd ever encountered.

When they'd explored nearly the entire keep, Gabriel headed to the one special place—indoors, that is—he thought Paige would love best.

"Where are you taking me?" she asked.

Gabriel glanced down at her and wagged his brows. "The east tower."

Paige's face turned white and she slowed her steps. "I don't think I want to go to the place you died," she said quietly.

Gabriel looked at her and shook his head. "Nay, lass. That happened in the west tower." He bent his head forward. "It would bother you so much to see it?" He himself never ventured there anymore. 'Twas full of bad memories, or worse—no memories at all.

Paige pushed her hands into the pockets of her jeans and nodded. She looked up at him and held his gaze for a handful of seconds, those purple-mooned eyes boring into his. "Yes, it would bother me a lot."

A lump formed in Gabriel's throat and he swallowed past it. "I canna recall anyone being bothered by it in quite some time, lass," he said.

They walked in comfortable silence until they reached the hidden steps leading upward. Gabriel gave a curt nod toward the single, narrow door. "In you go," he instructed.

Paige lifted one brow, then opened the door. It creaked and groaned on old hinges, and she peered into the blackened stairwell. "Gosh, it's dark in there." She turned around. "Spiders?"

Gabriel grinned. "Mayhap. Craigmire doesna go up here much anymore. Bad knees." He inclined his head. "Grasp the rope there as you climb, and hold on tightly." Christ, if the girl fell he'd in no way be able to stop her.

She did as he asked, and began the ascent. "It's so dark in here," she whispered.

"I'll move ahead of you." Gabriel did, and remained as close as he could without Paige passing through him. "Better?" he asked, and glanced down at her.

"Much," she said, and Gabriel could easily see her blush.

At the top, he inclined his head. "Open this door and I'll meet you on the other side." With that, he sifted through the aged wood and waited.

Paige felt her mouth slide open as she watched the sexy ghost disappear right through the door. Three days ago, she wouldn't have ever entertained the thought of anything like sexy medieval spirits existing.

Now? The man consumed her every thought.

She'd never admit it.

"Paige MacDonald?" Gabriel called from the other side. "I'm waiting."

Smiling to herself, Paige drew a deep breath, opened the door and peeked inside.

A gasp escaped her. She couldn't help it. The room's beauty stunned her.

The beauty of the man perched on the sill in front of eight adjoining picture windows stunned her even more.

A corner tower, the windows started at hip height and rose ten feet. Eight panels in all, there was an unobstructed view of the land surrounding Gorloch. Although still gray and furiously storming outside, the brightness of the sheets of snow illuminated the chamber in a strange, surreal sort of light. The sills were wide planks of polished wood—wide enough for a person's backside to sit and stare outside. A cavernous fireplace stood at the far end of the tower room, and floor-to-ceiling shelves filled with books stood at the other. And before the windows was a long, plush sectional sofa made of dark, buttery-soft leather. Several pillows in various dark colors were thrown casually atop the cushions.

And her warrior sat staring. Smiling.

Her warrior?

A smile pulled at her mouth, just looking at Gabriel. He looked pleased with himself, as though he'd just given her the most precious of gifts. She knew she didn't have a poker face. Her appreciation probably stretched from one corner of her mouth to the other.

"I take it you like the view?"

Paige stared. His legs were spread in a totally guy fashion, big-booted feet braced against the floor as Gabriel sat on the sill. His rugged red-and-black plaid—he pronounced it *played*—draped easily over his chiseled frame, and long dark hair hung over each broad, bare shoulder. His arms were crossed over his muscled chest, and those intriguing tattoos encircling both rocky biceps caught her eye, as well as the laced leather cuffs at each wrist. The hilt of his enormous sword poked up from behind him, where he kept it sheathed in a long, laced leather scabbard.

When her eyes finally rested on his face, her insides did a flip. Those intense green eyes, framed by the longest, blackest lashes she'd ever seen on a man, held tightly on to hers. A dusting of dark stubble grazed Gabriel's cut jaw, and the most luscious lips she'd ever noticed on a man pulled up at both corners, making the dimples in his cheeks pit deeply.

All in all, the man seriously did it for her.

"Paige? The view?" he said, his voice low and deep.

Slowly, and with more courage than she ever thought to muster up before, Paige walked closer. Her eyes didn't leave Gabriel's once. "Breathtaking."

"Aye," he answered, a distinct twinkle in his eye. His gaze traveled slowly to her feet, then even slower back to her gaze. "I have to agree wholeheartedly wi' you, Paige MacDonald."

Paige stopped before him, smiled, then looked away, the heat of embarrassment making her courage quickly disappear.

Gabriel chuckled lightly, then cleared his throat. He pointed out the large window they sat before. "If you peer hard enough through all that blasted snow, you'll find the pond. 'Tis frozen through and through by now. And just there"—he pointed farther to the right—"is a woodland path that Craigmire's wife takes on her mornin' walks." He smiled. "Like a sprite, she is, fast movin' and full of life for such an old gel." He grinned down at Paige. "The kirk ruins are along the path. 'Tis quite somethin' in the summer when the wildflowers and greenery grow lush all through it."

Though the landscape was covered in white, the tall Scots pines rose tall and mighty over the drifts and rock. She could vaguely see the outline of the pond. "It's all so beautiful," she said in a whisper, more for herself than for Gabriel. She looked at him and smiled.

"Indeed it is," he answered in that deep, soft brogue. His eyes searched hers. "I've got to know more about you, Paige MacDonald. Whilst you slept I thought of nothing else."

She swallowed past the lump in her throat, and then she gave another nervous smile.

"What's so funny?" he asked, and drew closer.

"I think I could listen to you talk all day," she confessed.

His grin widened. "You fancy my speech, aye?"

Paige nodded and shifted on the sill. "I like the way your *about* sounds like *aboot*, and the way your *R*'s roll. It's a beautiful accent."

He gave a light chuckle. "Then I shall endeavor to speak until you fall asleep this eve." He gave a mock-stern look. "But only after you've answered several of my questions. Agreed?"

Paige smiled and gave a nod. "All right."

Inclining his head, Gabriel rose. "To the sofa then?"

"Aye, to the sofa."

Gabriel's booming laugh echoed through the tower room.

They settled onto the sofa, with just enough space apart that

Gabriel's thigh and hers didn't touch. They faced the mammoth panels of windows, and Paige rested her head back against the plush leather cushion. "Okay, I'm ready."

Without missing a beat, Gabriel began. "Why have you no man, Paige?"

She turned her head and looked; she saw the sincere question in his ghostly green eyes. Her face and neck immediately heated up, and inside, she cringed. "It hasn't been my choice, you know," she said softly. "I guess I'm just not one of those types of girls."

"What type?" he asked.

She shrugged. "The ones guys radar in on. Flirtatious, sexy, easily approachable. I'm not any of those things. I don't drink, and I don't like to hang out at the bars. I'm a little shy, so maybe that comes off as uninterested. I don't know, it feels too fake, I guess. I tried flirting once, and to my humiliation, I failed miserably. And I blush so easily, it's a little embarrassing." She stared at her nails. "Maybe I give off a 'leave me alone' air. I'm not really sure. If I do, I don't mean to. I'm always so busy with work or with projects at the museum—"

"Look at me, Paige."

Slowly, she looked up and met his gaze. "I talk a lot when I'm nervous or upset."

A slow smile lifted his sensual mouth, and he cocked his head, studying her so intensely, it made her squirm.

"What?" she finally asked, wondering what he was thinking.

"You really dunna see it, do you?" he asked. Complete and utter amazement tinged the question.

"See what?" she said.

He studied her for several more seconds, before locking his gaze onto hers. "Just how beautiful you truly are."

There went the heat flash again, crawling up her neck and

spreading across her cheeks. She looked away. "You don't have to say stuff like that, Gabriel. I'm completely fine with the way I am. Just plain ole Paige MacDonald. Now with a broken nose and a pair of black eyes."

A deep, soft chuckle sounded from Gabriel, and Paige glanced at him. "What's so funny?"

Gabriel scrubbed his jaw, scratched the back of his neck, and looked at her. "Do you know what I've wanted to do for the past fifteen hours or so?"

Butterflies began anew in Paige's stomach, and she swallowed. "Strangle me for putting you in a bad predicament?"

"Nay," he said quietly, and leaned closer. "I've wanted badly to kiss you, Paige MacDonald. Just to see if those lips tasted as good as they looked."

God, she'd wanted the very same thing.

Slowly, the corners of Gabriel's mouth lifted.

Paige swallowed again. Hard. "Did I just say that out loud?" How on earth could a ghost kiss a live being? How could she say something out loud and not mean to?

Gabriel leaned closer still. "I'm going to kiss you now, the only way I can," he said, and lowered his head. "Hold verra still."

With her heart thumping, she did.

Chapter Seven

Paige froze, her heart hammering with anticipation, unsure what to expect. Gabriel's green eyes darkened as he drew painfully close, and his gaze never strayed. They stayed locked onto hers. Intense. Sincere. *Determined.*

Unbelievable. And *unbelievably sexy.*

Then he lowered his head and settled his mouth over hers. A strange, pleasurable sensation tingled the sensitive skin, turning her lips warm, and making her heart race.

Lifting his hand, Gabriel traced the outline of her jaw with his knuckles, and more sensations erupted. She'd never felt so alive, so wanted.

All from a ghostly kiss, without any real contact.

"Part your lips," he commanded gently, in almost a whisper.

Paige did, and Gabriel turned his attention to first her top lip, where he kissed briefly, then to her lower lip. With a sensual taste of his tongue, he lingered there, the tingling sensation overwhelming her senses. His fingers traced her throat, and Paige's heart pounded out of control. Her hands grasped the throw pillow and clenched it tightly in her fists. And just when she thought her ragged breathing would cause her to pass out, Gabriel slowly pulled back.

Paige noticed his breathing came hard and fast, too. She'd never wanted to touch something—someone—as badly as she wanted to touch Gabriel. It almost hurt not to. She knew what would happen if she did.

Together, they stared, face-to-face, and simply breathed. Well, it looked like Gabriel breathed, anyway . . .

"Christ, woman," he finally said, his voice deep, his brogue heavy, and his eyes searching her face as if he'd found something long lost. "Christ." He lifted a finger and traced each of her blacked eyes.

Paige felt the heat rise from her neck.

Gabriel glanced away, rose from his seat, and walked to the windows.

Paige stared after him. Fear grabbed her insides, and she glanced around the chamber, unsure what she'd done wrong. She was scared to ask. "I'm sorry," she said quietly. She stared at her hands, still gripping the pillow as if her life depended on it. Finally, she stood. "I, um, do you want me to leave?" She barely even heard the words herself and she'd been the one to say them.

Gabriel rubbed the back of his neck, shook his head, then turned to face her. In two strides he stood before her, towered over her, and somehow crowded the cavernous chamber with his enigmatic ghostly presence. A somber expression filled his eyes, and with one knuckle, he traced Paige's jaw. It left her skin tingling. "Just the opposite, lass," he said, nearly in a whisper. "I never want you to leave." He smiled, and Paige could tell it was forced. "But I willna waste what paltry amount of time I have with you cryin' over time we dunna have. What else shall we endeavor to do this day? The dungeon, mayhap?" He tapped the tip of her nose. "Now there's an adventure you'll no' want to miss—"

"Can you do that again?" Paige asked, barely above a whisper.

She looked up at him, certain her face was as red as a beet. She swallowed all humility. "Please?"

Gabriel blinked. He stared at her, studied every inch of her face with the most intense expression. Then, he smiled. "Move to the windows and sit down."

"Why?" she asked, barely breathing.

His intense stare nearly made her legs lock. "I fear your legs willna be able to steady you well enough."

Paige gulped and backed toward the window. "Oh."

Gabriel followed. Smiling.

When the backs of her knees touched the window seat, Paige slowly lowered her bottom until she felt the cool, solid wood beneath her. Her hands gripped the lip of the seat on either side of her thighs, and she watched Gabriel closely.

"Lean back," he said, his voice deep, heavily brogued, and commanding.

She did, and the icy glass seeped through her sweater.

Slowly, and without breaking his gaze, Gabriel placed a hand on each side of her head and braced himself. He drew close, the depths of his green eyes turning dark.

Paige's heart nearly stopped.

Then, his mouth moved over hers, and the tingling sensation started anew. Wherever Gabriel's lips touched, her skin numbly burned, and it made her insides flame. She gripped the wooden seat so tightly, her fingers ached, and without a command, she parted her lips.

A low growl emanated from somewhere deep within Gabriel, and Paige felt his urgency in the air around them. It all but snapped with electricity, and it heightened her already sensitive senses. His kiss became more intense, and he crossed over her solid plane as his fervor grew. Finally, he pulled back, staring hard at her. He closed his eyes and lowered his head, his lips close to her ear.

"I'm sorry, lass," he said, barely above a whisper. His chest rose and fell as if he actually could breathe. "I didna mean to lose control."

Paige's own breath came fast, as well, and her heart thumped hard beneath her ribs. Slowly, she lifted a hand to rest against the line of his jaw. Low in her stomach, her insides burned with need. "Pretend you can actually feel my hand on your face, Gabriel," she said softly. "And pretend I'm forcing you to look at me."

He did, and looked at her.

"Again," she whispered.

Gabriel's heart softened at her timid command. At the same time, his need for the virtual stranger with the blackened eyes and bandaged nose nearly consumed him. As he studied her, he knew then it wasn't her physical beauty that disturbed him so much, that made him want her more than any woman he'd ever known, or that had made him crave a woman's intimate touch with all his ghostly might.

'Twas her soul. He could see it as clearly as he could the purple moons beneath her wide blue eyes.

With a deep breath, he lowered his mouth to hers. Reining in the primitive passion he felt for her, he kissed her slowly, thoroughly, and he could tell by the way her head fell back, her lips parted, and the sigh on her breath, that she felt the verra same way.

At least, he hoped.

When he tried to pull away, she followed, not allowing it, and with a deep chuckle at her enthusiasm, he continued right on kissing her the best way he knew how.

She seemed to fancy it. A lot.

Finally, Paige lifted her hand to his jaw and pulled back. She stared, eyes glassy with need. "That's got to top all kisses in the history of kisses," she said softly.

Gabriel chuckled. "Is that so? And when have you last been kissed by a ghosty, lass?"

Paige shook her head. "No, I mean in the history of *all* kisses. If you can do that as a spirit, I can't imagine what you'd do," she searched for words, "in another, well—"

"If I were a live man?" he finished.

Slowly, she nodded and looked down in her lap. Her hands, now together, grasped one another tightly.

Gabriel cocked his head. "Look at me."

Paige raised her head and did.

"I cannot change what I am, lass," he said. "I dunna know exactly what I feel, so let's just say I am verra grateful that yon car out there stranded you here. I've no' felt this way in centuries." *Ever,* truth be told, but he kept that to himself. He gave a smile. "Besides, 'tis good that I'm in such a paltry form, lest you be bested of every stitch of clothing and thrown atop yon sofa for me takin', propriety be damned. Aye?"

The shade of red Paige MacDonald turned made the purple moons beneath her eyes seem pitch black. She returned the smile. "You are a very big flirt, Gabriel Munro."

He grinned. She had no idea just how serious he truly was. He decided best now no' to let her know. "Guilty as charged, Ms. MacDonald. So right. Are you ready for a trip to the dungeon after all?"

Paige nodded, and Gabriel stepped back. She stood and shoved her hands into her pockets.

He thought she looked rather sexy standing there, passion set deep in her purple-rimmed eyes and bandaged nose, her white teeth worrying her luscious lips.

It made him want her even more.

"Yes," she said, and rubbed her arms. "I'm ready for the dungeon now."

With a nod, Gabriel led the way. At the door, they both stopped, and he looked down at her.

A somber look filled her eyes.

"Just so you know, lass," he said, just before disappearing through the wood. "I didna want to stop."

As he faded through the door, he saw Paige MacDonald's eyes widen.

That was answer enough for him.

And for some reason, it made his heart lighter than it'd been in centuries—mayhap in his entire life.

Paige stared at the empty spot Gabriel Munro had just occupied. Unconsciously, she lifted her fingertips to her lips.

How had the spirit of a man gained access to her heart so fast? She'd all but broken the wooden seat she'd gripped so tightly. He'd awakened a searing passion inside her that she knew had never even been touched before. A man who couldn't even actually feel, had no physical substance, had made her shake with need. She shook even *now*, thinking of it.

She could only imagine how intensely passionate he'd be,

were he alive. How would those big hands feel against her skin?

That brought on an entirely new shuddering.

Paige turned the door handle and stepped into the darkened staircase. Gabriel was there, grinning. Waiting.

With a shake of her head, Paige followed the sexy spirit down to the great hall. Every other step, he'd turned his head to glance at her, making sure she held tightly on to the rope, she imagined.

Or to make sure she followed at all.

One thing Paige knew, and the thought stunned her every time it crossed her mind. Which, in fact, was all the time.

It wasn't Gabriel's sexiness, or his boldness in unusual but highly erotic kissing, or the passion he awakened inside her that made her thoughts return to him constantly. It wasn't her insanely acute attraction. Not at all.

It was something way deeper than that. Something she felt clear to her *soul*.

Chapter Eight

"It will be the Yuletide in two days," said Gabriel. He picked at his plaid, but didn't look at her. "What did you wish for this past Yule eve?"

They sat in the great hall on a long, plush sofa before the roaring fire Gabriel had helped Paige make. While she'd physically made it, Gabriel had instructed her how, step by step. It was a good fire, she thought, casting toasty warmth to the cavernous room.

She glanced at him, and she wondered if the intensity of his green eyes would ever stop making her feel light-headed. "Wish for?"

"Aye, wish for." He cocked his head and scrubbed his jaw. "Dunna you wish for things on the Yule Eve, then?"

Paige thought. "No, I never have. You?"

A soft chuckle escaped him. "Nay, I ceased wishin' centuries ago." He lowered his head and stared at her. "What were you doin' last Eve?"

Paige shrugged. "I worked until closing. Then I finished a project I'd been working on."

"Then?" Gabriel lifted his big hand close to hers, and with a long finger traced the outline of her knuckles.

"I drove home, ordered Chinese, and watched TV until I fell

asleep on the sofa." The thought, spoken aloud, sounded even worse than when she'd actually experienced it. She turned her face toward Gabriel and gave a slight grin. "Pathetic, huh?"

The thought made her want to cry.

He looked at her, searched her face, his eyes seemingly caressing each feature. "No' nearly as pathetic as watching another family's Yuletide whilst invisible and wishing mightily to be a part o' it." His hand rose to her face, and that same strong finger slid along her jaw, making it tingle. He moved closer. "And so tell me, Paige MacDonald. What is it you wish for this Yule Eve, then?"

Only one thing came to mind as she stared long and hard at Gabriel Munro's dark brows, square jaw, and astounding green eyes. Just one thing would make her entire life complete. The fact that she knew, deep in her soul, after only knowing the ghost of a twelfth-century Scottish warrior for such a short period of time that she might actually have feelings for him stunned her beyond words. So instead, she thought that one wish.

His life. She wished for Gabriel's life back.

But that could never happen. He'd died: murdered centuries ago. All that remained was his soul, his spirit, and for that she was more than grateful.

Lifting a hand, she covered his and sighed. "I'd be selfish if I wished for anything more than what I have right now," she said. Her own words shocked her; never before had she felt so free, so confident, so not shy. "I'm spending Christmas in a beautiful castle in the breathtaking Highlands of Scotland with an even more breathtaking man." She boldly searched his eyes. "I've never felt so lucky in all my life."

Gabriel's ghostly insides all but shook. Had he a live heart beating inside his flimsy existence, it surely would have melted at the lass's words. He could do little more than gape at her, and use every ounce of strength not to try and kiss her, in truth. He'd no' be able to stay within her physical boundaries now if he tried. So soft and heartfelt were her words, he didna wish to change her mood by asking more of her.

By asking her to stay with him always.

Never had he felt so powerfully for a mortal as he did Paige MacDonald. He'd grown fond of Craigmire and his family over the years since they'd taken over Gorloch, but no one else. No one, save Paige.

And it scared the bloody hell out of him.

He looked at her now, with her shorn fair hair, bright blue eyes, and purple-black half-moons beneath them. She smiled at him, and it made his heart shudder even more.

You've fallen for her, fool, he told himself silently. *Now what in bloody hell are you goin' to do about it? You, a ghosty, and her, a beautiful mortal. What do you have to offer her?*

"I know something else I'd love," Paige said suddenly, interrupting Gabriel from his dark reverie. She quickly rose from the sofa and moved to stand directly before the blazing hearth.

He looked at her. She was saving him, he warranted. She could tell he tussled with his words. Mayhap she even thought him no' to want her round, or worse—that he'd no' fancied her confession.

How very far from the truth that was.

Gabriel followed her and stood behind her. "And what is that?" he said.

"A Christmas tree," she said. She held her hands before the fire and rubbed them together. She didna turn round to face him. "Do you think we could find one?"

Paige MacDonald enchanted him, yet he couldna tell her. Although he felt a deep connection, he didna wish to frighten her away by tellin' her such. He barely understood it himself. He'd wait, just a bit longer, and see how events turned.

"Aye," he said, whispering in her ear. "We indeed can find one."

She turned and gave him a smile, and it made his puir knees wobbly. "Do you think the snow has slowed enough for me to go outside and chop one down?"

Gabriel studied Paige's eager face, and smiled in return. "Nay, lass. No need for you to chop anything down"—he inclined his head—"no' that you could swing an ax against a mighty Scots pine with those wee arms o' yours."

She scowled, and he laughed.

"Follow me," he said, and inclined his head again, this time toward the front door. "Let's see just how fierce the storm blows. If no' too badly, we'll venture outside and you can show me what sort o' tree you like."

One fair brow lifted in question. "What are you up to?" she asked, grinning.

"Och, lass," he said. "You shall see."

Together they made their way across the candlelit hall and to the front entrance. When Paige stopped at the front door, hand grasping the handle, he gave an encouraging nod.

Ever so gently, she cracked open the door and peeked out.

Then she opened the door wider and turned, smiling. "Still snowing, but not as hard," she said, excitement making her pitch higher. Her eyes begged him. "Let's go. Please?"

Gabriel fought back a full-throated laugh. He gave a short nod to the cloak closet. "Get that woolly o' Craigmire's first and put it on. His Wellies are in there, as well. Pull them on over your own boots. And go where I say, aye?"

"Aye," she said, already in the closet. She stepped out pulling on Craigmire's wool cloak. It swallowed her wee frame. Then she pulled on Craigmire's boots. "I'm ready."

Gabriel grinned and shook his head. "Out the door wi' you, then. And mind where you walk, gel. No more falls, aye? And we'll no' go far. 'Tis still too bloody cold out here for you to be traipsin' about too far."

She turned and smiled. "Don't worry. This time I'm not running for my life."

They walked side by side to the edge of the wood in the slow-falling snow. Drifts were piled up waist-high in some spots, and Gabriel guided Paige down the covered lane. She stayed just where he told her, thank the saints, until they reached the tall pines and firs. He kept stealing glances at Paige, whose woolen hood from Craigmire's cloak now had a frosting of white atop it. Her wee face peeked out from within.

"It's so beautiful here," she said, and then drew a deep breath. "It smells so clean here. Sweet." She glanced at him. "I love everything about it."

The words *I love everythin' about you* were on his lips, but he stopped them from fallin' out. The last thing he wanted to do was scare the lass off.

"I'm verra glad, then," he said instead. "So what tree do you fancy?"

They followed the slight trail into the wood, where the snow had fought to enter and only vaguely managed. He watched Paige look about, and when her eyes lit upon the verra tree she fancied, he could tell; she all but hopped about like a bairn.

"That one," she said, pointing to a tall fir. "Gosh, it's lovely." She turned her head and looked up at him. "There's no way I'd cut something that beautiful down, even if my arms weren't so wee."

Gabriel leaned closer, dragging his knuckles as close to the line of her jaw as he could. Gently, he traced her lower lip with his thumb. "You need no' worry, Paige MacDonald," he said quietly. "I've got a surprise for you."

Her throat moved as she swallowed, and her eyes widened as they stared into his. "You're going to kiss me again?"

Studying every inch of her face, he met her gaze. "Aye, I am." And, he did.

Paige's eyes softened as he lowered his mouth to hers, and the sigh she released when their essence melded once again nearly made him groan out loud. In his mind he had substance, could feel the soft plush skin of her lips, could imagine shoving his fingers through her hair and gripping tightly the back of her neck to hold her in just the right position whilst he kissed her senseless. As he softly tasted her he imagined her body beneath his palms, the feel of her breasts in his hands, and just what it would feel like to have Paige's hands on *him*.

Then, he *did* groan out loud.

And in the next second, he fell straight through her.

Paige gasped as Gabriel righted himself. He froze, his back to her now, and cursed in his ancient tongue.

A giggle erupted behind him.

Slowly, he turned round, only to find Paige MacDonald with a hand slapped over her mouth. But her eyes danced merrily, and Gabriel simply stared.

"Oops," she said behind her cupped hand, her voice muffled, her little blackened eyes crinkling in the corners. "Sorry."

Gabriel couldna have helped his grin, even if he'd tried. Which, he didna.

In one step he was before her, so close their bodies were nearly one. "Take your hand away."

Paige's eyes widened as she did as he asked.

Then Gabriel lowered his head more and kissed her slowly. When Paige released a sigh, he moved his mouth to her ear. "We'll finish this tonight," he said in a whisper. "For now, let's get you back inside before you freeze."

Chapter Nine

The moment they stepped inside the great hall, the lights flickered on. Almost a disappointment, Paige thought. She liked the ambience of the candles in such a dark, medieval place.

"You can douse them if it pleases you," Gabriel said.

She looked at him. "How did you know I was thinking that same thing?"

He shrugged, and grinned, dimples pitting both cheeks. "I sort of hoped, I suppose. 'Tis what I prefer, too."

Paige glanced up at the wooden rafters, with the enormous stag antler chandeliers on opposite sides of the hall now ablaze. "Do you think the electricity will stay on now?" she asked.

"Aye, I imagine so." Gabriel stood with legs braced wide, eyes at first glued to the floor. Then they lifted and stared directly at her. "I imagine the phone lines are workin' as well, if you fancy callin' for a cabbie?"

Paige's heart leapt. "Do you want me to?"

Gabriel studied her face, and she all but squirmed from the scrutiny of it. Something else laced his features, though, and Paige could have sworn it was *uncertainty*. "I dunna wish for you to do anythin' you dunna want to do, Paige MacDonald." He grazed her jaw with one finger. "And I dunna wish to sound as selfish as I truly am, but aye—I want nothin' more than for you to stay, despite the power returning." He moved closer still. "Will you still spend the Yuletide with me?"

Paige swallowed past the lump lodged in her throat and stared right back. She couldn't have torn her gaze from Gabriel's, even if she'd tried. "I would love nothing more," she said, her voice soft, even to her own ears.

A visible sigh of relief escaped Gabriel's sensual lips, and the smile he gave her made her insides turn to mush. "Thank you," he simply said.

Paige didn't even know what to say to that. Nothing at all came to mind to suffice just how grateful she truly was.

Paige drew a deep breath. "I'm going to go have a fast shower, just in case the power decides to go out again," she said, and made for the stairs. At the first step, she turned. Gabriel hadn't moved an inch. He stood there, staring. No smile, but the muscle in his jaw moved.

His green eyes darkened as he watched her.

Paige cleared her throat. "I'll be right back." She didn't wait for him to respond. She took off up the stairs.

Behind her, a deep, low chuckle sounded until she reached her room and shut the door.

Quickly, Paige chose her favorite pair of faded boot-cut jeans and a long-sleeved garnet cashmere sweater, and she laid them across the bed while she showered. Standing beneath the hot stream, she closed her eyes and let the water fall over her until the bathroom filled with haze. The soap smelled of lavender and vanilla, as did the shampoo, and both created a calm she hadn't experienced in, well, never.

Or was it the fact that the spirit of a nine-hundred-year-old Highlander awaited her in the great hall?

Paige thought perhaps it was the latter.

Only when the water began to run cool did she finish up. Wrapping her hair in one towel, she draped the other over herself, brushed her teeth, and inspected her face. Gently, she touched the sensitive purple-and-black skin beneath her eyes and eyelids, her slightly swollen forehead and the narrow strips of tape across the bridge of her nose. At least her nose wasn't crooked. How on earth could Gabriel think for a second she was attractive? Before the broken nose, she was plain. Now? Plain, broken and bruised.

He didn't seem to mind so much.

With a shrug, Paige decided not to ask herself any more unanswerable questions. She dried her hair, didn't bother with makeup at all since she already sported a nice shade of purple on her eyes, and dressed. Pulling on her boots, she eased out of the room.

And nearly ran straight through Gabriel.

He had waited in the corridor, leaning against the stone wall, arms crossed over his bulky chest.

Grinning.

Well, at first grinning. His eyes took on a decidedly darker tone once he inspected her closely. His gaze started at the top of her head, traveled slowly down to her booted feet, then even slower back up until their eyes met and locked.

Gabriel nearly tripped over his own booted feet as he straightened. He quickly imagined his stupid self, legs sprawled and plaid bunched up round his waist.

Paige MacDonald was the most beautiful creature he'd ever laid eyes on. After so many lonely years of stalking the halls of Gorloch, how had he become so bloody lucky as to encounter such a lass? No' only that, but gain her trust in such a short amount o' time? They got along as though they'd known one another for the whole of their lives. As if they were a perfect fit.

'Twas beyond his reasoning.

He'd thank the saints daily for his good fortune for the remaining of his existence.

"You scared me," Paige said, although mirth laced her alluring voice. "I thought you were downstairs waiting on me."

Gabriel smiled and drew closer. "I found I couldna wait any longer." He studied her. "Christ, you're fetchin', Paige Mac-Donald."

He then thoroughly enjoyed watching her neck and cheeks turn the same color as her jumper.

"I've got two big black eyes," she said quietly, batting her lashes. "I look like a raccoon."

"And a fine raccoon you are," he said. He inclined his head. "I've a surprise for you, and once we reach the end of the passageway, I want you to close your eyes."

Her pixie nose, now bandaged at the bridge, crinkled. "What have you been up to while I was showering?"

He lowered his head to her ear. "You shall see," he whispered, and could have sworn he smelled the sweet scent of lavender.

"I cannot wait," she answered.

Together they walked the length of the candlelit corridor.

A few yards from the end, Gabriel brought Paige up short. "Here's far enough, lass. Now, do exactly as I say, aye?"

She looked at him and nodded.

"And close your lovely eyes," he whispered against her ear.

She shuddered, met his gaze, then closed her eyes.

Gabriel thought he could stare at her for several centuries looking just as she did at that moment.

"Now," he said sternly. "I want you to grasp the handrail and dunna let go," he said.

She did exactly as he asked, her eyes pinched tightly shut. A slight smile pulled at her mouth, and he had a powerful desire to stop just as they were and kiss her. Instead, he continued on.

"Verra good, lass. Now slowly take the steps until I tell you to cease."

"Okay," she said, excitement in her voice.

Somehow, it pleased Gabriel to think mayhap he had put it there.

When she reached about midway down, he stopped her. "Just there, Paige. Now," he said, and once again drew close to her ear and whispered, "open your eyes."

With a deep breath, she did.

"Oh," she said in a voice so light, Gabriel barely heard it. "Wow . . ."

Gabriel watched the glow in her blue eyes as she drank in the sight before her. Christ, how he hoped he'd done a fine job. 'Twas many a Yuletides past since he'd thoroughly enjoyed the holiday, but he remembered his fondest. And with that memory, he'd created a Yuletide for Paige.

"I can't stop staring at it all," she said, her eyes sweeping the great hall. Finally, she looked up at him. "It's like something straight out of a fairy tale, Gabriel."

He swallowed past the lump in his throat at his name on her tongue. "'Tis my gift to you," he said. "An image, nothin' more, but for you all the same."

Her gaze returned to the hall. "Can we go down?"

"Whatever you wish," he returned.

Together they walked down the stairs.

Paige could do little more than stare at the conjured scene before her. Joining the decorations Craigmire's wife had put up were boughs and boughs of Scots pine, pine cones, and nuts weaved in long garlands and draped across every surface including the hearth and swagged over every doorway. A tall fir that looked exactly like the one she'd picked out in the wood earlier sat in the far corner of the great hall, and it, too, had small garlands of nuts and candles wrapped from tip to stump. A thick wrap of plaid, the same pattern and color as the one Gabriel wore, swaddled the base of the tree. What looked to be hand-blown glass ornaments hung here and there, as well as tiny silver bells. The glow of the candles gave the great hall an amber hue—a much different hue than the real candles. *Amazing.*

"It's the most beautiful Christmas I've ever seen," she said softly, then looked at Gabriel. "How could you know?"

Gabriel cocked his head. "Know what, lass?"

She blinked, then smiled. "That this is a Christmas straight out of my dreams." She glanced at the spot between her boots. "Although I have to confess, you're a Christmas surprise that I hadn't counted on at all."

Suddenly, he was so close, her body tingled with his energy. "Is it a surprise that you're pleased about, Paige MacDonald?"

Paige collected what little courage she possessed and looked up to meet Gabriel's questioning gaze. "I've spent most of my adult life alone, never really belonging. I merely wanted to be around people this year, perhaps sort of *feel* like I belong in some strange way." She shook her head. "Never, ever did I expect to feel this. Or you." Without looking at him, Paige took the remaining steps and wandered amongst his conjured Christmas. His gift to her.

She didn't trust herself to look at him. What had she just confessed? He probably thought she was a lunatic. Not only had she accepted his ghostly existence, but she'd just basically admitted to being in—

"Paige, stop," Gabriel said, suddenly right behind her.

She stopped, breathed, and stared at a flickering candle set within the enormous Christmas tree until her vision blurred.

"How do you feel?" he asked quietly.

She couldn't bring herself to answer.

"Look at me," Gabriel said, his voice deep, the brogue heavy and sensual. "Please?"

With butterflies in her stomach, Paige slowly lifted her gaze.

The impact of what she saw in the depths of Gabriel's eyes nearly rocked her backward.

Taking a deep breath, Paige swallowed her fears and faced the enigmatic ghost of a Highlander warrior.

Chapter Ten

Gabriel felt badly for forcing Paige to tell her feelings. The girl stood there, staring straight back at him with more courage than she'd possessed a mere two days before, and he allowed it.

Christ, how he wanted to know how she felt.

Even if it meant making Paige MacDonald squirm for a moment or two.

He certainly knew how he felt. How, in such a short time, had he come to know it? But he did. And he prayed mightily she felt the same.

Paige MacDonald looked at her booted feet, drew a deep breath, then bravely stepped closer. She once more looked him square in the eye. No fear, Gabriel noticed now. Simple honesty.

His heart melted a bit more.

A slight smile tipped the corners of Paige's mouth. "I don't know if I'd be this bold, were you alive in the flesh," she said. "I think you being a ghost gives me more strength and courage. I'm really shy around men I'm attracted to. Probably because I know they're not usually attracted to me."

Gabriel said nothing. He wasna too happy to hear she'd been attracted to other men, but that couldna be helped, he supposed.

A gaggle of idiots, those modern men, and all the better for himself, he thought. He held his breath—such as it was—and waited.

She assessed him head to toe, and seemed to concentrate mightily on her words. Almost as if they surprised her, too. She shrugged. "I don't know, but for the very first time in my life I feel wanted." She tipped her head back, lifted her wee hand, and grazed the line of his jaw. "And thanks to a single, solitary look from you. I feel as though I've known you my whole life, Gabriel." She laughed softly. "I feel comfortable around you; all of my senses are heightened. I feel alive." She again shrugged. "And I also feel as though it was meant for me to book a self-driving tour of the Scottish Highlands in the dead of winter, and that it was meant for my car to die and for me to find my way here, to Gorloch." She wrapped her arms around herself and blushed that appealing shade of red. "To find my way to you."

Gabriel's heart pounded fast and hard in its ghostly cage. Every nerve ending that really didna exist hummed with pent-up emotions. He clenched his fists, since the alternative was to make a feeble and useless attempt to grab Paige up in his arms and devour her. He drew a deep breath, because he knew if he wanted any sort of physical bond with her, he'd have to go painfully slow. He didna wish to keep making a pitiful grab for her, only to fall through her.

Slowly, he lifted his hand and traced the sweeping line of fair hair that hung beside Paige's jaw. With the pad of his thumb he smoothed both darkened circles beneath her eyes. Then he traced her lush lips with his fingers.

He'd never wanted to touch a woman so fiercely in all his existence, dead or alive.

"I am a selfish man, Paige MacDonald, for it pleases me to know you've been alone all this time." He placed a knuckle beneath her chin. "Look up at me."

She did.

"I now understand why I died when I did, and why I've roamed Gorloch for all these centuries past." He lowered his mouth to hers and brushed over them once. "I've been waiting for you, Paige. You were meant to be mine."

Paige's insides shook with something. An overwhelming sense of joy? Fear? Uncertainty?

Love?

She didn't know, and didn't want to *try* to know. Not now. All she wanted to do now was to listen to Gabriel's deep, accented voice wash over her with words she never dreamed she'd ever hear, from anyone.

Especially from someone like Gabriel Munro.

Her fingers itched to grab onto him, pull him to her, and never let him go.

Even though Paige couldn't really experience the touch of his mouth on her skin, she *felt it*, inside. On the surface, nerve endings tingled, and she knew it was from Gabriel's spirited energy. Yet in her imagination, she could easily picture and sense his strong lips grazing hers; his tongue brushing against her own; and his mouth moving in slow, erotic kisses over her jaw, her ear, and down her throat. Even his uneven breathing sounded real.

It made her shiver.

It made her *groan* . . .

"Christ, Paige," Gabriel said, in nearly a growl. "You're drivin' me daft, lass." He pulled back and searched her eyes. "I've ne'er wanted so badly to have a woman as badly as I want you." He shut his eyes, then looked at her. "We've got to figure out something else to occupy our time, lass," he said, although the grin on his face looked strained. "I fear I shall lose control and make a daft fool o' myself otherwise."

Paige shuddered at his words, and to be honest, she thought she just might self-combust and make a fool of her own self. She connected with Gabriel so deeply; it was almost as if he truly could touch her. She barely trusted her voice, so she cleared her throat and nodded. "Okay." Taking a deep breath, she asked, "What do you suggest?"

Gabriel's green eyes turned dark, smoky. One brow lifted, and two dimples pitted his cheeks.

Paige felt her skin grow hot.

Gabriel laughed. "Right, lass. Do you feel up to a midwinter's walk through the wood? I can only go as far as the Gorloch property line, but there's another fine path that Craigmire's wife takes. Afterward, we've got to get some food in that growling belly," he said, pointing at her stomach. "Mayhap then we could watch a movie?"

Paige stared in disbelief. "You watch movies?"

Gabriel shrugged and grinned. "Aye, loads of them. Especially the American movies. *Die Hard* is one of my favorites. Craigmire has quite a collection of fine DVDs."

Paige looked at him, then burst out laughing.

A sexy smile stretched across Gabriel's even sexier face. "What's so funny, lass?"

Paige shook her head and glanced at the roaring fire in the hearth. "Only *I* would stumble across the man of my dreams, only to find he's a spirit of nearly nine hundred years *and* he watches modern American movies."

"Is that what I am?" he asked quietly, then lowered his head to catch her gaze. "The man o' your dreams?"

Paige bravely met his stare. She'd not admit anything else. "Absolutely."

An indescribable expression—perhaps one of amazement—

crossed Gabriel's face, and then he smiled. It was stunning. "That is by far the verra best Yuletide wish come true, indeed. Come, then. Let's get you bundled up for our midwinter's walk before it gets too dark."

Minutes later, Paige was encased in the thick wool of Craigmire's coat, two pairs of woolen socks, Craigmire's Wellies, a scarf, and her thick knitted hat pulled over her ears.

"Ready?" she said, taking the last of the steps down to the great hall.

Gabriel smiled and shook his head. "You look like a wee fairy drowning in a sea o' wool." He drew close. "You look a mite more fetchin' in that woolly than Craigmire does, I'll warrant," he said. "Too bad Mrs. Craigmire took her wee coat. 'Twould have fit you perfectly."

Paige glanced at him. He laughed.

"To the wood?" he said.

With a chuckle, Paige opened the door and stepped out into the frozen Highland air. "Always."

As they followed the same path they'd taken earlier to pick out a tree, they walked in comfortable silence. Paige's boots crunching through the powdery snow broke the wintry quiet of Gorloch. It struck her how she made the only noise, and that in another time, Gabriel's big booted feet would have joined hers in the crunching.

Slowly and as covertly as possible, Paige slipped a glance at the tall Highlander walking next to her. Just as easily as if he were alive and well, he moved with a heavy sort of grace that she didn't really expect. That long plaid wrapped about his shoulder, hips, and waist and connected by a brooch, and those worn boots that reached his knees—they all seemed as much a part of him as her jeans were of her. His arms and chest were bare and muscular, and his dark hair hung loose and wild below his shoulders. A fine dusting of like-colored dark hair dusted his forearms, and ropelike veins twisted up and around his hands and wrists, all the way up to his biceps and across each shoulder to his chest.

Gabriel Munro was absolutely the most magnificent man she'd ever laid eyes on.

And he was all hers. . . .

She could hardly believe it.

"Och, how I'd trade me tricks o' conjurin' for one o' mind-readin'," Gabriel said, breaking into her thoughts. "I have a feelin' I'd fancy what I found."

Paige gave a nervous laugh and stepped over a snow-laden branch. "I'm very glad you can't. I'd be way too embarrassed."

"Is that so?" he said, chuckling. "'Tis too intriguing to let go. Tell me. What were you thinking?"

Paige looked first at her surroundings, and how the grayness of the winter's day had seeped into the late afternoon. Everything was gray and white, with a splash of dark green from the Scots pines and brown from a pine cone or exposed branch.

"You're stalling."

Paige gave a light laugh. "You're absolutely right, and I'll keep my embarrassing thoughts to myself, thank you very much."

"Hmm," he said as they entered a small clearing. "A lass with a verra strong will. 'Tis a fine quality I admire." He leaned in close and brushed his mouth close to her ear. "'Tis a quality that stirs me."

Paige knew then she turned the absolute brightest red she'd ever turned.

Gabriel confirmed it with a booming laugh that echoed through the snow-covered pine boughs.

At the clearing, Gabriel pointed out a large rock for Paige to sit on. She did, and he leaned in close to her.

"See you there," he said, pointing toward a narrow stream. "Be verra quiet, so you dunna scare it off."

Paige stared through the gray mist and her eyes landed on a Highland stag. Magnificent, shaggy, and red, it stood with its head erect and ears forward, staring into the bramble, awaiting the least small sound. With its black cloven foot, it pawed at the ground then lowered its head to search for a buried blade of grass in the snow.

"Beautiful," Paige said as she breathed a sigh, intrigued by a wild buck nestled in the loveliest of winter settings.

"Indeed," Gabriel whispered, very close.

Paige looked up into Gabriel's eyes and smiled.

Chapter Eleven

After he'd insisted Paige make herself some supper, the wee girl had finally eaten a meal of soup from the pantry and a sandwich made of cheese and bread that she'd fried in butter on the stovetop. Gabriel had shown her Craigmire's secret hiding place where the old man hid his chocolate-topped digestives from his wife, and Paige had eaten a handful of those, too.

With the teapot full and plenty o' sugar and cream, they were finally ready to settle down with a movie. Gabriel watched Paige now as she searched the bottom shelf o' Craigmire's massive selection on hands and knees, with her delectable little rump in the air.

Gabriel felt as though he'd choke.

"Oh! I've never watched this one before," she said, and sat back on her heels and looked at him. "Have you?"

Gabriel walked over and knelt down. He peered at the selection and grinned. "Och, aye." He cocked his head. "You've never watched *It's a Wonderful Life* before? 'Tis a tradition—so says Craigmire's wife."

Paige rose, clutching the DVD case to her chest. "Yes, I know it is. But I've never had anyone to have a tradition with." She smiled. "Can we watch it?"

Her pleading blue eyes softened him more than he'd ever admit to another soul. Damn, how his kin would roar, had they been around to see how such a wee lass could turn him to porridge with a simple look.

"Paige MacDonald, I would endeavor to do anything you asked, as long as you continued to look at me with such longing in those beautiful eyes." He smiled. "A tradition is just the first of many things I wish to start with you."

She stood there smiling at him for several seconds, then turned, removed the DVD from the case, and started the movie. Plopping down in the center of the sofa, she pulled her legs up to her chest and patted the spot beside her. "Come on. It's about to start."

She could have verra well said "Don one of the gowns of Craigmire's wife and dance on the battlements," and he would have done so, gladly. Instead, he moved to the sofa, sat close to the woman who'd come to mean more to him in a few short days than anyone he'd ever known in his existence, and watched a modern film in which a lanky man named George Bailey learned a very valuable lesson: Be thankful for what you have.

Gabriel knew just what the man felt. Indeed, he was thankful. He'd roam another handful of centuries if it meant finding Paige MacDonald. The wait had been well worth it. He'd never been happier in his life. Or "unlife."

By the end of the film, tears rolled down Paige's cheeks. With the back of her hands, she wiped her eyes and looked up at Gabriel. "I loved it," she said quietly.

I love you was on the tip of Gabriel's tongue. Christ almighty, it nearly burned him to keep the words inside that he wished to say so badly. But he feared he'd frighten her off with such an endearment. He had a bloody hard time believing he felt so strongly in such a small amount o' time. But, damnation, he did. Didna he? Is it truly what he felt? Or was it merely blinding lust that drove him?

He'd wait until he figured it out himself.

"Another?" Paige said, grinning. "I haven't just sat and watched movies all night in, well, I don't think I ever have. If I did, I don't remember it being this much fun."

Gabriel smiled, and so they did just that. They watched two movies in all, nearly four hours of movie madness. Paige MacDonald was definitely a lass after his own heart. Her verra first choices were some of his favorites. They watched the The Mummy followed by Raiders of the Lost Ark. Fine Yuletide films, he'd thought. He'd no been verra fond o' how Paige's eyes had lightened at the heroes, but he'd given a good, manly scowl, just to let her know of his displeasure.

It had garnered him a tinkling laugh from Paige.

How, though, had a modern girl no' watched those films, yet he, a twelfth-century warrior, had?

'Twas mind-boggling.

And he was passin' glad he'd watched them with her first.

But truth be told, he'd had enough movies for one eve. He wanted nothin' more than to have Paige MacDonald all to himself. So they wandered up to the west tower, to sit before the long windows and stare out into the winter's night. She'd stopped by her room first and had changed into what she'd referred to as jammies, which consisted of baggy red trousers and an even baggier black jumper that buttoned up the front. Both pieces appeared powerfully soft. The one thing Gabriel found himself thanking the saints for was that the top button seemed to have fallen off, leaving a good amount of Paige's throat exposed.

He'd decided right then to keep his lecherous thoughts to himself. For now, anyway . . .

Paige sat on the window seat, knees pulled to her chest, and a warm wool wrap around her shoulders. They'd turned out the lights, and she'd lit only a few candles. They threw the room into a lovely amber glow, much like Gabriel's conjured candles. She'd built a small fire in the hearth, just enough to keep her warm.

And the sweetest, sexiest man God ever created—in any century—sat directly across from her. Staring. At *her.*

It made her insides jump with excitement.

Her face growing warm at the thought, she turned her head and glanced out at the midwinter's night.

"'Tis a wondrously clear sky, aye?" Gabriel said.

Paige nodded and continued to stare. "It is." A blanket of white covered the lands of Gorloch. A light dusting of snow drifted down in tiny flakes from the sky. "The moon makes everything look a little blue," she said absently. "It truly is like a dreamy winter wonderland."

"Aye, 'tis a grand Highland Yuletide moon indeed."

After a moment of silence, Paige looked up. Gabriel's gaze penetrated her, and she smiled and wrapped her arms around her knees. "Are you staring at my raccoon eyes?"

He pulled close and peered even closer. "Aye, and they're turning all sorts of lovely shades." His brows furrowed. "Are you sure you're well?"

Paige gave a light laugh. "Yes, I'm positive. It only hurts when I touch it."

"Well," he said, standing and moving before her. "Dunna touch it."

Paige smiled. "Yes, sir."

Without a word, and without breaking his gaze, Gabriel moved from his seat to hers. Bracing his hands on either side of her on the sill, he bent at the waist and lowered his head until his lips brushed her ear. "I'm verra sorry, lass," he whispered, "but I canna seem to keep my mouth off o' you."

Paige's eyes drifted shut at the erotic Highland whisper. "Oh," she said, her voice cracking, as his lips moved to her jaw, "that's okay."

With a soft, deep chuckle, Gabriel continued to make her shiver with kisses along her throat and her chin, and then he settled his mouth over hers. "Open," he said.

Paige slowly parted her lips, and Gabriel's moved erotically over hers, easing his tongue against each corner of her mouth, and then tasting her lips as if he truly could feel them. Her skin tingled and warmed, and she squirmed in the window seat as a pleasurable fire burned in her stomach.

His mouth moved back to her ear. "I want to see more o' you," he whispered, his voice deep, accented. Then his head pulled back, just a fraction, and his eyes met hers.

Paige's heart raced as she lifted her fingers first to her clan pin necklace, which she slipped off and over her head. She set it on the cushion beside her. Then, to the buttons on her night shirt, but she kept her gaze riveted on Gabriel's. Slowly, she released each one until the silky black top fell open. She didn't care that she'd blushed a furious shade of red. All she wanted was Gabriel's eyes and ghostly lips against her skin. When she leaned back against the window seat cushion, the slinky material slid ever so slowly over her breasts, and she simply stared, and breathed.

Gabriel's mouth lowered to hers, and he let one strong hand slowly drag over her jaw, down the column of her throat, and over her collarbone. Easing to the floor on his knees, his hand shook as he traced the swell of her breast with one finger, and her skin burned with need. He drew back and stared, his eyes dark with passion, and his mouth followed the path of his finger, slowly and erotically. Paige gasped a slight sigh, her breath coming fast. "Gabriel," she whispered.

His sensual lips, barely there but causing enough current to make her skin tingle, moved back up her throat and to her lips. He kissed her slowly there and long.

"Christ, woman," he said hoarsely in her ear. "Christ, you're so beautiful."

Together they sat for several moments, neither saying a word, simply breathing. Paige's hands moved to her shirt and buttoned the front. She looked at Gabriel.

"You're amazing," she whispered, and smiled.

His eyes remained darkly passion-filled.

After a few more moments, Gabriel inclined his head, a devilish look in his eyes. "You're lookin' weary, lass. I'll sit wi' you on the sofa, if you wish."

Paige stifled a yawn. "I do wish. Thank you." She grasped her necklace and placed it back on, tucking it down into her night shirt.

Together, they moved to the sofa. "Here," he said, "you can lie down and I'll sit behind you."

Paige grinned, fluffed a couple of pillows midway on the sofa, giving Gabriel enough room to sit at her head without falling through her, and laid down. After he settled in behind her, she looked up at him.

The beauty of his ghostly face, so rugged, so strongly cut, nearly made her gasp.

"I honestly cannot believe this is all happening to me. Me, of all people," she said, and slowly shook her head. "A few days ago I was running from you, scared out of my mind. Now? I'm all comfy and curled up beside you." She peered at him. "Don't you think it's all a bit bizarre?"

Gabriel rubbed his jaw with his hand and gave the slightest of smiles that made his dimples deepen.

She didn't think she'd ever grow tired of looking at those sexy marks in his cheeks.

Then, he lowered his hand and traced the outline of her nose, her forehead, and then her lips.

"I suppose I'm at that point where I'm fearful to ask too many questions of it, Paige MacDonald." His finger ran over her knuckles. "I'm too afraid I may blink and find you've suddenly gone."

In the back of her mind, she'd thought of little else that day. Leaving. *She didn't want to.* But she didn't live in Scotland, after all. She wasn't a citizen. Her job was in America.

Along with her lonely, boring, one-bedroom apartment life.

Besides. Gabriel didn't own Gorloch, and while she had plenty of money saved to buy herself a place, she could only stay six months with a working visa.

Not that Gabriel Munro had asked her to stay. Sure, he'd said he didn't want her to ever leave, but it wasn't the same thing.

"Me thinks you are havin' wicked thoughts runnin' through that lovely head o' yours, what with such a grumpy expression on your face." He stroked the line of her jaw. "What are you thinkin'?"

Paige stared straight into Gabriel Munro's mesmerizing green eyes. And lied.

"Nothing. I'm just taking everything in, I suppose." She stifled a yawn. "I'm so comfortable here, I think I could fall asleep just listening to your accent."

A deep chuckle sounded behind her. "Shall I say *aye* over and over then?"

Paige giggled. "Please. The more the merrier. And say something that has lots of *r*'s in it, too."

Gabriel laughed, and then settled down to tell Paige tales of days gone by. Vivid stories of his youth, his wild warring days, of cattle raids and skirmishes with other clans, of his mother and father, and brothers.

Before long, Paige's eyes began to drift closed.

Somehow, though, she still felt the pleasant tingling against her skin wherever Gabriel touched her. It calmed her, aroused her, and as she slipped into slumber, the thought of actually being physically touched by Gabriel Munro made her shiver.

Just before his deep, strangely medieval accent lulled her fast asleep.

Some time later, Paige's eyes fluttered open. The light in the room told her that she'd slept through the night, and it was now morning. Christmas Eve day.

It had been forever since she'd felt such excitement.

Sitting up, she rubbed her eyes and immediately searched for Gabriel. She found him perched on the windowsill, looking out. She ran a hand through her hair. "Good morning."

For several seconds, Gabriel said nothing. He simply sat staring out into the morning mist. His back was rigid, his shoulders pulled back sharply. His fists were tightly clenched. In his profile, she saw his jaw was set.

And immediately, Paige felt something had changed. Something, and she'd not a clue what, had happened.

Fear made her stomach uneasy.

"Gabriel, is something wrong?" she asked hesitantly.

After several long, painful moments, he turned and looked her directly in the eye. His gaze was fixed and hard, and it made Paige's throat tighten.

"You deceived me."

Paige blinked, shocked. "Excuse me?"

"Your clan pin, Paige." He inclined his head to her chest, where at some point during the night, her family heirloom had escaped her nightshirt and fallen out. "You're from the Gorloch Clan Mac-Donalds, Paige. Silver sword, winged creature in the center, with an amber stone. The verra same. The verra ones who *murdered me!*" he yelled. He drew in a deep breath and closed his eyes.

"I, I didn't—" she began.

"It doesna matter," he said quietly. He looked up. "You must leave. Now." He pushed up from the sill and walked past her, his stare hard and full of disgust. "Pack your belongings, call a taxi, and go."

With that, he disappeared through the wall.

Paige's breath caught in her throat, and she moved to the window and stared out into the early morning. Tears burned her eyes, and she tried to breathe normally, but it just wouldn't happen.

Resting her forehead gently against the cold glass, her thoughts consumed her. She'd not been responsible for his death. Never, ever would she have allowed it, had she been alive back then. She'd have done anything to save him.

She *loved* him.

Tears spilled over her lids and onto her hand. Slowly, she wiped them with her fingers, and wiped her eyes.

She hadn't known Gabriel Munro for long, but in two things, she was positive: one, she loved him. And two, once he made his mind up, there was no changing it. She'd known how strongly he'd felt from the very beginning, about *those* MacDonalds. She'd known she was from that same clan. Her granny had told her tales. She'd *known*.

And yet she'd kept it from him, had been too scared to tell him what she knew. The truth.

Paige wiped her eyes again, for the tears now seemed to be a constant leak.

Gabriel was right. She *had* deceived him. And she'd now pay a severe price.

With a deep breath, she eased herself down from the west tower, changed, packed her few belongings, and called a taxi.

As the car pulled away, she turned in her seat to see Gorloch castle for the last time.

Just before the castle disappeared from view, she saw the figure of a mighty Highlander standing on the battlements.

It looked as though she was destined to spend yet another Christmas alone after all.

Paige silently cried until she reached Inverness.

Chapter Twelve

Paige tugged the collar of her coat up, shoved her hands deep into the pockets, and trudged up the busy Inverness sidewalk. Last-minute Christmas Eve shoppers had already started the day, scrambling around from shop to shop, looking for that just-right present for their loved ones.

Quickly, she blinked and took a deep breath. She'd told herself not to cry anymore. She promised this to herself.

She was also fast believing that she had *lied* to herself.

After the taxi had dropped her off at Allister's bed-and-breakfast, where the young couple, Ally—short for Allister, a high-energy, handsome, ginger-haired Highlander—and his sweet wife, had welcomed her and settled her in, she'd decided to take a long walk along the main shopping street in Inverness. She had nothing to purchase, but she couldn't stand the idea of sitting alone with nothing but her thoughts.

Thoughts that continuously returned to a twelfth-century Highland warrior.

She'd been walking now for nearly three hours. First, along the banks of the River Ness. Inver, as she'd learned from Ally, meant *mouth of river* in Gaelic. Hence, Inver-Ness. The snow had stopped falling, and the scenery was breathtaking. The cold felt brisk against her cheeks, and as always, a heady, sweet scent clung to the air.

It almost seemed perfect.

But without Gabriel, nothing seemed right.

An inviting used-book store boasting coffee and tea came into view, and Paige decided to grab a cup and sit for a while, perhaps buy a book to read. She pushed the door and a small bell tinkled, reminding her of Zuzu Bailey in the movie she'd just watched with her ghost of a warrior.

Every time a bell rings, an angel gets her wings . . .

Paige wondered if it were true.

Inside the small stone-walled store, with dark wooden rafters overhead, a fire burned in a whitewashed hearth, making the intimate store warm and toasty. The scent of freshly brewed coffee and pastries filled the air, and Paige walked to the counter where three others stood in line. As she waited, she glanced around, noticing the other patrons standing at various bookshelves, browsing the selections.

Then, she saw him. Almost as if she were watching an old projector film, she moved toward a man standing at a bookshelf, book in hand. Paige couldn't take her eyes off him, and unable to stop herself, she moved closer. Wearing a gray woolen coat that hung to just below his knees, he had long, dark hair pulled back at the nape, with a small braid on either temple. Big, muscular, with a strong jaw and dark brows, he was an impossibly gorgeous man. His head was down, reading the pages of a book he'd just picked up.

From her angle, the man looked so much like Gabriel, he could have easily been his twin.

"Gabriel?" She thought she'd said it silently, but apparently not. And she didn't realize how close she'd gotten until he looked up at her, and she got a good look at his face, full-on.

Her eyes widened, and she covered her mouth.

"Lass?" the man said, setting the book down and grabbing her arm gently. "Are you ill? You look as though you've seen a ghost."

Mortified, Paige's eyes filled with tears. "I'm sorry. You look just like someone I knew." She pulled out of his grasp and turned, heading out of the store.

Moments later, as she headed down the street, her arm was once again grasped. Paige turned, looked up, and stared at Gabriel's look-alike. His dark brows were drawn over the most brilliant, intense pair of silvery eyes she'd ever seen. Different in color than Gabriel's, yet eerily the same.

"What name did you call me?" he said quietly. His unique eyes searched hers, and he didn't loosen his grip on her elbow.

Paige stared up at him, confused. "Gabriel. Look, I'm sorry. I was mistaken."

The man released her arm, but didn't walk away. "Nay, lass," he said, his voice deep, accent heavy, just like Gabriel's. "My name is Ethan Munro. How do you know this other lad, Gabriel?"

Paige blinked. Could it be possible that Ethan was a descendant of Gabriel? They had to be—they looked like twin brothers. Although Gabriel looked older. Not in years, but in centuries . . .

"We look just alike, aye?" he said.

He was *grinning*.

Paige stared up at the man's intense gray eyes. "You wouldn't believe me if I told you."

The man's smile stretched across his painfully handsome face. "Try me." He inclined his head toward the path by the river.

With a sigh, Paige agreed and walked with Ethan Munro down the path by the River Ness. She barely had to say anything at all. Just agree. She left out the part about how she'd somehow fallen in love with a spirit, and in only a few days. But she told him everything else, right down to her broken nose.

He seemed to know an awful lot about her ghost.

And then he told her the most fascinating tale she'd ever heard, save the very one she'd just experienced. And had she not experienced it with Gabriel, she'd never have believed a word that Ethan had said.

Apparently, he and his kinsmen had been *enchanted* for more than seven hundred years before Ethan's wife, American mystery novelist Amelia Landry, had leased their haunted tower house for the summer. She'd helped them solve an old mystery—the very one that had enchanted them in the first place. They had been made to live as a spirit, with no substance, for most of the day, and then gain substance at twilight. *Weird.*

The man she was staring at, probably gaping at, was nearly as old as Gabriel, he said. "So, you're not only Gabriel's descendant, but you're from the fourteenth century?" She shook her head and sighed. "I'm not saying that out loud again."

Ethan stared down at her, then chuckled. "Aye, you're right. And damn me, but I simply canna believe it. The stories are true, and my own kin has been livin' a ride's day away for centuries."

"What stories?" Paige asked.

"Our clan had always heard of Gabriel Munro's unfortunate demise, and that he'd gone to his grave thinkin' the MacDonalds had been the ones to put him there. But we were bound to our land, as is he. Gabriel, being murdered at Gorloch, remained at Gorloch. And we were bound to our Munro lands." He shook his dark head. "'Twasna so, lass. The stories, I mean."

That stopped Paige in her tracks. "What?"

Ethan Munro stopped as well, and shoved his hands into the pockets of his coat. "Aye, 'twas an unfortunate thing, his death. It was rumored his verra best mate told him the lies, knowin' Gabriel would go after the MacDonalds on his own. Even filched a MacDonald clan pin to leave behind. Back then, it didna take much to start up a clan war." He smiled down at her. "Or a war o' your own."

"What were the lies over?" she asked.

Ethan sighed. "The usual. A lass."

"Oh."

Ethan inclined his head, much in the same way Gabriel did, and looked at her. "So why are you here, on the Yule's Eve, all alone? What made you leave Gorloch?"

Paige looked up, then lifted her heirloom from beneath her sweater. "Gabriel saw this while I was asleep." She blushed. "He didn't even give me time to explain."

"Explain what, lass?" he said, studying the pin.

"That, well, I didn't have anything to do with his death, even if I was from *that* clan o' MacDonalds." She said that last bit as Gabriel would have said it, and Ethan laughed.

"Aye, well understand this: In our day, centuries ago, clans weren't the verra best at gatherin' and embracin'. 'Twas more of a challenge to remain enemies." He shrugged. "The MacDonalds were a powerful lot." He stared at her. "But they were no' responsible for Gabriel's death."

"I see," she said quietly. "I'm pretty sure Gabriel couldn't be convinced of that."

For several long seconds, Ethan Munro studied Paige. She squirmed, shifted her weight, and finally, after the heat rose on her cheeks, she looked him in the eye. "What?"

Ethan grinned. "You're in love wi' him, aye?"

The heat beneath her skin grew hotter, and she frowned. She hadn't even admitted it to Gabriel. "Yes. Very much. Not that it matters now, and I don't know if he feels the same. We never, well, I just." She sighed. "He doesn't know how I feel."

A slow grin crossed Ethan's face, and he pulled out his cell phone. "You dunna worry about that, lass. Aye? You leave it in my hands." He grazed her jaw with a knuckle. "Trust me. I vow you willna regret it."

Gabriel stared across the snow-laden grounds of Gorloch. The wind had stilled and the flakes had ceased falling.

And the one thing that had come to mean the verra most to him was a bloody MacDonald.

And she'd deceived him.

He frowned, pushed off the parapet, and swore.

Inside, he paced, his thoughts running dark. How he'd fallen in love wi' a bloody MacDonald was beyond his reasoning. He should have sensed that filthy clan within her, no matter how beautiful she was.

MacDonalds were known for their cleverness.

She'd certainly proven that fact.

But fallen in love wi' her, he had, and now he wished mightily to have her back. He'd been a fool—

A car door slammed shut, and Gabriel jumped. So deep into his black thoughts was he that he hadna even heard the approach. For a moment, his heart betrayed him and leapt.

Had Paige returned to him?

He frowned. Even if she had, he'd have to make her leave. Wouldna he? He couldna allow his heart to open to one of *those* . . .

Just then, the front entrance banged open. Gabriel materialized just as fast, and when his eyes clapped onto the three big men standing in the foyer, *uninvited*, Gabriel pulled up short. He stared, angry at their trespassing; then he could do little more than gape.

He didna have time to do much of anything else before the one who looked just like himself began to speak.

"No need to play your ghosty tricks on us, man," he said, crossing his arms over his chest. His men did the like. "So stay put where we can see you. We're your kin, Gabriel Munro, born nearly a century after you. I'm Ethan. This is a cousin, Aiden, and me brother, Rob. We were enchanted for centuries, trapped on Munro lands. We'd heard stories about your murder, but ne'er thought you existed as a spirit, here."

Gabriel simply stared, and scowled. He didna say a word.

Ethan Munro made up for the both of them.

"You've been wrong all these centuries, and I want you to keep your tongue in your head and let me tell you the truth of it. 'Twas no' a MacDonald who stole your life." Ethan came closer. "'Twas your best mate, Padrick. 'Twas no' thing more than he wanting your woman. But his desire turned to murder when she tried to fight him off. He didna wish to be blamed for it and knew there was tension betwixt the Munros and MacDonalds. He filched a clan pin and left it for you to find." He stepped closer, as did his kinsmen. "You did, and at his urgin', you blamed the MacDonalds and swore revenge." He shook his head, those silver eyes boring into his. "You didna take long before you'd hacked your way through nearly all o' the MacDonalds close by. But one got away, lad."

"Aye," Gabriel finally said, anger nearly boiling out of him. "And I would have gotten his skinny arse, as well, had he no' hid in the bloody east tower. He stabbed me wi' me own blade whilst I slept!"

Ethan frowned and hollered back. "How do you think he managed to hide up in yon tower, man? Are you so bloody blind that you canna see how Padrick deceived you?"

The one named Aiden stepped forward. "He feared your wrath

much more than he treasured your kinship. After you were killed, he carried that lie round wi' him until days before he died himself."

"Aye," said Rob. "He wanted a clear conscience before meeting God, so he told one o' your brother's sons."

"And the tale was passed down ever since," finished Ethan.

Gabriel looked at his kin. Emotions ran rampant through him. A week ago, and he'd no one but Craigmire and his wife. Now? He had kin.

He'd *had* Paige MacDonald, as well, but he'd run her off. He'd lost her. And he was a bleedin' idiot.

Then, he met the silvery stare of Ethan. "How did you know to find me here?"

Ethan grinned. "I encountered a gorgeous, melancholy lass in the book café in Inverness earlier this morn." He shrugged. "At first I thought 'twas my dashing good looks and fine form that caused her to gape and wander up to me."

Rob and Aiden chuckled.

"But I soon learned 'twas *you* she saw in me, and the likeness stunned her so badly, she couldna help but approach, whispering your name," Ethan said. "It didna take long to convince her o' the unique situation we faced."

It didna take long to convince Gabriel, either.

Ethan and his kin—his verra own family—had been enchanted? The thought stunned him.

Yet, it didna. Although it did sound more believable than his own paltry tale of murder and ghostliness.

Gabriel pinched the bridge of his nose and shoved a hand through his hair. After a few solid Gaelic curses, he looked at his cousin. "I am an idiot."

Ethan smiled and stroked his chin. "You were deceived, cousin, but no' by Paige MacDonald. Not by any MacDonald."

"I ousted her from here," Gabriel said, and cursed again. "I'm verra sure she'd sooner throw herself from the battlements than return here, to me."

Aiden stepped forward and frowned. "Do you know what it means to have a fine, mortal, modern lass accept you for what and who you are, and love you irrevocably?" He shook his head. "'Tis a gift, man. A bloody gift you shouldna look away from. That indeed would make you an idiot, in truth."

Did he say *love*?

"We'll leave you now to mend the rest o' your mess," said Ethan, and headed for the door. The others followed. "But if you throw Paige MacDonald out o' your home again, 'tis your own demise. There are plenty o' live Munros who'd gladly offer for her attentions."

Gabriel blinked.

The three Munros laughed.

"We'll be back, cousin," Ethan said with a grin. "Happy Yuletide."

And then they slammed the door.

Gabriel simply stared at the solid oak. His heart pounded, and his mouth suddenly ran dry. He dared to hope.

Car doors slammed shut, the engine started, and the vehicle started off down the path, away from Gorloch.

As Gabriel stood there, dazed by the latest events, wondering just how to get Paige MacDonald back to Gorloch and staring at the door, a small knock sounded from the other side. His insides locked up.

He didna even have to look. He knew who it was.

He didna know whether to shout for joy, or run for shame.

Instead of either, he drew in a deep breath as he readied to pass through the door.

Chapter Thirteen

Paige's heart beat faster and faster with each passing second. From the moment she'd met Ethan and his kin, and on the drive back to Gorloch, she'd wanted to weep. She held it in, though.

She was scared.

Scared that, no matter how very differently the tale went, Gabriel would still begrudge her for not telling him she was of *those* MacDonalds from the very beginning. Ethan had insisted that he knew the heart of his kin better than any, and that Gabriel would indeed appreciate them bringing her back to Gorloch.

She knocked.

And immediately, the handsome, green-eyed warrior came through the wood and stood by her side. His chest rose and fell rapidly, as though he struggled to breathe.

She knew the feeling.

"Paige," he said, searching her face. "Christ, Paige, I'm verra sorry. I dunna know what to say."

Paige stared up into his pleading face.

She loved the way his *sorry* sounded like *soddy* in that deep, ancient Highland accent. "I should have told you from the start that I suspected my clan was *the* clan." She looked down at the spot between her boots, and Gabriel's ghostly ones that looked nearly as substantial as her own. "I didn't want you to send me away."

Several moments of silence stretched between them, and with each breath Paige could see the frost puff out before her lips. The wind had stopped, as had the sprinkle of snow. Everything was white and bright, the air clean and fresh.

"Look at me, Paige MacDonald."

With tears burning in her eyes, she slowly raised her head and met Gabriel's gaze.

"I regret more than anythin', askin' you to leave. Even if your clan had been responsible for my demise, 'twasna you, and I'm verra sorry." He ducked his head closer and whispered, "I wish nothin' more than for you to stay. 'Tis the Yuletide Eve, dunna forget." His eyes sought hers. "I'm beggin' you to stay here with me. Please?"

Paige's heart thumped heavily with joy. "I wouldn't want to be anywhere else," she said softly. "Thank you."

He stepped closer and braced himself with one arm on the stone wall behind her head. His eyes scanned her face. "I want to kiss you powerfully bad, lass. Can I?"

Paige didn't trust her voice. She nodded.

A slow smile lifted the corners of Gabriel's mouth, and the dimples returned in both cheeks as he lowered his head. Paige sighed as his lips brushed over hers, then again, and then lingered while he explored her mouth the only way he could. Everywhere he touched her left a delicious searing in its path.

She never wanted him to stop.

But after a few moments, he did. Slowly, he moved his lips close to her ear. "I am verra glad you're here," he whispered. "The emptiness is once more gone." He pulled back and looked at her. "Come. Let us begin enjoying our Yule, aye?"

Paige smiled and nodded. She wanted so badly to throw her arms around his neck, press her mouth to his, and feel the pressure of his strength as he squeezed her into a warm, enveloping hug. Instead, she lifted a hand and grazed the line of his jaw and smiled.

She couldn't think of a single thing to say.

And somehow, Gabriel seemed to sense that. His smile widened, as if he knew she was happier now than she'd ever been, and that he was responsible for it. Together they walked through Gorloch's front entrance and up to the room she'd leased. Setting her things on the floor in a corner, Paige turned and glanced at Gabriel.

"Can you ice-skate?" he asked.

She smiled. "I haven't since I was a kid."

Gabriel inclined his dark head. "Then come. Your wee feet look as though they'd fit right into a pair belonging to Craigmire's wife. They're in the mudroom, behind the larder."

Paige grinned. "And how will I skate through days of snowfall?"

"Och, a smart lassy you are. The family from the next estate just had it scraped for their wee ones to use on the Yuletide, so we'd best use it now whilst we're still alone."

"Clever," she said. "And what will you wear?"

As they hurried down the passageway, Gabriel chuckled. "I dunna need blades, Paige MacDonald. I can float." He wiggled his brows. "Ghost, remember?"

How could she ever forget?

The funny thing was, she couldn't care less.

"Okay. No laughing," Paige said, a mock frown stretching over her pixielike features. "I mean it."

Gabriel stared down at the lass who'd come to mean more than life itself, and in such a short amount o' time.

'Twas miraculous at best.

He couldna take his eyes off her . . .

Wearing Craigmire's bulky wool coat, Paige had Mrs. Craigmire's ice skates laced up, a pair o' those fetchin' jeans that hugged her in the most intimate of ways, and that crazy multicolored hat pulled down over her wee ears. Above two black-and-purple moons, blue eyes shown brightly back at him.

He thought she'd never looked so endearing.

"Well?" she repeated, and pushed off the bench she'd sat upon to lace up the skates. "Deal?"

Gabriel grinned and stroked his jaw. "Nay, lass. I canna make such an agreement." He shrugged. "I suspect 'twill be too much to laugh at. I willna be able to help myself."

Paige scowled, and Gabriel chuckled. Then she eased from the bench and stepped onto the small, freshly scraped frozen pond, just behind the castle's west wall. Large drifts of snow sat pushed up on the edges.

With arms out like a bird, she glanced at him. "I hope I don't break anything else."

Gabriel moved out onto the ice with her, keeping his eyes locked with hers. "Take it slow, lass. Mayhap with your wings spread as such, you willna fall."

Together they moved in a slow circle round the pond, and after two passes, Paige stood upright and elegant, gliding just as smoothly as a ghosty herself. A slight billow of white puffed out before her lips with each breath, and when she smiled at Gabriel, he thought the beauty of it would melt the whole bloody pond. He couldna take his eyes from her for nearly an hour.

"Why are you looking at me like that?" she asked.

Gabriel swung in front of her, moving his big booted feet over the ice as though skating. He faced her, and grinned. "Because you are beautiful, what wi' that wee red nose." No' to mention he'd seen more o' her and hadn't been able to get that eve out o' his head.

"Hmm," she answered, and the she smiled. "Oh, look. It's starting to snow again."

Gabriel glanced at the sky. "Aye, so it is." He pulled closer, and looked down. "It will be dark soon. Have you skated enough?"

With a graceful twirl, she stopped, the blade of her skates scraping the ice. "Sure." She smiled even wider. "It's Christmas Eve, you know."

Gabriel watched excitement dance in her blue eyes. "Aye, indeed I do."

He had a surprise for her. Actually, 'twas a bit o' a surprise for himself, as well. And he couldna wait to bestow it upon her. "Come, then, you wee little bottomless pit. I hear your poor belly growling again."

Paige skated to the edge of the pond, stepped off, and moved to the bench. With one knee raised, she unlaced her skates.

"'Tis wi' regret that I cannot prepare a Yule Eve supper for you, Paige MacDonald," he said. "I should have had Ethan call—"

She looked up, and the expression in her eyes softened Gabriel's heart even more. "Honestly, Gabriel, I don't need so much fuss. I am perfectly content eating whatever." She took off her other skate and pulled on Craigmire's Wellies. Then, she smiled. "As long as it's with you."

That sentence alone gave Gabriel the verra courage he needed to bestow Paige her Yuletide gift. "As with me, lass," he said quietly. He dropped down onto the bench beside her and met her shy gaze. "Had I the substance, I'd toss you in yon snow pile and kiss you breathless."

Paige visibly gulped. Then, once she'd turned several shades of red and pink, she gave a bashful smile. "I'd let you, too."

Gabriel shifted his head to one side, lowered his mouth to hers, and grazed her lips. How he could lose himself in a mind's-eye vision of what it might actually feel like to have those soft-looking lips moving fervently beneath his, to have her hands push through his hair, and to feel her tongue against his. After a moment, he pulled back. "You're makin' me daft again, lass. Inside. Now." He grinned. "Your lips are blue."

With a tinkling laugh, Paige gathered Mrs. Craigmire's skates, and together they walked back to the castle. They spent the rest of the daylight hours walking about the halls, in the larder where he insisted Paige prepare a filling Yuletide supper—no' just a grilled cheese sandwich and soup. She'd found a Cornish hen in the freezer, a few yams and other vegetables, as well as a frozen custard pie Craigmire had purchased from Tesco and hidden from his wife.

Once the hen had finished baking, they sat down to eat. Gabriel conjured up a mixture of candles and ornaments for the meal, and Paige had glowed with excitement.

As she poked her fork into a baked yam, she glanced at Gabriel. "I feel funny, sitting here eating while you can't."

Gabriel watched her mouth delicately close over the fork and chew the yam. Then she lifted her glass of wine and drank. "I enjoy watching you eat. Besides. I've no' eaten in centuries. Trust me—this suffices as the closest thing to actually tasting food."

She smiled and before long, finished eating. "I'm stuffed."

"Miracles never cease round here," he said, and grinned.

His stomach twisted into knots. 'Twas nearly time for Paige's gift, and damn him, but he was as skittish as a whelp meetin' his first virgin.

Bloody hell.

"What's wrong?" she asked, and cocked her head to the side to study his face. "You look ill."

He forced a smile. "'Tis impossible, that. Come." He inclined his head. "Let's worry about the dishes later. I've a mind to sit with you before the fire."

"Hmm," she said, tapping a finger to her temple. "Wash dishes, or sit before a roaring fire on Christmas Eve with the handsomest Highlander in the universe." She rolled her eyes, then grinned. "Okay. Let's go."

That somehow eased his mind, and Gabriel laughed. Together they walked to the great hall, he watched helplessly as Paige stoked the fire she'd built earlier, and then they sat.

"'Twill be the Yuletide in a couple o' hours," he said.

"Yes," she answered, staring into the flames. She looked at her hands. "I wish I had something more appealing to wear tonight." She glanced at him and smiled. "I hadn't counted on having an occasion to dress up for."

"You're perfect the way you are," he assured her, and traced the curve of her hair with a finger. "Absolutely perfect."

She shyly looked away.

And it was then Gabriel drew in a deep, long breath, and turned to face her.

'Twas now or never . . .

Chapter Fourteen

Paige turned her head and studied Gabriel's profile. He *did* look ill. Something was bothering him.

It made her seriously nervous.

Then, he turned fully toward her.

"You've changed my life, Paige MacDonald," he said quietly, grazing the top of her knuckles with one long finger. "I canna remember the last time I looked forward to the day, or the sunset, sunrise." He smiled. "Or snowfall, as much as I do now. Before, 'twas merely goin' through motions of unlife. 'Tis what I do, and there's no gettin' round it." He moved closer, and stroked her jaw with his knuckles. "Until now. Now, with you, I'm experiencin' everythin' as though for the verra first time. It's all new, fresh." He grazed her lips. "I dunna want you to leave, Paige."

She looked at him, waiting.

His eyes softened as they locked with hers. "And I dunna wish for you to just be my guest, or my companion."

She swallowed past the large lump in her throat.

Lowering his head, he moved his mouth to her ear. "I am in love wi' you, Paige MacDonald." He pulled back, just enough to look her in the eye, and her heart lurched. "I know 'tis fast, but I feel as though we were meant to be together, as though you were sent here." He smiled. "Just for me."

Paige blinked, swallowed, and opened her mouth to speak, but Gabriel placed a single finger over her lips. "Shh, love, I need to finish."

She waited, tears already burning her eyes.

"I canna live without you, Paige." Sincerity burned deep in his green eyes. "I know 'tis daft soundin'," he began, as he closed his eyes for a moment, then opened them again. "But will you wed me, Paige MacDonald?" He stroked her jaw, her lips, her throat. "Will you wed the spirit of an aged warrior? You know I've nothin' to offer but my undyin' love for you—"

"Shh," Paige said, placing her fingers over his lips to hush him. She searched his face, looked deeply into his eyes and saw nothing but pure, raw honesty and sincere love.

So surprised by it, she gasped.

"Oh, Gabriel," she whispered in awe. "You've more to offer than anyone." She placed a hand over his heart, and for a second, she imagined his smooth skin stretched tight over rock-hard muscle and the steady thump of his heart beneath her palm. "Your soul," she said, again whispering, not trusting her voice to be any louder. "I am so in love with you," she said, and moved her mouth close to his ear. "I will wed you, Gabriel Munro." She stroked his jaw. "And I would love to be your wife."

Paige saw many things cross Gabriel's face. Relief, joy, love—all things she herself felt. His smile began with nothing more than his dimples pitting his cheeks. The longer he stared at her, searching her eyes, the wider his smile grew. Finally, he threw back his head and laughed, the sexy, deep sound echoing throughout Gorloch's great hall.

Paige felt her own smile pulling at her mouth, and she simply watched in awe as her Highlander moved close, placed a hand on either side of her head, which rested on sofa cushions, and looked her dead in the eye.

Suddenly, his smile faded, replaced by something else entirely. She couldn't exactly put a finger on it.

"Are you sure you can stand livin' with someone for the rest of your days who cannot physically touch you? Or satisfy you in the ways a husband satisfies his woman?" he asked. "Truly?"

Paige sought his eyes, eager to put his fears at ease. "You touch me in ways you cannot fathom, Gabriel Munro. Everything else, we'll learn together."

Leaning forward until their lips brushed together, Gabriel whispered, "Christ, I love you, woman."

And he kissed her. Paige's lips tingled, and her insides burned as Gabriel moved his mouth over hers; then he pulled back and stared at her.

"I am truly the luckiest man, alive or no'," he said.

Paige smiled, and then blinked. She stared hard, and then her mouth went dry and her throat tightened.

"What's wrong, Paige?" Gabriel asked.

Paige continued to stare. "You're . . . you don't look as solid as before." She frowned. "Is something happening?"

Gabriel glanced down at his arm, then the rest of his body. Quickly, he rose and turned, stomped each foot, and then met Paige's gaze. "Och, Christ, no."

Paige was up on her feet as though she'd been struck by lightning. "What is it?"

Gabriel's somber expression made her stomach knot with fear. "What is it, Gabriel? Please!"

He locked his eyes to hers and moved close. "I had no idea, love," he said, a sadness tingeing his voice. "Christ, I didna know."

"Know *what?*" Paige said, all but shouting.

Gabriel's image grew more and more translucent.

Then, it struck her.

"No!" she said, her voice cracking. "Gabriel, please."

"Paige, *shh*," he said, and met her gaze squarely. His voice shook as he spoke. "I will always love you, lass," he said gently, his form fast fading into the amber light of the great hall. "I will always be wi' you."

Paige lifted a hand and caressed his jaw. "I will always be with you," she returned, then gave a wan smile. "Mrs. Munro. It sounds perfect."

He was vaguely there now, his outline barely visible. "It does indeed, my wife." His smile was the very last to go. "You're mine forever, Paige." He whispered, *"Dunna forget that. . . ."*

And then, he was gone.

Leaving Paige in Gorloch's great hall all alone.

Paige looked around the empty hall, her heart feeling equally as void. Slowly, she lowered herself to the cushion and sank back.

Tears rolled down her face uncontrollably, and she wiped them with the back of her hand. She hugged herself, her insides physically hurting, and she pulled her knees up and wrapped her arms around them.

Nothing but a wintry Yuletide Eve wind rushed through the stone cracks of Gorloch, leaving Paige alone.

Her heart already ached for the man she'd come to love irrevocably in a few short days.

She wasn't sure how long she'd been sitting there, but the tears had stopped and she'd finally been able to catch her breath. She'd gotten up, washed and dried the dishes, and simply wandered the halls, even grabbed Craigmire's coat, slipped it on, and traipsed up to the battlements to look out over the snow-laden, moon-bathed land.

Christmas Eve in the Highlands. Still ruggedly beautiful, but now it meant much, much more to her than just lovely countryside or a special land filled with turbulent and proud history.

In that same country, that same turbulence, a man had once been born. He'd lived a short life before dying a violent, treacherous death. His unsettled spirit had roamed for nearly nine hundred years, and then they'd met. She, Paige MacDonald, a lonely museum curator with no family, no love. And he, the ghost of a fierce warrior.

Together they'd found love. Contentment.

Raw ecstasy.

Paige blinked through a new set of tears, and the icy cold winter's night froze the liquid on her cheeks. Swiping them with her sleeve, she left the battlements and made her way back to the great hall. Without much thought at all, she grabbed the thick wool blanket from the back of the sofa, wrapped herself up, and lay before the Yule fire.

There, on what had been the happiest night of her life, in a medieval castle where she'd recently been proposed to by a handsome twelfth-century Highland warrior, she silently cried herself to sleep.

The sound of car doors slamming and loud, deep voices drew Paige out of her slumber. Slowly, she cracked open her eyes. She sat up even more slowly. The fire had long since been extinguished, the hall had grown cold, and her body felt stiff and achy.

Then the memory of losing the only man she'd ever loved rushed back, and her heart cracked in half again.

A heavy fist banged on the front door, and Paige jumped. She rose and stared. *Who could it be?*

"Paige?" a deep voice hollered. "Open up, lass!"

Ethan Munro. Oh, God, she'd have to tell them they'd just lost their kinsman.

Wiping her eyes, she made her way to the front door and opened it. Big, handsome Ethan stood there grinning, surrounded by others that looked a whole lot like him.

"Yuletide greetings, Ms. MacDonald!" said Ethan, and he grasped her hand in his and pressed a kiss to her knuckles.

Standing next to him, an attractive woman with long, straight blond hair smiled, a sweet toddler in each hand. "Hi, Paige. I'm Amelia." She inclined her head. "Ethan's wife." She looked at the guys on either side of her. "I hope you don't mind?" She turned the little ones loose, and they ran inside.

Paige swallowed a lump in her throat. "Um"—she glanced at Ethan—"of course not. I need to speak with you, please?"

Ethan pressed his lips together, as if trying to stifle a smile. "Of course." He grasped her elbow gently and pulled her close to the stairs. The others filed in and made their way to the sofa. Several large Highlanders plopped down and sprawled out.

It made Paige miss Gabriel even more.

"What's the matter, lass?" Ethan asked.

Paige drew a deep breath, forcing the tears to remain at bay. "Gabriel's gone, Ethan."

Ethan merely stared at her.

"He proposed to me last night," her voice cracked, "and I accepted, and then . . ."

"You did say aye, did you no'?"

That voice came from the doorway.

She looked up. Ethan grinned, and his silvery eyes danced with merriment. He inclined his head in the direction of the front door.

Slowly, Paige turned her head and looked.

Quite suddenly, her heart jumped to her throat, and she gasped. She felt her mouth slide open, and she simply gaped.

Standing in the doorway was Gabriel Munro, dressed in a black sweater, jeans, boots, and a brown leather jacket, half of his hair pulled back and secured at the nape. Green eyes stared at her with so much intensity, she started to shake.

"Gabriel?" she said hesitantly.

He smiled. Dimples pitted his cheeks.

Paige squealed and took off, drawing up short just before plowing straight through him. Her breath coming fast, she met his gaze.

It was different, his gaze. Stronger. More intense than it was before. He stared down at her now with an absolute predatory gaze.

"Are you no' going to embrace your fiancé?" asked Ethan.

Paige glanced at him. "What?"

Just as Ethan, with a big hand on her backside, pushed her straight at Gabriel.

Paige gasped and squealed.

Just as Gabriel caught her, lifted her right off the floor, and brought his mouth a mere inch from hers.

Again, Paige's mouth slid open, speechless.

"I vow you're givin' me an invitation, what wi' your sweet mouth parted," he whispered.

With her hands, Paige slid her palms along Gabriel's arms, then his shoulders, then one on each of his jaws.

"How can this be?" Paige asked, mostly to herself. Then, she fixed her gaze onto Gabriel's.

He apparently could wait no more.

With a low groan, he crushed his mouth to hers, and the sensation of his warm lips pressed to hers and then his velvety tongue caressing against her own made her heart thunder. His arms enveloped her, big hands molding to her back, her neck, and pulling her mouth closer still.

Vaguely, in the background, Paige heard the Munro clan whoop and holler.

Without thinking, she shoved her hands through Gabriel's hair and kissed him back with just as much fervor as he did. She all but wrapped her legs around his waist, and it was only when she felt his large hands cup her bottom that she heard Ethan's deep, strong voice.

"All right, then, that's enough laddie," he said, and suddenly she was pulled out of Gabriel's arms. "That shall come only after the nuptials have been voiced."

Paige glanced up at Ethan, who wiggled his brows.

Gabriel shoved Ethan away and enveloped Paige's body in his arms once more.

He looked down at her. "We've plenty o' time for answers, but I'll say this just to douse your obvious curiosity." He kissed her again. "'Twas my hatred of the MacDonalds that kept me here all these centuries past." He kissed her again. "And 'twas no' only my own recognition of my mistake, but your love and my acceptance o' it that gave me redemption." With two strong hands, he adjusted the angle of her face just so, leaned in to kiss her, and then stopped. His eyes searched her face, and Paige completely forgot there was a medieval hall full of Munros. "Say it again, Paige MacDonald," he whispered, and grazed his thumb along her bottom lip.

She shuddered. God, it felt better than she'd even imagined.

"Say it."

Slowly, she smiled, and slid her arms about his waist. "I love you, Gabriel Munro," she said softly. "And yes, I will wed you."

The thunderous boom of Munro males echoing in the great hall was deafening, and Paige threaded her hands through Gabriel's hair and pulled his mouth the rest of the way to hers. A groan escaped him, and she knew only she'd heard it, and they kissed their very first Yuletide kiss.

Her silent wish had come true. She'd not cared one whit how her Highlander had returned to her. Only that he had.

That he'd returned in the flesh and blood of his earthly body was more than a plus. It was a miracle.

And she'd thank God and the Powers That Be for such a miracle for the rest of her days.

"Do you think you can accept my rowdy kinsmen as well?" Gabriel said, close to her ear. The feeling had been delicious when he was a spirit. Now? It made her quake uncontrollably.

"Oh, yes," she answered. "Gladly."

In one fatal moment, she'd lost her love.

Hours later, she'd not only been given that love back, but in the flesh, as well as an entire family.

Paige knew then there wasn't a soul as lucky as her.

"Welcome to the family," said Amelia, who'd come to stand close. "I'm so happy to have another girl around."

Paige smiled. "Thank you."

The rest of Christmas Day flew by. The Munros, who had employed a husband and wife to cook for their large clan, brought them to Gorloch to prepare the holiday feast. Turkey, dressing, potatoes, yams—the works—had been prepared. Presents had been brought, as well, and the two young Munros had played until each had fallen asleep beneath the very real tree all the men had gone out and chopped down.

Paige thought she'd never seen more food consumed in her life as when the Munros had sat down to dinner.

Gabriel had sat directly across from her, and he'd not once taken his penetrating green gaze from hers. He ate, but not with as much fervor as one would think a soul could eat after not having one single bite for centuries on end.

He looked starved for something else entirely different.

Later that night, Gabriel whisked Paige off to be alone—not an easy thing with several large medieval Highlanders determined to make sure Paige kept her innocence intact.

Somehow, though, they managed to make it to the west tower. Without a word, Gabriel led Paige to the sofa, sat her down, then lit what candles remained in the room. Outside, a Christmas night snow fell. Gabriel settled down beside her, pulled her into his arms, and sighed.

"I fear that if I close my eyes, this will all disappear," he said in his thick Scottish burr. He pressed his lips to her temples and nudged her cheek with his mouth. "Are you still sure? About becoming my wife?"

Paige turned in his arms to look at him. She stroked his cheek, his jaw, and then his hair. "I've never been surer about anything in my life," she said.

Gabriel grinned and gathered her close. "When?"

With her head to his warm chest, Paige smiled. "The sooner the better. I don't think I can take your kin hovering over us for much longer."

A deep rumble started in Gabriel's chest as he chuckled. "Hogmanay, then. 'Twill give you enough time?"

Paige sighed, content. "I've waited for you my whole life, Gabriel Munro. I suppose I can wait another week."

Lowering his head, he moved his mouth to her ear. "I vow

I canna wait," he said, his deep voice washing over her. She shuddered.

Neither could she.

They spent several hours before the long windows, watching the Christmas night snowfall, wrapped in one another's arms.

Paige thought she couldn't get much happier.

That is, until Gabriel Munro tucked her hair behind her ears, tilted her head, and covered her mouth with his . . .

Chapter Fifteen

Paige glanced in the mirror at herself.

She could hardly believe it was her.

Amelia had helped her plan everything. Paige had decided to wed at the Munros' ancestral ruins, at the small abbey there on the property. Ethan had gained a permit just to allow it, and he'd acquired a priest for the ceremony, as well. Small though the wedding was, the other she Munro had not wanted Paige to miss out on one single bride's moment. They'd bonded quite fast and had shopped for only a day before finding what Paige thought was the perfect bridal gown.

She stared at it now and wondered how Gabriel would like it.

She hadn't seen her fiancé in almost two days. The other Munros had whisked him away for a bit o' rousin'.

He'd truly looked as though he'd rather not have gone.

Running her hand down the soft lines of the simple antique white shift, she stared at her image. Sleeveless, it had beautiful pearls sewn to the bodice, and the low-scooped back buttoned from the middle to just below her hips.

Gabriel was going to have a heck of a time, what with his big fingers.

Paige blushed at the thought.

319

Gently, she eased her feet into like-colored mules, and she drew a deep breath as she applied the smallest amount of lipstick. Staring at her image, she tucked her hair behind her ears and tapped her powder brush at the fading purple moons under her eyes.

"Oh, now I think I'm going to just die," said Amelia, stepping into the room. She looked her over with a big grin. "Honestly, you are the most gorgeous bride I've ever seen, bruised eyes and all."

Paige smiled. "Thanks." She picked up her headpiece; a small pearl clip with a chin-length chiffon skirt.

"Here, let me help you with that," Amelia said, and adjusted it to Paige's head. She smiled. "There. Perfect."

Paige glanced in the mirror, then at Amelia. "Thank you. For everything."

Amelia smiled. "You are more than welcome, future Mrs. Paige Munro." She cocked her head. "No regrets about quitting the Smithsonian? I mean, that's a pretty cool place."

Paige smiled. "No regrets. I've worked more hours in my twenties than most people work their entire lifetime. I'm ready for a change."

Amelia grinned. "That you've saved most of that money really helps," she said. "Ethan tells me you've an inheritance as well?"

Paige nodded. "Yes. My grandmother left me a healthy sum. I just saved it right along with the rest." She smiled. "I am still speechless over yours and Ethan's gift. A castle?" She shook her head. "It's too much, Amelia."

Amelia laughed. "Are you kidding? Ethan would do anything to keep Gabriel and you close. Besides, it's just a small tower house, close to ours. And you'll need to do some renovations."

Paige grasped her cousin to be and hugged her tightly. "Thank you. Again."

"Och, are you sure you wish to wed that lunkhead cousin o' mine? I'll gladly take you, lass."

Paige and Amelia both jumped as Aiden stuck his head in the door. He grinned.

"Sorry," Paige said. "But I'm afraid I'll have to choose the lunkhead. Thanks, though."

Aiden Munro burst out laughing. "Right. Well he'll lay me flat if I dunna bring you to the abbey right away. He's used Ethan's mobile to call at least three times in the last twenty minutes. 'Tis time."

Aiden walked over to Paige and draped her antique white shawl over her shoulders. He jutted out an arm to her and Amelia. "Let's go then, loves."

It took less than twenty minutes to reach the Munro ruins. Truly, they weren't nearly as ruinous as Gabriel had thought them to be. The abbey had been restored to a lovely medieval building.

Ethan met them at the abbey's entrance, and as Paige stepped out of Aiden's Rover, she drew a deep, calming breath. The snow had stopped for several days now, and a crisp, clean scent filled the air. Hogmanay, nearly midnight. Gabriel had insisted on the time, and she'd heartily agreed.

"Are you ready, cousin to be?" Ethan asked, offering Paige his arm with a smile.

Paige smiled up at him. "I am," she said. He kissed her cheek and led her into the kirk.

Raftered ceilings, six lovely stain-glassed arched windows, and dark wooden benches filled the small kirk. Tiny candles covered the surfaces on either side, as well as the altar. Munros filled the benches, Mr. and Mrs. Craigmire sat with them, and a priest awaited her at the front.

As did the handsomest man she'd ever laid eyes on. Gabriel

sported a billowy white shirt beneath his sexy red-and-black Munro plaid. Black boots, polished and gleaming, reached his knees.

"Breathe, lass," whispered Ethan.

Then he walked her to Gabriel.

Ethan placed Paige's hand in Gabriel's, then moved to his cousin's other side. Amelia stood for Paige.

The ceremony was short, spoken first in Gaelic, then in English.

The priest looked first at Gabriel. "Will you take this woman as your beloved, to forever protect and cherish until you breathe no more?"

Gabriel's eyes softened as he squeezed Paige's hands. "Aye, I will."

"And you, lass," the priest said. "Will you take this man as your beloved, to forever protect and cherish until you breathe no more?"

Paige felt a tear slide down her face, and she smiled at Gabriel. "Yes, I will."

"The rings?"

They'd agreed on simple platinum bands, and as Gabriel pushed hers gently over her finger, his green eyes softened. She followed, placing the wide band on Gabriel's finger.

"Kiss her, then, man," said the priest. "She's yours."

Gabriel's eyes grew dark as he lifted the small chiffon veil and pushed it from Paige's face. With both hands, he angled her face just so, then lowered his mouth to her ear. "You're mine."

Then, he kissed her.

And she kissed him back.

They were in an ancient kirk, after all, so the kiss was kept short. Much shorter than Paige would have liked.

Congratulations were passed around the small kirk, with many a Munro hugging and slapping their joy, and finally, Amelia came to her side.

"Welcome to the family," she said, and pulled Paige into a fierce hug. "Now the Craigmires are visiting us for a few days, so you two will have Gorloch to yourselves."

"Oh," said Paige, and felt her skin grow warm. "Thanks."

"The official reception is next week, and it's unavoidable, I'm afraid," she continued. "In case you didn't realize it, you've entered into a strange and elite world of mortals marrying medievals."

Paige laughed. "Yeah, I see that."

"Well," Amelia continued. "One of the biggest and loudest medieval men you'll ever want to meet has caught wind of the wedding, not to mention more ghosts than you can wrap your brain around. His name's Dreadmoor, and, well, you'll see. They want a reception. Demand it, actually."

Paige grinned. "Sounds fun."

"Just you wait. Now, until then." Amelia turned and latched onto her husband. "We've stocked the fridge at Gorloch with everything you two will need." She grinned. "I promise, no one will bother you."

Paige gulped.

Ethan laughed.

"Can I please have my wife now?"

Paige turned and Gabriel pulled her close. "Ready?" he said, his voice steady.

She stared into his stormy green depths. "I think so."

Another chuckle from Ethan, just before his wife elbowed him in the stomach.

"Okay," Amelia said. "Directions for Gorloch are already programmed in," she said, nodding toward the Rover. "Cell phone in the glove box. Call if you need anything."

"She won't," growled Gabriel, tugging Paige away. "Come, Mrs. Munro."

Paige waved goodbye to her new family and hurried toward the Rover, her husband all but dragging her.

She didn't think they'd get to Gorloch soon enough.

Gabriel couldna keep his eyes off his wife.

His *wife*.

He could hardly believe 'twas true.

They reached Gorloch in less than half an hour.

Paige stopped the Rover and turned off the ignition. She drew a deep breath and smiled. "Here we are."

Gabriel grinned at his bride, jumped out, and ran to the other side to collect her. He easily scooped her up.

Neither said a word as he carried her inside. Gently, Gabriel set her down.

"Are you hungry?" he asked, lacing his fingers through hers.

Paige shyly shook her head and leaned into him. "Maybe later."

That's all the urging Gabriel needed. He latched the bolt on the front door and tucked Paige's hand in the crook of his arm. He smiled down at her, and together they climbed the steps.

They'd have made it to Paige's chamber earlier, but he hadn't been able to quit pulling her to a stop, pressing her to the wall, and kissing her senseless.

Rather, 'twas he who was senseless. He couldna get enough o' her.

The castle was quiet, except for the wind blowing through the cracks in the stone. Once inside, Gabriel lit several candles, then knelt and built up a roaring fire. When he turned, his bride still stood directly where he'd left her, near the door. He rose and walked to her. With his hand, he lifted her chin until their eyes met.

"Is somethin' wrong?" he asked, feeling her unease.

Paige's eyes softened. "Nothing's wrong." She lifted her hand to his jaw. "Everything's perfect."

With that, Gabriel pulled her close, sliding his hand round her waist, the other hand cupping the back of her head. He lowered his mouth to hers and settled there, tasting first her top lip, then the bottom. Already a fire burned within him, he wanted her so badly. So much so, it pained him.

Slowly, as they kissed, Gabriel guided her back, toward the bed.

Lifting his head, Gabriel searched his bride's face. Her eyes had darkened with passion; her lips, plump from his kisses. "Christ, Paige Munro," he said, grazing her throat with his fingertips. "Christ."

Without a word, Paige slowly unbuttoned the white linen shirt and loosened it from his plaid. Gabriel stood statue still, waiting. Her fingers trailed his abdomen, and he suddenly felt powerfully grateful for his fine form, as she eased her hands over each muscle there and then explored the ones on his back and over his chest.

It all but drove him daft.

Then, her hands covered his, and she moved them to her shawl. He needed no coercing as he unclasped the paltry piece of cloth and tossed it aside, leaving her delicate shoulders bare. He lowered his head and pressed his lips to her collarbone, and she sighed.

That small sound alone nearly drove him over the edge.

With the wood crackling in the hearth, Gabriel slowly turned Paige round and began to loosen the buttons on her gown. Once he'd reached the last one, he pushed the silky material from her, and it pooled around her feet. Another shift, made of even flimsier cloth, still clung to her, and he pushed it away as well. A small swath of silken cloth covered her breasts and bottom, and he sucked in a breath as he took in her slight form, so different from his own. As tenderly as possible, he turned her round to face him, then lifted her to the bed. With one hand, he unclasped the pin holding his plaid together, and it fell in a pool of linen atop his wife's gown.

Paige's eyes remained locked onto his.

Quickly, he kicked off his boots and the rest of his garb, slid her shoes from her feet, then joined her. With one arm, he braced himself over her. Paige's eyes were wide and glassy, and Gabriel found he couldna stop touching her. Skin that felt like velvet beneath his hands made him shudder with anticipation, and he dragged his fingers over her collar, down her arms, and over her flat stomach, her hips, and then, she reached for him and pulled him down.

As soon as their bodies touched, Gabriel came undone, his hands left nothing undiscovered, and the fire burning low in Paige's stomach all but scorched her. She ran her hands over his bare back, tracing the muscles there, and when his mouth came down on hers, she kissed him back with a fury she hadn't known she possessed.

At first, Gabriel kissed her hard, frenzied, as though a wild and feral animal. Suddenly, he stopped, and rested his forehead against hers.

"I'm verra sorry, love," he said, out of breath. "I canna seem to control myself."

Paige's own breathing was ragged, and she held on to him. "I don't want you to," she said.

He drew back and looked at her. A small smile pulled at his mouth. "Aye?"

She smiled and pulled his head down to her. "I want you *now*," she whispered. "I can't wait any longer."

When Gabriel pulled back and locked his gaze onto hers, she smiled, gathered her courage, and unclasped her bra. His eyes darkened and he pushed the material aside.

"Christ, Paige," he said, wonder in his voice. "You're beautiful." His eyes softened, then turned stormy. "And you're all *mine*."

Paige held her breath as he lowered his head to hers, and when their mouths met, the frenzy began again, and this time, Paige met Gabriel's with equal passion. He tasted every inch of her, his mouth moving erotically over her lips, her throat, and her breasts. When his warm tongue touched the sensitive peaks, she groaned and arched into him. Gabriel trailed erotic kisses down her stomach and ribs, and then his fingers hooked the silken panties and pulled them off. They joined the pile of wedding clothes on the floor.

He came to her then, once more holding his weight on one arm, his other free hand skimming her skin, touching her in places and with a passion Paige had never before known. Stretched over her, he kissed her gently, softly, his tongue tasting her lips, her teeth, her chin. He looked like an ancient warrior, with his long hair hanging loose around his chiseled chest and broad shoulders, those sexy tattoos encircling his biceps.

With one hand, Paige wrapped her fingers through that long hair and pulled. "Now," she whispered, and looked at him, pleading. "Please."

Gabriel kissed her once more, then slowly lifted his head.

"Dunna close your eyes, Mrs. Munro," he said, his voice a hoarse whisper. "Watch."

With his hips, Gabriel nudged her legs to accommodate him, and then he entered her, hot, hard, and completely delicious. Paige gasped at the tightness.

She hadn't expected that.

Gabriel's eyes widened, and he froze. "You've never?"

Although there was a slight bit of discomfort, it wasn't nearly like what she'd heard about as a teenager. "Does that bother you?" she asked, wondering if he preferred someone experienced.

Gabriel closed his eyes, muttered something unintelligible, then looked at her. "I love you, Paige Munro," he said, and slowly began to move inside her. "You truly are mine. Forever." He lowered his head to her ear. "'Twill only hurt for a moment."

With his eyes locked onto hers, Gabriel moved deeper, slowly at first, but when Paige wrapped her legs around his waist, twisted his hair between her fingers, pulled, and said *now*, his thrusts became faster, desperate, and all at once Paige exploded inside, tiny fragments of shattered glass scattering behind her eyelids as Gabriel pleasured her. Wave after wave crashed over her as her first orgasm consumed her, and the moment she groaned and arched, he joined her, a low, deep growl emanating from his throat as he discovered his own pleasure. Slowly, they eased, they moved together, and Gabriel rolled to his back, taking Paige with him. He settled her atop him, still deep inside her. Wrapping his arms about her, he brought her to his chest.

Paige felt his heart thundering beneath her ear, and his large hands skimmed her spine. He pressed his lips to her temple and cuddled her in a tight embrace.

"I am your first," he finally said, when his breathing had returned to normal.

Paige pushed up and looked at her husband, her chin on his chest. "You are my *last*."

A slow smile spread over Gabriel's face, his dimples pitting deeply. "Never in my wildest dreams could I have ever dreamt up such a tale as this," he said, tracing her wedding band with his finger. He pushed her hair behind her ears. "I would gladly wait for you again, no matter the centuries." He brought her close. "I love you, Paige Munro," he mouthed against her lips. "Always."

Paige suckled his lips, caressed his stubbled jaw with her fingertips, and gently nipped his tongue. She cupped his face, and met his gaze. "I think I was meant to be Mrs. Gabriel Munro," she said softly. "I will love you always."

With a grin, Gabriel turned her onto her back, lowered his head, and kissed her thoroughly. Gently at first, and then passion took over, and his hands found even more places on her body to explore.

Just as their pleasure surged again, he lowered his mouth to her ear, suckled her lobe, and whispered, "Watch, love," that thick Highland brogue making her shudder. "Watch what you do to me."

Paige locked her eyes to her husband's, smiled, and did just that.

About the Authors

Dawn Halliday has held various jobs from bookselling to teaching inner-city children to acting, but she's never put down the pen. She lives in California with her husband and three children.

Sophie Renwick works as a nurse. She lives in Ontario, Canada, with her husband and daughter.

Cindy Miles is a romance writer by day and a trauma nurse by night. Witnessing near-death experiences as a nurse coupled with a lifelong interest in ghosts has given her mysterious and whimsical romances a special twist. She lives in Savannah, Georgia, with her husband and two children.